THE IMPORTANCE OF BULLDOGS

- A Novel

Ellen Davidson Levine

Terroir Ink

A Terroir Ink First Edition

The Importance of Bulldogs – a Novel

Copyright © 2010 by Ellen Davidson Levine

Cover design by A-Vibe Web Development (http://avibeweb.com)
Cover photo by Rick Levine © 2010

Author photo by Prechtel Photo

Library of Congress Catologing-in-Publication Data is available upon request

ISBN-13: 978-0-9844839-2-1
ISBN-10: 0-9844839-2-6

In Memory of Max

ACKNOWLEDGMENTS

My gratitude to those who read and commented on the several drafts of this novel, and to my writers group for adopting Ruby Doobie. Thanks to friends and family for your love and encouragement. Thanks to Rick, for everything.

For all the edits, encouragement and wisdom, special thanks to the Frogs. I am also grateful for the support and patience of friends and family and my office mates, Bella and Jack

CHAPTER 1

I was speeding down Seven Hills Road in my rickety VW Golf on my way to commit suicide.

Since early morning I'd been on the verge of doing something desperate. For hours, I'd aimlessly traveled the back roads of the Willamette Valley, going nowhere. I had nowhere to go. Forty-five years old and I had no home, no job, no one who cared if I lived or died. All I had was a decrepit car with an almost-empty gas tank and a suitcase-full of dirty laundry on the back seat.

The Golf crested the seventh hill of Seven Hills Road. It was dusk. I switched on the headlights. In front of me, the steep road dropped to the valley floor like a terrifying rollercoaster ride. With no protective barrier along the edge, the narrow road left no room for bad driving. Perfect.

I pressed my foot on the accelerator, flirting with the idea of death. The car lurched forward and the speedometer needle twitched nervously as the car picked up speed. 65, 70, 72, 75. At 80 mph, the car started to shimmy and shake like a giant vibrator. My body throbbed with anticipation. I was breathing hard. One turn of the steering wheel would take me over the edge to a fiery climax at the bottom of the ravine. The ultimate orgasm. A sexy way to go.

Midway down the hill, the headlights lit up a blurry bulk, where the road flattened out. *Shit.* A deer maybe, or a cow. I stomped on the brakes. The car swerved. It fishtailed right, left, right, but didn't slow. Tires shrieking like banshees, the Golf hurtled down the road. The shape took form. A person. *Ohmygodaperson.* I knew the car couldn't stop in time.

With my last strength, I jerked the steering wheel. This wasn't a game of tempting fate anymore. This was real. I squeezed my eyes shut. Either I was going to kill someone or I was going to go off the cliff and crash and die and I didn't want to look. I went limp with regret and guilt and dread and other emotions I couldn't begin to name.

The sharp stink of burning rubber bit my nose like smelling salts. My head snapped up. My eyes fluttered open. I felt a knifing pain in the place where my neck met my right shoulder. As I reached to massage the tender spot, I became aware of the absence of sound. The Golf was quiet and still. The car had stalled and come to a stop at the bottom of the road, on a large dirt pullout. Several feet away, a plump, middle-aged woman stood in the middle of the road. She had a broad grin on her face. I turned the ignition off and gingerly got out of the car, ignoring the twinge of pain in my neck.

"What the hell's wrong with you? Are you crazy or something?" I slammed the car door shut, adding an exclamation point to my angry words. "You could've been killed."

"You're an angel," the woman said, keeping her smile and ignoring my tirade. "I was so scared I'd be out here all night. And then you came along."

Her words made me regret my rage. I offered an apologetic smile. "Are you all right?"

"Yes. I am now. You?"

"I think so." My tongue stumbled on the words as if they were pebbles.

Her face brightened with another smile. "I'm MaryLou Hunter," she said, offering her hand. She was overweight and short, about my height, and several years my senior, in her early or mid-fifties. Her pale face was framed by frizzy brown hair. Her eyes were the color of dark chocolate.

"Ruby. Ruby Dubin." I shook her hand.

"Ruby, you're an answer to my prayers." She gestured at the white van standing in the left lane about twenty feet down the road. "It won't start. I don't know what to do."

The sky had gone completely dark. The moon and stars were hidden behind a layer of storm clouds. I had to walk closer to see that the Honda minivan was slumped on the rim of the right tire. The van was scraped and banged up on that side, with the door pushed in and the side window nothing but shards of glass. The headlamp on the passenger side was also shattered, the windshield had a web of cracks and there were dents and scrapes across the front of the van too.

"There were some rocks lying in the road." MaryLou's voice came from behind me. "It was like they attacked me."

I glanced around. I didn't see any rocks nearby and the damage seemed worse than what a couple of rocks would inflict, unless they were boulders. Mentally, I shrugged. I had bigger worries. My near-death experience hadn't fixed any of my problems. I wasn't sure yet if I was relieved to be alive or sorry not to have ended it all. Until I figured out the answer, I'd just keep doing the next thing to do. "I guess we'd better move the van out of the road," I said, turning to look at MaryLou.

"You're right. I didn't even think of that." MaryLou stepped forward and wrapped me in her arms. "See? It's just cosmic that you showed up."

We walked around the van to the driver's side. MaryLou opened the door. There was glass on the passenger seat but the driver's side was okay. She got behind the wheel and turned the ignition. Immediately, a deafening banging and clanging filled the air, the clatter of metal on metal. I muffled my ears with my hands, my heart thumping madly.

"Shut it off," I yelled.

MaryLou nodded and kept her hands over her ears.

I screamed. "Off."

Again, she nodded and her ears stayed covered.

I sighed. My neck ached and I felt suddenly tired and empty. All I wanted was a place to lie down. Instead, I was standing in the middle of the road with this nice but totally airhead woman, both of us in danger of permanent hearing loss. I reached across and turned the ignition key to off, silencing the deafening noise.

"Oh, Ruby, thank you." MaryLou lowered her arms and gave me a wide smile. "I don't know why I didn't do that." I stood aside to let MaryLou get out of the van. We stood staring at the crippled car for a few minutes. "What do we do now?" MaryLou asked.

"We have to push it."

Moving the van was easier said than done, even after we remembered to release the emergency brake. The dark, lonely spot on Seven Hills Road sounded like the birthing room in a maternity ward, what with all the grunting, groaning and gasping as we labored to push the van across the road to the wide turnout where my Golf was parked. I was shaky and tired. My neck and shoulder muscles ached. Not only was the van heavy and cumbersome but a light rain turned everything slick, including the road.

"Can't get a good grip," MaryLou said, stepping back from the van. "It's too slippery."

"Reminds me of how I lost my job," I said.

"What do you mean?"

We were both out of breath, although the van had only budged a few inches. We agreed to take a quick break while I related the story about how, three months ago, I got fired from ARF, the Animal Rescue Foundation.

"Soon as I showed up to work" I told her, "my boss started barking instructions at me." My boss, Mr. HDW, was not a nice man. The public thought he was a kind, charitable, animal-loving guy. Behind the scenes, Mr. Harold D. Williams was a mean-spirited bully. Everyone working at ARF feared and hated him and the dogs did too. The aggressive dogs growled, others whimpered and cowered when he took one of his infrequent walks through the kennel area.

"My assignment that day was to bathe Finn McCool, an Irish wolfhound big as a Shetland pony. Unfortunately, Mr. HDW forgot to share a small detail with me. The giant dog was normally a sweetheart but he hated water."

MaryLou's lips formed an "O" and I could tell by the sparkle in her eyes, she was anticipating the story's punch line.

"The moment I turned the sprayer on him, Finn broke loose. He ran amok, slipping and sliding, flinging water everywhere. The kennel erupted in a frenzy of barking dogs. I chased after Finn, while Mr. HDW stood at the door, shrieking 'Catch him, catch him'." I remembered how HDW's face flushed with anger when I told him he was scaring poor Finn even more. "Catch the dog," he ordered. "Then I want to see you in my office."

"So?" MaryLou said, nudging me from my thoughts.

"So, it took the rest of the morning for me to coax the scared dog into his kennel. When I finally walked through HDW's office door, disheveled and exhausted, he was at his desk, leaning back in the chair, hands clasped on his chest, as if in prayer. And then, in a really sarcastic voice, he asked me to give him one good explanation for what happened out there."

"Creep. What did you tell him," MaryLou asked.

"I told him I'd lost my McCool." I looked away, suddenly embarrassed by the story. "He fired me on the spot."

"That's so unfair," MaryLou said. "He shouldn't have blamed you like that."

"Unfair." I shrugged. "Story of my life."

"Oh, Ruby. It doesn't have to be."

What she said startled me. What did she mean? Personally, I hadn't observed anything fair in my life and I'd been around almost half a century. It wasn't fair that one flippant remark had started my downward spiral, from jobless to homeless to hopeless. It wasn't fair that everyone I'd trusted and loved had let me down. It wasn't fair my luck was so bad. Once, I thought having my birthday on January 1 made me special, I thought it was a lucky sign that I would turn fifty on January 1, 2000, the same day the calendar would flip into a new century. Lately, I'd starting hearing some people call that date Y2K. They predicted all kinds of disasters. No need to commit suicide. Just wait 'til the end of the world. Happy birthday.

"Ruby, your life could be perfect if you'd let it." There was such conviction in her voice. I wondered if MaryLou might know something I didn't. I searched her face for answers but I couldn't decipher anything from the wide smile she offered me.

The faint sound of a car in the distance reminded us of the urgency of our task. We had to get the van out of the road. With renewed energy, we leaned against the van and shoved. It didn't move.

"This isn't working." I stood up and rubbed the back of my neck. Pain was like a boa constrictor, wrapping around me and squeezing hard.

MaryLou shook her head. She gasped a response. "We. Can. Do it. Together. Now."

Once again, we pushed the van, grunting with effort. Miraculously, the van moved. It glided slowly across the blacktop and onto the dirt, stopping not far from where we'd been aiming. MaryLou and I grabbed each other. We jumped up and down. We danced a joyful jig. In that moment, I felt a powerful connection between MaryLou and me. The night's events had bonded us.

We'd forgotten the approaching car. Just then, it whooshed past, spraying us with dirty water from the road. I looked down at my wet, mud-splattered jacket and jeans and then at MaryLou's black pants, mud-brown from the knees to the hem.

"A muddy mess," MaryLou said, plucking at the wet cloth of her pant leg where it clung to her skin.

I twirled and posed like a clumsy fashion model. "Every well-dressed woman wants clothes designed by Mud-damn Mess."

MaryLou laughed first and I couldn't resist her happiness. I broke into laughter that wouldn't stop. The more I laughed, the harder MaryLou laughed. And that made me laugh more. My eyes watered, my nose ran, I gasped for breath and I couldn't stop. I don't know how many times we managed to quiet ourselves, only to succumb to another round of hysterical laughter. Finally, after much deep breathing, wiping of eyes, and pressing together of lips to hold back stray giggles, we calmed down enough to inspect the damages, using a flashlight I got from the Golf's glove compartment. MaryLou's van hunched to one side, a wounded beast. I pointed the flashlight back down the road, measuring the distance we'd pushed the van. Bits of glass sparkled in the circle of light. I still didn't see any rocks, even alongside the road.

"I dread telling Devin. He already thinks I'm the worst driver," MaryLou said, "This is my second accident in a week."

"You can probably get it fixed," I said.

MaryLou blinked, thinking about what I'd said. After a moment she waved her hand in the air. "No," she said. "I didn't really like driving it that much anyway."

Mentally, I raised eyebrows. For me, a broken down automobile had always been a calamity that required scraping up enough money to patch the car, and then hoping it would run for another few thousand miles.

MaryLou interrupted my thoughts. "Can you take me home?"

I took a deep breath. "I don't know. Gas tank's almost empty." Not to mention that I didn't have the money to fill it. I got depressed again, thinking of everything I needed and didn't have.

MaryLou leaned towards me and gently touched my arm. "As thanks for rescuing me, I'd love to buy you a tank of gas. There's a gas station just a couple miles from here."

I shook my head. "I couldn't."

"Please." Her hand pressed a little harder on my arm. "I insist. It's the least I can do."

"Okay. Thank you." I was too embarrassed to look her in the eye.

We collected MaryLou's purse and several packages from the van, crowded everything into the Golf, and took off. The empty tank warning light glowed red as we entered the small town, which was nothing more than a few scattered houses and a convenience store with a couple of gas pumps out front. I slowed the car, turned into the brightly lit parking lot and parked by one of the pumps.

"I'll go pay," MaryLou said. She got out of the car, yoo-hooing the attendant. I watched the two of them in the rearview mirror as they stood together, talking, while the man unscrewed the gas cap, unlocked the hose, inserted it in the tank and clicked the nozzle in place. In Oregon, it's illegal to pump your own gas. Over the years, a few people have tried to change the law. Personally, I hope Oregonians never get dumb enough to vote for getting out in the weather, inhaling gas fumes, dirtying their hands and then trudging to the cashier's booth to stand in line in order to pay the same high price as before. I thought about how cool it was to live where self-serve was against the law.

Right away, the irony grabbed me by the gut and twisted hard. My stomach felt sick and my hands starting to shake. I'd been close to never filling a gas tank again, either self-serve or full-serve. I wrapped my fingers around the steering wheel to steady them and deep-breathed until I didn't feel like throwing up.

Mary Lou got back in the car. "I don't live too far from here." She gestured vaguely. "Just a couple of miles back the way we came."

I've since figured out that the phrases "not too far" and "just a couple of miles" mean nothing in rural-speak. Country roads are narrow and often curvy. Every mile is filled with hazards. By day, you might round a bend only to find your way blocked by a tractor bumping along at 10 mph. By night, legions of deer, skunk and possum wait at the side of the road to fling themselves in front of oncoming cars.

After many assurances that her house was just a little further, we pulled into MaryLou's driveway. Gigantic rhododendron bushes lined the asphalt driveway as it wound up the hill. At the top, a weedy, overgrown lawn surrounded a rambling faux-Tuscan villa with a prominent four-car garage. The home's Mediterranean-style stucco and tile seemed out of place in the soggy winter landscape.

I pulled the car close to the path leading to the front door and turned the engine off, to conserve gas. "Well," I said, "It's been quite a night." My neck gave a sharp twinge and I reached to massage it.

"Why don't you come in, let me give you a cup of coffee or something." She lifted her left arm, flicked on the car's inside light and tugged at her sleeve, displaying a dainty watch with a gold band and tiny diamond chips circling the watch face. "Oh my goodness. It's almost 10:30. You can't go driving around at this time of night. You'll stay here tonight."

"I couldn't possibly," I protested. I could hear my Aunt Elaine in my voice, being polite even if it meant turning down a warm bed when I had nowhere else to sleep except my car.

"Ruby, don't be silly. It's no problem. No problem at all. Please." MaryLou's dark brown eyes looked straight into mine. She broke the gaze first, turning to open the car door and step out.

Mesmerized, I got out of the Golf and followed her.

CHAPTER 2

T he house was dark. MaryLou ushered me through the front entry, across the living room and down a long carpeted hallway to the guest bedroom, flicking on every light switch she passed until the house was bright as a day in July. While MaryLou hustled off to find me pajamas and towels, I stood in the doorway and surveyed the small guest bedroom.

The room was crowded with an old-fashioned mahogany bedroom set. The bed had a massive headboard and was flanked on either side by large, doily-covered side tables. The white chenille bedspread, the fussy, dark furniture and the doilies made me think of Aunt Elaine's bedroom. I remembered how I'd climb into the big bed for comfort when I had bad dreams.

I pulled off my muddy jeans and sweater, leaving them in a heap on the floor. I don't remember lying down but when I awakened, I was sprawled across the bed, covered by a blanket MaryLou must have spread over me. In the morning light filtering through the sheer curtains, I could see pajamas, towels and my laundered clothes neatly piled on the bureau where she'd left them. My chest and arms felt sore and bruised, but my neck wasn't hot with pain any-more. I got up and dressed, found the bathroom, then wandered down the long hallway, following a spicy coffee smell to the cheerful yellow kitchen. A coffee-maker on the counter was just finishing the last gurgles of its brew cycle.

I grabbed one of the mugs that had been set out and filled it to the brim. The coffee was a dark roast, nice and strong. I took it black. Carefully, I carried the mug across the room and settled into a chair at the pine table in the alcove. I was halfway through my second helping of coffee when MaryLou came in, poured herself a mug and sat down opposite me.

"You had a good rest," MaryLou said. She was wearing a pink fleece bath-robe and fuzzy, powder blue slippers. She had dark circles under her eyes. I wondered if she'd slept much. "This is my family," she said, pointing at the side wall.

I inspected the gold-framed photograph. A man, a woman and two children were seated around the very table upon which my elbows rested. They all wore red sweaters with white snowflakes dancing across the chest. It took me a moment to recognize MaryLou in the slender woman with soft, shoulder length hair. A good-looking man with a thin face and high cheek bones had his arm around her. Even in the photo, the man's eyes glittered with intensity. The children sat on either side, the girl next to her father and the boy by his mother. Only MaryLou and the boy were smiling.

"Lyman," MaryLou said. "And that's Devinda. And Devin." I followed her finger, looking first at the boy with a Tom Sawyer grin and then the little girl, sitting on her father's knee. The girl was small and thin and her face was unusually sharp-featured for a child. Like her name, Devinda was a diminutive of her father.

"The kids were driving me nuts, so Devin, bless his heart, took them camping for the weekend," MaryLou said. She told me to make myself comfortable while she phoned a towing service and arranged to rent a car. "There's another car in the garage. It's Devin's, an old 1956 Chevy he's been restoring for years," MaryLou called over her shoulder as she disappeared into another room.

I sat there thinking about 1956 Chevys, Dickie Norwood, my Aunt Elaine and my Uncle Mike.

Aunt Elaine, the woman who raised me, was the opposite of her older sister, my mother. Aunt Elaine was unfashionable and dumpy. I take after her, at least in the looks department. My aunt went to church every week and prayed every day. All it got her was a lousy marriage, an abandoned kid and a long painful death from cancer of the uterus. And yet, up to the day she died, Aunt Elaine believed her prayers would destroy the cancer, bring back her health and make her life wonderful.

Before my aunt died I bought into the whole belief thing myself. When she got sick, I tried everything I could think of to convince God to save her. I became the perfect young lady my aunt had always wanted me to be. I studied hard in school and got straight A's. I stopped saying swear words. I used proper grammar. I wouldn't fool around with my boyfriend Dickie anymore. Of course, he broke up with me and started dating my best friend Sandy. Even then, I tried to think only good and pure thoughts about Dickie and Sandy, instead of imagining their excruciatingly painful death in a fiery car crash that also totaled Dickie's electric blue '56 Chevy which I'm sure he loved more than he ever cared about Sandy or me.

When Aunt Elaine's cancer wouldn't stop spreading I offered my life in exchange for hers, praying morning and night for her recovery. She died early one morning, alone in her hospital room. I didn't find out until I got home from school that afternoon and found Uncle Mike waiting to tell me. It was just a few days after my sixteenth birthday. That's when I figured out there was no pay-off for being religious.

The night after my aunt's funeral I had a fight with my Uncle, which ended when I declared he was to blame for Aunt Elaine's death and slammed out of the house. I went to my friend Annie's house and got drunk on cheap wine. I decided to be as bad as I could be, my way of giving God - and Uncle Mike - the finger. I made it out of high school and floated through two years of college but when I finally flunked out of Portland State, Uncle Mike told me I couldn't get any more money. The terms of my aunt's will specified that he was in charge of the funds until I graduated from college or he died, whichever came first. Naturally, we had a huge blow-up. I stopped returning his calls, didn't answer his letters and eventually lost touch with him. Twenty-five years and two failed marriages later, I regretted my foolishness. After all, Uncle Mike was the closest thing to family I had. And I wasn't sure if he was alive or if he would even want to see me again.

My almost-suicide had apparently awakened ghosts from my past. I waggled my head to shake off haunted memories. Looking for a distraction, I wandered into the large family room adjoining the kitchen. A velvet brown sofa stretched along the wall, well-worn and comfortable looking. Two overstuffed chairs faced the couch. In the center, a massive Spanish oak coffee table was littered with newspapers, a little girl's powder blue jacket, a battered library book titled *Science for the Curious* and some toys. I flipped the book open. It was checked out to Lyman Hunter from the Roseville Middle School Library. Next to the book, a headless Barbie doll with a narrow waist and swollen boobs raised its arms in supplication as if it were praying for a new head, or maybe breast-reduction surgery.

Looking up and away from the macabre toy, I inspected the walls. They were covered with gold-framed, ten-by-twelve photographic portraits of the children, especially Devinda. I stared at photo after photo, intrigued and repulsed by the way the little girl posed for the camera, head tilted coyly, eyelids sleepy and half-closed, a secretive smile on her rosebud lips. I rubbed my neck. The pain had returned.

"Devin loves taking pictures of the kids." MaryLou stood just slightly behind me. When I turned to look at her, she gave me a wide smile. She wore a black jacket over a tailored white blouse and she'd put lipstick on. A few scarlet flecks were caught on her front teeth.

"Your daughter likes to pose, doesn't she?" My face flushed warmly as the words spilled out. I hadn't meant to reveal my judgment about Devinda's portraits.

MaryLou laughed and shook her head. "Isn't she cute? She wants to be a movie star. And she adores being on stage with me."

"On stage? You're an actress?"

"I thought you knew." MaryLou waved a hand in the air, brushing the words away. "I didn't mean that. I shouldn't assume everyone knows who I am."

"Who are you?"

"Have you heard of SETII?"

I wondered why she was changing the subject. "Sure. It's a planet or something."

MaryLou smiled. "You're funny, Ruby. SETII stands for Seeking Energy, Truth and Infinity, Incorporated. SETII is really who I am."

The radiance on MaryLou's face reminded me of the uplifted faces in religious paintings. Despite the sarcastic comment that rose to my lips, I felt jealousy, wishing I believed in something so much I would glow.

"SETII could help you," she added softly. "We all need someone who cares about us, don't we? SETII is about caring."

I gulped, swallowing the emotion that tightened my throat. Was I that obvious? Did I act that needy?

Suddenly, there was a snorting and snuffling, like a wild boar was loose in the house. A brown and white bulldog lumbered into the room. Inches from me, he came to a halt. Like any bulldog, he could easily be mistaken for a fairytale beast, with his barrel-chest and large head, his wrinkled snout and drooping jowls and especially the mean-looking lower canines jutting from his mouth. This dog was a classic English bulldog, so ugly he was cute. He lifted his head to inspect me with sad, intelligent eyes.

I gave him time to sniff me out. When I could tell by the tilt of his ears he approved, I bent to scratch him on a spot right above his tail, the same place my Uncle Mike's bulldog Clarence liked to be scratched. The dog sighed and plopped in a heap by my feet.

"Look at that. He likes you," MaryLou said. "We got him for the kids but he's just no good around them. I can't trust him." She finger-combed her hair, a gesture of hers that was already familiar. "Maybe you should take him."

The dog raised his head and looked at me, as if he were imploring me to say yes.

I shook my head. "I can barely take care of myself at the moment. I wouldn't be able to give him a home or feed him or anything."

"Ruby, listen. It wasn't just chance that brought you here." MaryLou's voice vibrated with feeling. "You chose to answer the call I put out into the universe. I need you as much as I think you need me." She gave my arm a light touch. "You need a place to stay, don't you?"

I rubbed the back of my neck. "Well. Yes."

"Ruby, it's perfect." She gripped my arm tighter. "I need a caretaker for my upper property. You can live in the cabin rent-free for keeping an eye on things."

"You don't know anything about me." And I didn't know much about her either. "I've never been a caretaker. I wouldn't know the first thing about fixing anything or whatever caretakers do."

"You think I'm nuts, don't you?" MaryLou smiled. "I'm not, I promise you. The caretaking is no big deal." She waved her hand in the air, a fairy godmother turning the pumpkin into a golden carriage. "Besides," she continued, "your job interview started when you helped me last night. I knew right away we were meant to be in each other's life."

I didn't say anything. I felt off-balance, the same as if I were standing at the edge of the sea with the tide going out and the sand slipping from under my toes.

"Ruby, listen to me. What do you have to lose? Give it a try for a week or two and then we'll see. Let me show you the cabin at least. It's up the road a mile or so. Cowboy hasn't cleared all his stuff out yet but I know he won't mind. Just come look at it."

The flood of her words swirled around my head. It had been a long time since someone cared enough to boss me around. "Okay," I said.

CHAPTER 3

Struggling to keep up with her, I followed MaryLou along a narrow path that cut through the field behind her house. MaryLou's outfit - black velvet, wide-leg pants, white blouse and black leather jacket - seemed incompatible with the setting. But on her feet she wore a pair of scuffed Nikes and she kept a steady pace, gliding smoothly along the path, while I stumbled clumsily over every twig and rock that littered the way.

After a bit, the path angled up a hillside thick with weeds and scrub oak and, here and there, age-blackened tree stumps from an old clear-cut. When I finally reached the top of the hill, I paused to catch my breath.

"Yoo hoo." MaryLou stood at the edge of a heavily-wooded area about a half-city block below me. She waved, turned away, and disappeared into the trees. I caught flashes of her black jacket between the tree trunks as I picked my way carefully down the hill and followed her into the dense patch of woods. The old trees towered above me. Some sunlight filtered through the branches but mostly it was dark as dusk and the smells were damp and earthy.

I caught sight of MaryLou just as the narrow path flattened and came out of the trees. I hurried forward, right into the ambush of monster blackberry vines. Barbed tendrils grabbed at my pants. Thorns pierced the sleeve of my sweater and slashed my arm. I pried myself free - *ouch, ouch, shit, ouch* – and suffered more scratches and slight blood loss when a thorn stabbed the ring finger on my left hand.

A bit further on, the path ended at a small footbridge that was merely a few slime-covered wooden planks stretched across the creek. Water rushed noisily below but MaryLou didn't break her stride, crossing in a few quick steps. She stopped and waited for me.

I hesitated, nervous about slipping on the mossy wood. Despite the fast moving water, the creek was neither deep nor wide, but the rocky bed looked lethal. Keeping my eyes on the creek bank only three or four feet away, I urged myself forward and moved carefully and slowly across the bridge. Not until I stepped safely on the opposite bank did I lift up my eyes. I could hardly believe the incredible setting in front of me. Like an idyllic model for a Thomas Kinkade painting, a log cabin nestled comfortably in a stand of pine. All it lacked was the curl of smoke drifting from the chimney.

"Wait 'til you see inside," MaryLou said, noticing my wide-eyed appreciation. "You're going to be thrilled."

Obediently, I tagged after her but instead of the joy MaryLou predicted, every step closer to the cabin made me more uneasy. This was too good to be true. There was a catch. Like the caretaker job. The first time something broke, she'd find out how incompetent I was and kick me out. Nervously, I watched MaryLou struggle to open the locked door, trying one key and then another with no success. A part of me hoped she couldn't open the door, as if that would keep me from the inevitable bad ending.

"Ruby, come here." MaryLou thrust the key ring into my reluctant hand. "You try."

I narrowed my eyes, looked at the opening and made the obvious choice, an old-fashioned brass key. It clicked smoothly into the lock.

"I knew it. Listen," MaryLou said, excitement bubbling in her voice. "You were meant to be here. You intuitively picked the right key to unlock the door."

I was beginning to understand this was a typical MaryLou thing to say, so I didn't argue with her.

The door opened to reveal a bright and airy sitting room. Bookcases lined the walls. To my immediate left, a brown plaid sofa sat alone, facing the room. Two recliner chairs, arranged in front of a south-facing window, overlooked an overgrown vegetable garden. A door on the far side of the room opened into a small kitchen and eating area, painted a cheerful canary yellow with sky blue trim. Except for an old-fashioned black rotary dial telephone, there was no sign of a television, radio or even a record player.

To the right, another opening revealed a hallway leading to the bedroom. Tucked at the end of the hallway, like an afterthought, was a closet-sized bathroom with the sweet and sour smell of shaving cream and mold. I wandered into the bedroom. A king-sized bed, stripped of its bedclothes, took up most of the space. Opposite the bed a large window had a view of the tall trees. A small chest of drawers in the corner of the room held a framed photograph of a man dressed in cowboy shirt, jeans, and boots, his arm possessively draped on the shoulders of a petite blond. They were standing on the front porch of this very cabin. I crossed the room and picked up the photo for closer inspection. The woman gazed at the man with an adoring gleam in her eyes. He was facing straight ahead, squinting at the camera. At the bottom of the photo, someone with the back-slant of a left-hander had scribbled a message: "To Cowboy with all my love! Alice. XXOO." The "i" in "Alice" was dotted with a heart.

I returned to the front room where MaryLou waited. "Are you sure this Cowboy guy is going to be okay with me staying here?" I said.

It wasn't that I didn't love the place from the moment I crossed the bridge and saw the charming cabin perched at the edge of an enchanted forest. It's just that life had made me a firm believer in the principle that if it sounds too good to be true then it is too good to be true. The free cabin and caretaker job MaryLou had offered in the whimsy of a moment would turn out to be another false promise. Maybe Cowboy and his girlfriend would return and kick me out. Maybe MaryLou expected more than I could do. Or maybe something I couldn't yet imagine would spoil this little paradise.

"Listen, don't worry about it." MaryLou waved her hand, dismissing my concern. "Cowboy's getting married to some rich girl named Tina or Trina or something. He's not coming back." She smiled. "I can tell you really like it here. You should give it a chance, Ruby. This was meant to be, I promise.'"

"I do love the cabin." Anyway, I had nowhere else to call home. I took a deep breath and exhaled loudly. "Whew. Okay, I'm your new caretaker. And I'll start work right away on the flowerbeds." I shivered with sudden excitement as I imagined myself clearing the weeds, freeing the flowers.

MaryLou laughed. "You're such a nut. It's only January." She seized me into a hug. "Oh, Ruby, I'm so happy. It'll be perfect. You'll see."

I hoped so.

We headed back to MaryLou's, this time taking the longer way along the paved road. As we neared the Hunter place, I saw a mud-splattered green SUV pull into the driveway.

MaryLou gave a little scream. "It's Devin and the kids." She scurried ahead to greet them. I caught up with her halfway up the steep driveway. She was

17

breathing hard. "Don't worry. I'm okay," she gasped as I approached. "I've got to get in shape."

She reminded me of the overweight man who brought his puppy to ARF, complaining the dog was hyperactive. When the volunteer on duty explained that puppies need to be walked and played with, he shook his head. "I can't keep it. Before I start walking a dog, I've got to start exercising." I decided against telling the story to MaryLou.

When we reached the top of the driveway, the SUV was pulled in front of the garage. A little girl I recognized from the photos came running helter-skelter to greet MaryLou. Devinda had on a dirty tee shirt, turquoise pedal-pushers and red tennies, no socks. "Mommy," she shrieked, wrapping her arms around MaryLou's hips.

MaryLou patted the top of her daughter's head. "Devinda, this is my new friend Ruby. Can you say hello?"

The girl regarded me with shrewd eyes. She said nothing.

MaryLou appeared not to notice. "Did you have a good time," she asked.

Devinda's face brightened. She chattered excitedly about the camping trip as we walked to the garage.

A boy slouched against the dirty SUV, hands thrust into the pockets of his jeans. He was skinny and taller than me already, and he had the gangly arms and legs of someone who still had a lot of growing to do. Although there was a shadowy hint of dark hair on his upper lip, his face still had a round, boyish look.

Just as I was wondering where MaryLou's husband might be, he emerged from the driver's side of the vehicle. He was taller than I'd imagined from the photograph in the dining room but it was easy to recognize his narrow face and pointy chin.

"Devin, this is Ruby," MaryLou said, gesturing at me.

"Ruby," he acknowledged tonelessly while his dark, hypnotic eyes appraised me. He gestured at the SUV. "Sorry I can't talk now," he said, "but I've got to get this unloaded. Devin turned away and began dragging gear out of the SUV, piling everything in the driveway.

MaryLou fluttered her hands. "You're not going to leave that stuff here, are you?"

Devin raised an eyebrow in her direction. "Lyman," he snapped. "Get this stuff inside."

Lyman paled. With deliberate slowness, he bent to gather the canvas and tent poles, all the while muttering curses and complaints. Devin ignored him.

"Devin," MaryLou said. "I need to tell you something."

Devin turned slowly. His arms fell to his sides. He stared at MaryLou as if he could see right inside her brain with his x-ray eyes. "What happened this time?"

"I wrecked the van last night. Coming back from Salem. It was an accident. I hit, well, I hit some rocks that were in the road."

"Again?"

"It was dusk and I couldn't see in time."

"You're all right?" Devin's voice held no emotion.

"Of course I am." She leaned over and planted a kiss on his cheek.

"Good. Now don't forget our appointment this afternoon."

"Appointment?"

Devin pressed his lips together and released them with a puff of frustration. "With Sykes, damn it."

"Oh, right. I didn't forget."

"I'm going up to shower and change." He looked at his watch. "We'll leave here in about an hour." He nodded at me. "Nice to meet you." Abruptly, he turned on his heels and marched into the house, shadowed by his daughter.

Lyman stood up. "Mom," he complained. "It's not fair. Devinda never has to do anything."

"She's just a little girl," MaryLou said. "She's not strong enough to carry that."

"Well, Dad was really mean to me. He made me . . . ."

"Lyman." MaryLou silenced him. "I don't want to hear it. Besides, Hunters always stick together. Right?"

"But Dad . . . ."

"Right?"

"Right," he said. He bent down and hefted the two large canvas bags and the tent poles onto his shoulders. Balancing the precarious burden, Lyman made his way to the house.

"Poor Devin. He's just exhausted." MaryLou waved her hand in the air. "He's been working day and night."

I nodded politely. Maybe that excused the way he'd spoken to his wife and son, but I wasn't sure. Still, I was puzzled by the force of my instant dislike of Devin. Maybe it was his name, so similar to devil. I wondered what MaryLou saw in him. But then, who was I to criticize another woman's choice in a man? MaryLou looked at me as if she knew what I was thinking. I struggled to say something neutral. "What does he do? I mean, what keeps him working day and night?"

"Money."

The rest of MaryLou's answer was cut off by the spine-chilling howl of a dog in pain. I spun in the direction of the unbearable noise. The house. Propelled forward, I ran up the steps and through the open door, almost tripping on the camping gear that was scattered across the floor. Lyman stood in the entryway, the bulldog hunched at his feet, quivering and submissive.

"You're pathetic," Lyman said. His voice was hard and sneering. "Pathetic," he repeated, drawing his right leg back, getting ready to kick the dog.

"Don't you dare," I shouted, startling the boy. He teetered, arms windmilling crazily, lost his balance and thudded against the wall.

For the moment, I didn't much care what happened to him. I gave the frightened dog time to remember me by sniffing my pants leg and then my fingers. I knelt down, one hand rubbing the soft brown fur behind his ears while I explored for bruises with the other hand, just in case Lyman had already landed a few kicks before I came into the house.

"What's going on here?" It was a man's voice, harsh and demanding. Devin's voice.

I continued my examination, whispering in the dog's ears, telling him he was a good boy, telling him he'd be okay. I heard MaryLou come into the house. She was breathing hard.

"Lyman." Devin's angry voice again. "I asked you what's going on here. Talk."

"Nothing. Nothing's going on. The dog was in the way and I tripped over him is all."

I glanced up, meeting the boy's eyes. He stared back, his eyes sending a silent plea not to say anything. Hiding the gesture from everyone else, I pointed at him and then at me, signaling that this was between us. We would deal with it later. Lyman gave me a quick nod of agreement.

"Devin dear, let it go. It was an accident," said MaryLou.

"The boy is pathetic." Devin turned and retreated from the room.

MaryLou crouched next to me. "Is Snoopy okay?"

That clinched it. I knew beyond a doubt the dog didn't belong in this house. An English bulldog named Snoopy is a dog that's misunderstood. Snoopy in the comics is a Beagle. Beagles are a cute, smart breed. They have a lively curiosity and a good nose for tracking, which sometimes leads them to wander far astray. Bulldogs are loyal and have many other fine qualities to make up for their generally sloppy, smelly and noisy habits, but one thing they aren't good at is snoopiness. The bulldog's squashed-in nose pretty much eliminates the skill to track a scent with any reliability. Anyway, a bulldog generally prefers comfort over adventure. Over most anything, in fact. For a bulldog, Clarence was a way better name than Snoopy.

Clarence Oddbody, my Uncle's bulldog, was named after a character in my aunt's favorite movie. From the day Uncle Mike brought him home, Clarence greeted me at the door every day after school, grinning widely, his tongue dripping from the side of his mouth. That dog gave a sympathetic ear to many of my growing-up woes. Most of all, he was devoted to Uncle Mike, who didn't mind scratching Clarence for hours on end on the special place just above his stubby tail. In return, Clarence accompanied my uncle on long, slow walks to who-knows-where, although the dog clearly preferred to be indoors. Snoring loud as a chainsaw, all the while launching stink-bomb farts, Clarence would sprawl in front of the living room heater vent in winter and under the big fan in the hallway in summer, always keeping an ear open for Aunt Elaine. Clarence carefully avoided her, knowing that she barely tolerated his existence in the house and would seize on any misbehavior as an excuse to banish him. That's why it was so weird that Clarence died the same week my aunt did. Weird and sad.

It was because of Clarence Oddbody that I told MaryLou I'd take the dog up to the cabin with me. She immediately claimed some kind of canine kismet had brought us together. Whatever the reason, the bulldog was sitting in the passenger seat when I pulled the VW into the parking space by the cabin. On the way over, I'd explained the name change. "No more Snoopy. From now on, you're officially Clarence the Second." I swear he smiled, although maybe he was only trying to breathe.

That night, Clarence II curled up on the bedroom rug while I stretched luxuriously on the big bed, soothed by the lullaby of Clarence's asthmatic snuffling. It was a homecoming, of sorts.

The next morning, Clarence was still snoring loudly when I climbed out of bed and went into the kitchen. Cowboy's pantry yielded an unopened three-pound can of off-the-shelf coffee. If I stayed, I'd have to find some decent brew. Fifteen minutes later, after a luxuriously hot shower, I rummaged through my small, battered suitcase for something decent to wear. The cleanest and least rumpled clothes were my black jeans and a long-sleeved shirt, red with lacy trim at the neckline. I dressed, ran a comb through my short hair, drank a cup of coffee and pretended I wasn't hungry. MaryLou had promised to pick me up at 8:30 for a tour of nearby West Yamhill – the closest laundromat and gas station plus the Quik-Stop Market - and then Salem, about 25 miles to the south. Maybe I'd get something to eat then.

I went back in the bedroom for my shoes. Clarence II was still asleep. "Time to get up, you lazybones." I gently nudged him with my bare foot. Clarence woke with a start, whimpering and cowering like a lost kitten. My body got the point before my brain did, bringing me to my knees, my arms encircling the dog's oversized head. Except for the fur and the funky Bulldog odor, it was like hugging a bowling ball. "I'm so sorry," I whispered. "I'll never hurt you. I promise."

Right away, Clarence forgave me, licking the side of my face with a long sandpapery tongue. Our love fest was cut short by the blare of a car horn. I leapt up, mentally checking my list. Clarence Two had water, food and he'd already discovered the doggie door cut into the kitchen wall, so I said a fond farewell, grabbed my jacket and purse, and hurried down the path.

In the parking area below the cabin, the Hunter's dirty green SUV rumbled impatiently. MaryLou was behind the wheel. She was wearing a purple jacket over a lavender blouse and dark pants. "I hope you don't mind if we switch things around," she said, as I settled into the passenger seat. "I need to go to the office for a teeny bit. I'm supposed to be there by 9:00" She glanced at her watch. "No problem."

Before I got the seatbelt snapped shut, the SUV was headed down the road. MaryLou drove fast and casually, the steering wheel cupped loosely in her left hand. Her right hand clutched a coffee mug.

"How was your night at the cabin?"

"I loved it. And Clarence did too."

"Clarence?" MaryLou turned to look at me just as we rounded a sharp curve. The Explorer began to glide into the other lane. MaryLou took a quick sip of coffee, set the cup into its holder and turned the steering wheel just in time. The SUV lurched back to safety.

I let my breath out before answering her. "Snoopy. I renamed him Clarence. Hope you don't mind."

"Of course not. He was probably meant to be named Clarence anyway. He just needed you to come along and know that." She glanced at me. "Anyway, tell me how your first night in the cabin was."

"It was wonderful. I slept great. The bed is so comfortable." I hesitated. "I'm really grateful, MaryLou, don't think I'm not. But I really do want to earn my keep and I'm still not sure what you expect of me."

MaryLou concentrated on the road. We were nearing the outskirts of the small city and traffic was getting heavier. Finally, she shrugged. "Don't worry about it. Just live in the cabin. Make sure the property's okay. And, I don't know, maybe fix stuff that needs it." She smiled broadly. "You see how perfect it is? You have a home and now you have a dog. You were meant for each other."

I laughed. "I guess you could put it that way." After all, I'd had a similar thought, although with a less cosmic slant.

MaryLou was always pushing the cosmic plan, the SETII way. When she talked about SETII, her face glowed like a full moon in summer and I wanted to believe her. And yet, life taught me early to be suspicious. A few months after I was born, my mother packed me into a taxi already stuffed with baby blankets, diapers and a Raggedy Ann doll, and delivered me to the two-story house bordered by a white picket fence where her childless sister and brother-in-law lived, my Aunt Elaine and Uncle Mike. The next morning my parents flew to the Orient and then the Philippines and then somewhere else, visiting me only once a year, when they had to come home anyway. It was something to do with business or taxes, I can't recall which. They died in a plane crash, somewhere in the Pacific when I was 12.

Marsha, my mother, was blonde and thin as a movie star. To this day, the merest whiff of Chanel #5 makes me think of her. My father, Arthur Dubin, as in Dubin Lumber, was born with plenty of money to throw away, which is what he did with the entire Dubin fortune. He was slim and elegant, the perfect match for my mother. I always think of him flicking his wrist to check his watch, impatient to be off to the next more exciting event, whatever it might be. I received no inheritance from my parents, neither money nor looks. My hair's dark brown with more and more wiry grey mixed in these days. And I'm 5'3" and pear-shaped. My wide hips and strong legs give me the kind of womanly figure popular in primitive art rather than the anorexic look so highly valued these days.

"We're here," MaryLou said, interrupting my mental trip. "I can hardly wait to show you around SETII."

CHAPTER 4

We parked at the curb in front of a two-story Victorian painted mint green with lavender trim, a surprisingly elegant combination. A wooden sign planted in the front yard announced that SETI, Inc. was on the first floor and Capitol Investment Enterprises was upstairs. The tree-lined street was quiet, although it was only a few blocks to the State Capitol Mall. The shiny gold dome of the State Capitol building was visible over the treetops. I followed MaryLou up the wide front steps of the house, through the open door and into a large vestibule, dimly lit by an ornate fixture on the wall.

"This is it," MaryLou gestured a hand vaguely at the room. Her other hand was busy pawing through her briefcase-sized leather purse. She went to the door immediately on our right. A bronze plaque on the door told me this was the entry for SETII. "Hold on a sec'," MaryLou said. "I can't find my keys." She seized the purse with both hands and bent to peer inside.

I took the opportunity to check things out. The floor was old-fashioned black and white tile. There were puffballs of dust in the corners. Streaks of mud - or something else brown - led to an oak staircase, which took up most of the opposite side of the entry hall. Devin's office was upstairs, but it was gloomy dark and I couldn't see anything past the landing. At the far end of the entry room, there was an oversized door with a thumbtacked sign. Big red letters warned "NO ENTRY." The sign was crooked. A lot of things could hide behind a door like that: - stairs to the basement, a bathroom or something less boring, like a dungeon, a torture chamber or a closet with a skeleton.

The jangle of keys startled me back to reality. MaryLou jabbed a key into the keyhole, jiggling the doorknob with her other hand until the door swung open. "Old-fashioned lock," she said, pulling her keys out and dropping them carelessly into her purse. "I think the only person it keeps out is me."

The door opened into a reception area, furnished with a beige metal file cabinet, a gray secretary's chair on wheels and a large desk of uncertain wood. A telephone with lots of buttons, a computer monitor and keyboard and a fax machine all waited quietly on the desk. A few uncomfortable-looking chairs lined the wall to the side of the desk. The room's best feature, in addition to the old oak flooring, was a floor-to-ceiling window behind the desk. With a wide view of the backyard, the window let in lots of natural light, even on this cloudy day.

"Come see my office," MaryLou said, leading me down a narrow hallway and into a spacious room done in Martha Stewart pastels. A large, shabby chic couch and some oversized upholstered chairs were grouped around an oak desk.

"Nice," I said. "You did a great job of decorating."

MaryLou nodded, distracted by a note she'd picked up from her desk. She stared at the small square of memo paper, biting thoughtfully at her lower lip. "I've got a call to make," she said. "Listen, you wait for me in the outer office and then I'll take you around and introduce you to everybody. Okay?" Without waiting for my answer, she picked up the receiver.

I went back down the hallway to the reception room, feeling strangely claustrophobic. On the desk the telephone blinked busily. The array of buttons and choices puzzled me. I was seriously lacking in technological savvy. I'd never faxed, e-mailed or surfed the internet. My jobs taught me other things. I knew about dogs. I learned about good wine waiting tables at a pricey Seattle restaurant. When I clerked at a bookstore, I learned to speed read between customers. Once, many years ago, I worked almost a whole season for a greenhouse operation in Southern Oregon, tending baby marijuana plants. The job ended after a week when my boss, a 21-year old rich kid from L.A., got busted. Luckily, the police chose my day off to surround the property, confiscate thousands of seedlings and arrest everyone they found. Unluckily, I never got paid. That job taught me it was better to stay legal.

"Ruby. Come meet everyone." MaryLou stood in the doorway. "I know you'll like them," she said, as she led the way. "They're all wonderful, wonderful people."

We went out to the vestibule. It was brighter now that a light was on upstairs. MaryLou opened the NO ENTRY door and gestured for me to follow. Laughter and the buttery smell of microwave popcorn wafted down a short corridor. I almost crashed into MaryLou when she stopped abruptly at the entry to a large, old-fashioned kitchen. The room seemed spacious even though it contained lots of cupboards and shelves and racks of pots and pans. There was also a banquet-sized table with a dozen or more straight-back chairs. A few people – two women and a man - were clustered at the far end of the table, chattering happily. At the sink, a grey-haired woman was bent over a stack of dirty dishes.

"Everybody, everybody." MaryLou held her right palm up. The noise stopped. I was struck by the way they all held the same attentive posture, the same polite smile. Even the woman at the sink shut off the faucet, wiped her hands on a towel, and stood quietly, listening. It was easy to figure out MaryLou was the boss here.

MaryLou put an arm around me, gently forcing me to stand beside her. "Ruby, this is the crew. Guys, this is Ruby, my new friend."

I flushed, warmed all over by her words and embarrassed to reveal such emotion.

Pointing to each of the people circling us, MaryLou made introductions. "Laura is the best idea person in the world," she said, gesturing at the short blonde woman on the left. MaryLou pointed at the other woman, a tall blonde. "And Janet knows about all the technical stuff." She swiveled her head, obviously searching for someone. "Where's Sondra?"

For a moment, I thought she meant the woman by the sink. I wondered why she hadn't been introduced yet.

"She's not here," Laura offered. Her voice was high and girlish.

"She doesn't usually come in this early," Janet said. Although her face revealed nothing, there was something in her tone of voice that made me think Janet didn't care much for Sondra, whoever she was.

"Oh well." MaryLou waved her hand. "You'll meet her later." She pointed at the man.

"Don't forget her," the man said. He nodded in the direction of the sink, where the gray-haired woman was once again scrubbing dishes.

"Oh. Sorry. Over there," MaryLou gestured, "is one of our SETII Betties. That one's Jaqi, I think."

The woman didn't turn around. Maybe she couldn't hear over the sound of the water splashing into the sink.

"And then there's moi," said the man, filling the awkward silence. "Barry Adams at your service," he added, bending to the waist in an elaborate bow. He was slim, medium height, with trimmed light brown hair and a face that was interesting more than it was handsome.

"And Barry. I would die without Barry. He writes my sermons."

I stiffened. "Sermons? Are you some kind of church?"

"No, no, no." The four-part harmony of denial was accompanied by synchronized headshakes and gestures. It was like watching a rock and roll group: MaryLou and The Crew.

"SETII is different." MaryLou's voice trembled with sincerity. "We seek to reclaim the power that belongs to each and every one of us. We call my messages a sermon because it's a word most people understand." Behind her, Barry, Janet, Laura, even the SETII Betty at the sink, nodded their agreement in a silent chorus.

As if MaryLou had cleared up my confusion, I nodded too. Personally, I wanted nothing more than to be done with the conversation. Alarms sounded in my brain, signaling escape time. This wasn't my kind of scene. I calculated the likelihood of finding my way back to the cabin to claim Clarence and my car. Not good. I hadn't paid enough attention to the route MaryLou took. I'd have to survive the day, get a ride back with MaryLou. I would leave in the evening. Better yet, I could enjoy one more night in that bed and leave first thing tomorrow morning.

"Back to work, all of you. Break's over." Devin appeared in the doorway at the other end of the room, his face twisted angrily. "We don't pay you to stand around doing nothing`."

Without a word, Janet and Laura and the older woman scuttled from the room like frightened mice, rushing past Devin with their heads turned to avoid eye contact. Barry followed more slowly. When he got to the doorway, he turned and extended his middle finger, pointing at Devin's back. Wondering how she'd react, I glanced at MaryLou. Like me, she stood facing Devin and she must have seen Barry's angry gesture. Her face revealed nothing.

"Who're you?" Devin glared at me. I took an involuntary step back, as if he'd shoved me.

"It's Ruby," MaryLou said. "You met her yesterday. She's staying at the cabin. Remember?"

"Yeah, yeah." Devin dismissed me with a shrug of his shoulders. "Listen, MaryLou. We've got to talk. Have you heard from him yet?"

MaryLou caught my eye and gave a helpless shrug. "Sorry, Ruby. Let me just give Devin a quick heads-up on some things."

Devin sighed and made a show of checking the time on his watch. "I haven't got all day." Emphasizing his point, he turned and left the room.

"I'll be up right away," Mary Lou called after him. I expected her to rush me back to the office area. Instead, she stood, staring at the empty doorway as if she could make Devin reappear. I was kind of glad she couldn't.

As if reading my mind, MaryLou sighed and turned to me. "You'll have to forgive Devin," she said. "He's under so much stress right now. He's not sleeping, not eating." She shook her head, raised her arms and combed her fingers through the frizzy hair. "I don't know. He's been impatient with all of us, even Devinda." Then she brightened, her eyes regaining a glow that colored her irises a rich purple-brown, matching the color of her jacket. "It'll work out. He's just breaking through another personal boundary and that can be a difficult time."

Personal boundary? Breaking through? If that was another way of saying Devin was an asshole, I agreed.

MaryLou glanced at her wristwatch. "We'll have lots of time before we have to pick up Devinda and Lyman and deliver them to soccer practice. And don't worry. I haven't forgotten my promise to give you a tour of Salem. I especially want to show the best places to go shopping."

She ushered me back to the small office. "I'll just be a minute," she said, darting out of the room. Moments later, I heard her pounding up the stairs.

I sat on the chair and twirled around to look out the window at the empty back yard. After awhile, I stared at the blank walls and I studied the zigzag path of a crack on the ceiling. I imagined a giant child drawing the line with a fine-tip pen. The shrill insistence of the telephone interrupted my reverie. It rang again. And again. I've never been able to resist a telephone ring. Gingerly, I pushed the button with the blinking light and picked up the receiver. "Good morning. SETII offices."

"MaryLou Hunter, please."

"Let me see if she's available," I said, thinking fast. "May I tell her who's calling?"

"Just tell her Sykes," he snapped. "She'll want to talk with me."

I formed my reply carefully, trying to sound as if I knew what I was doing. "Please hold. I'll see if I can reach her." My pointer finger hovered over the buttons like a UFO over the desert. Cautiously, I pressed HOLD, scanning the board for the next logical step. There it was - a red button labeled INTCOM. I held my breath and pressed the button firmly.

"Yes?"

Shit. It was Devin. "A Mr. Sykes for MaryLou. On line one."

Without a word, Devin cut me off. I sat and watched the line one button flicker brightly. It was fifteen minutes before the light faded. In the room above, there was a scream and then heavy footsteps. Was Devin pissed off again? Was he coming downstairs to yell at me? Maybe he was angry at me for forwarding the call. I sat behind the desk, uncertain what else to do. I was surprised when it was MaryLou who swooped into the office. She came up to the chair and gathered me in her arms.

"Ruby," she said, squeezing tightly, "I can do the show now, thanks to Mister."

Abruptly, she stopped talking and pulled away from me. The way her head tilted and her eyebrows contracted, I could almost hear her thinking about what to say. I knew when she figured it out too. I watched her face spread into a wide smile.

"Benefactor," she said. "Thanks to my benefactor. And you are my personal angel."

"Personal angel? What do you mean?" I resisted her enthusiasm. I felt suspicious again. What show was she talking about? And why did she hesitate to say the man's name? Stripes? Strikes? Sykes. That was it.

"You answered the phone."

I shrugged. "So?"

"Listen to me. We were going to ignore the phone because Devin didn't want any interruptions. But once again, you were the catalyst. You literally answered the call." MaryLou reached to give my cheek a gentle touch. "You were meant to be here, surely you can see that?"

I looked at her, unsure what to say. Was it cosmic that I'd answered the telephone because the ring of an unanswered phone makes me crazy, because I had nothing else to do, because I was trying to be helpful? "I thought maybe the call was for me," I said, hoping humor would shift the mood.

"I think it was, in a way," she said. "A call for you to stay here."

I shook my head. "I don't know."

MaryLou squeezed my arm. "If you weren't meant to be here, you'd be somewhere else."

I could tell she thought she'd said something wise and compelling. Personally, it was so illogical and yet so endearing that it gave me the giggles.

Taken aback at my laughter, MaryLou let go of my arm. She took a step back, somehow lost her footing and fell, hard enough to break a hip.

"MaryLou." I jumped up. The office chair skittered away on its wheels like a frightened animal. "Are you okay?"

"Yes, yes. I'm okay," she reassured me, struggling to push herself up. I offered her my hands and helped her to her feet. "You see how much I need you," she said, when we stood facing each other. "Thanks for the hand up."

"That goes both ways," I answered, thinking of Clarence and the cabin.

"Hi." We both swiveled our heads. Barry was standing in the doorway.

"Ah. Thank you, Barry," MaryLou said. She turned to me again. "I'm going be tied up for a bit so I asked Barry to show you around Salem, maybe take you to a grocery store. Whatever you need." She pressed a papery wad into my hand. I glanced down, saw it was folded bills, with a fifty on top. "Consider this an advance, to get you started." More hugs, one for me and one for Barry, and MaryLou fluttered from the room with no evidence she'd taken a hard fall to the floor only minutes before.

I turned to look at Barry. He offered me a toothy grin I wasn't sure how to interpret. Hand on my hip and arching an eyebrow, I gave him my Mae West imitation. "Hello, big boy. I understand you're my chauffeur." I winked. "Want to take me for a ride?"

"Don't mind if I do, don't mind if I do." His W.C. Fields drawl was right on.

I relaxed, in the same way a gazelle might let down her guard enough to graze the savannah while still keeping watch for the approach of hungry lions. One more mention of church, one more unpleasant encounter with Devin or one more anything else that came along and I'd take flight. For the time being, I'd maintain my policy of going with the flow. Or in this case, going with Barry.

CHAPTER 5

We took Barry's car, a red Mazda RX 7. As soon as we got in the car, he pulled open the ashtray to reveal a small ceramic pipe nestled inside. "Smoke?"

Surprised, but not unpleasantly, I took the pipe and plastic lighter he offered. The bowl of the pipe was cold when I cradled it in my palm. The car headed across the railroad tracks towards the center of town. We passed the pipe back and forth a few times along with meaningless chatter about the weather, which was moist and gray.

Just before we got to the Capitol Mall, Barry tucked the pipe away in the ashtray. I looked out the window as we rolled past the dignified government buildings. This was an off-year for the legislature which only meets in odd-numbered years, a fact I remembered from a sixth grade class trip to visit the Capitol. On the sidewalks, dark-suited women and men scurried along, toting bulging briefcases. They were outnumbered by clusters of scruffy homeless people and Goth street kids huddled by the steam venting from the building basements. Barry turned right, onto High Street. We drove along the edge of a large park. In the gray light, the stark branches of the trees looked burned and blackened.

"Hey," Barry said, pulling my attention back inside the car. "You won't tell MaryLou, will you?" He nodded his chin at the closed ashtray. "I mean, I believe in her and all, but you know how it is." He smiled wickedly. "We have to have our little secrets, don't we?"

I laughed at the exaggerated expression on his face. "I won't say a word. But maybe you can explain something."

"Sure." He glanced at me expectantly.

"What is SETII anyway? Is MaryLou some kind of preacher? And Devin, what's with him? Why is he so cranky?" My curiosity spilled over, threatening to drown Barry in a flood of questions.

"Whoa, one at a time." Barry flipped the blinker for a left, waited for several cars to pass, and turned into the parking lot of a large grocery store. "Ross Markets. They're fabulous," he said. He pulled into a parking spot and switched off the engine. "Now." He swiveled in the driver's seat and faced me. "Here's the deal. SETII is a way of thinking, a way to understand that we need chaos to create energy, and we need the truth to achieve infinity."

"Oh dear. I don't think I understood a word you just said."

He laughed. "Don't worry," he said. "You'll see. MaryLou's just incredible, a totally positive force of energy." Barry lowered his voice, even though it was just the two of us crowded into the little red car. "If you ask me, Devin's lucky MaryLou is his life partner. He needs her help so he can evolve from his darkness." Barry leaned forward. "And if you think Devin is uptight, wait until you meet Sondra."

"Who's Sondra?"

"Devin's sister. And MaryLou's assistant." He rolled his eyes. "Total chaos."

I nodded. I'd encouraged his gossip, thinking maybe I could glean some useful information. Unfortunately, like MaryLou, he had a large vocabulary of vague words. Personally, the world would be a better place if people said what they meant without hiding behind a bunch of abstractions. Or maybe I was stoned. I tried again. "So, is MaryLou a counselor?"

"Not exactly. She's really more like a guide who wants to share the insights she's gained. See, MaryLou is just way more advanced than most of us. And she's willing to share her knowledge so we can all evolve to a higher plane."

It didn't sound much different from the promises made by the preachers Aunt Elaine used to watch on daytime TV. Different words, same song. I decided to pursue a different question. "Do you know who Sykes is?"

Barry shook his head. "Uh uh."

"What about this show MaryLou's going to do. Do you know about that?"

"Sure do." Barry's face grew animated. His thick eyebrows moved up and down like dancing caterpillars. "MaryLou just found out she's going to have a show on Channel Twelve. Twelve is such a celestial number. Can you believe it?"

"Amazing." It was hard to be sarcastic with someone like Barry. His enthusiasm for SETII made him deaf to my cynicism. Besides, I couldn't help thinking back to yesterday. I couldn't deny I'd experienced something of MaryLou's special energy. She'd looked into my eyes and somehow known just what I needed. MaryLou had offered me a chance to start over. Like something in a fairy tale, she'd given me a dog and a key to the cabin in the woods.

"We'd better get moving," Barry reminded me. We got out of the car and walked across the parking lot to the market without saying anything more to each other. We both grabbed plastic baskets from the stack alongside the door and agreed to meet back at the car in a half-hour. Barry headed for the bakery. I grabbed a few basics, like peanut-butter, bread and eggs and then went searching for coffee, which I eventually discovered at the far corner of the store, near the beer and wine. I was still pondering whether to splurge on a bag of Alligheri's Italian Roast when Barry found me.

"Sorry I took so long," he said. "I had a hard time choosing." His basket was heaped with two bottles of champagne, a box of gourmet crackers, several packages of cheese and a small, pink bakery box. "Going to celebrate tonight. Just me and someone special." He wiggled his eyebrows comically. "The food's for after we celebrate. If you know what I mean."

"I vaguely remember about that stuff."

He smiled. "We'd better get moving. I need to get you back to MaryLou so I can get there before . . . ." Abruptly, Barry stopped talking and hesitated a few moments before he finished the sentence. "Before my special someone comes home." I thought it was strange, as if he'd either forgotten the special someone's name or was afraid to say it.

On the drive back, I decided I liked Barry. He had a deep voice, the kind used in car commercials because it sounds fatherly and reassuring. He was over the top about SETII but he had a playful side and a twinkle in his eyes. With his contradictions, he'd become a real person to me, instead of just one of MaryLou's Crew.

We got to the SETII office just in time to meet MaryLou coming out the front door. "We're late," she said, bustling down the sidewalk. "Sorry, Barry, no time to talk."

I tossed a quick thanks and wishes for a great celebration at Barry and rushed to catch up with MaryLou, the bag of food bouncing against my side. We reached the SUV at the same time. MaryLou's arm was thrust elbow-deep into her purse, digging for her keys. "Got them," she said, jangling the keys victoriously.

Unlike the morning's casual, one-handed drive, MaryLou raced the SUV across town as if she'd attended the Tonya Harding School of Aggressive Driving. Tonya was the '94 Olympic figure skater from Oregon who took the concept of winning-at-all-costs to a horrible extreme by having her competitor's legs hacked. I found myself white-knuckling the door handle until we veered onto a side street and came to a wrenching halt at the end of a long line of cars and trucks.

We were parked in front of Hoover Elementary School, a prison-like structure apparently designed by people who believed windows distract children from learning. A bell trilled. Kids swarmed out of the squat brick building onto the sidewalks and around the waiting vehicles.

"There she is. There's Devinda." MaryLou gestured at the waif-like child slouched in front of the flagpole. With an impatient sigh, MaryLou climbed out of the SUV and yoo-hooed loudly until she caught Devinda's attention.

The little girl was less enthusiastic than her mother. Slowly, she made her way to the SUV, a jacket dragging on the ground behind her. Her light brown hair was half-in and half-out of a ponytail clip. She was wearing turquoise pedal pushers, a yellow tee-shirt and Nike tennis shoes with no socks. Her clothes were filthy, as if she'd been rolling in the mud at recess time. Or maybe she'd been in a fight.

MaryLou didn't seem to notice. "Hurry up," she urged. "We're late for picking up your brother. It's soccer today."

"I didn't want to walk on the grass." Devinda's tone of voice was more Red Queen than seven-year old girl. "Grass is a living thing, just like us. Would you want someone walking on you?"

"It was very considerate of you to walk on the sidewalk, Devinda. But you could have walked faster." MaryLou slid behind the wheel, turning the key and the steering wheel almost simultaneously. The engine made a grinding noise and the SUV jerked forward, cutting diagonally across the two-lane street to make a sharp left at the end of the block, miraculously without killing us or anyone else.

"Mom. Tomorrow can I take the bus?" Devinda's voice was annoyingly whiney but I couldn't blame her for asking.

"Now, Devinda. We've had this discussion. Daddy doesn't want you riding the bus. It's not safe." MaryLou swiveled her head to look at Devinda in the back seat. "Devinda, you haven't said hello to Ruby. Where are your manners?"

I gave Devinda a friendly smile just as the SUV drifted into the right lane, cutting off a powder blue BMW. The Beemer's horn blasted a long complaint. My heart did aerobics as the SUV lurched to the left, correcting course. MaryLou stayed calm, staring through the windshield as if nothing had happened. "Devinda," she said, after another block or so. "I'm still waiting." At least this time she didn't turn her head.

After a few seconds, Devinda muttered a begrudging hello without as much as a glance in my direction. Instead, the little girl aimed angry eyes at MaryLou's back.

Lyman was waiting alone on the sidewalk in front of the middle school. He piled into the back of the SUV, smelling of sweat and bubble gum. He blew a pink bubble and eyed me cautiously. "Snoopy okay?"

"He's not Snoopy anymore," MaryLou chirped. "You'll never guess what his name is now."

"I decided to call him Clarence," I said.

Lyman stared at me.

"That's a stupid name," Devinda said.

Soccer practice was held at Bush Park, the same beautiful expanse of lawn and trees I'd admired earlier. As soon as the SUV stopped, the kids jumped out and ran off, heading for the bleachers and clumps of people I could see in the distance. MaryLou opened the door on her side. "I'd better stay with them until Devin gets here. He can bring the kids home."

"No problem. I'll just wait here." I leaned back against the seat and closed my eyes. I must have dozed off or I wouldn't have been startled by the rapping on the window. I jerked forward, breathless and pumped full of adrenaline, ready to defend myself from the moon-faced specter on the other side of the SUV window. I rubbed my eyes, trying to focus them.

"What do you want?" I called through the window.

The figure stepped back. She was a stout woman and short, maybe even shorter than me. Her long, dark hair was streaked with gray and she had on a white silky shirt and purple harem pants that didn't do a thing for her figure. Big breasts hung low on her chest, like an old peasant woman's. She made a megaphone of her hands. "Who're you?"

I opened the door and got out of the SUV. "I asked first," I said, smiling to soften my words.

She folded her arms across her chest and gave me a sharp, appraising look. "Sondra," she said. "Sondra Hunter. Who're you?"

Ah ha! The dreadful Sondra. I told her my name but didn't offer any more information.

Sondra started playing Twenty Questions. "You a friend of MaryLou's? I haven't seen you around before."

"We just met recently."

"Oh. Where're you from?"

I told her Portland, which is where I was born. She was framing another question when MaryLou showed up. The two women hugged. MaryLou's stylish outfit and well-groomed hair were a dramatic contrast to Sondra's messy retro look.

"I see you've met my new caretaker," MaryLou said.

"What about Cowboy?"

MaryLou dismissed Sondra's concern with an arm wave. "Cowboy's gone."

"He'll be back. He always comes back." Sondra turned to me. "You think you're up to caretaking 200 acres?" Her tone of voice made it obvious she didn't think so.

"Sondra. Ruby's already had her interview."

Sondra stepped back and lifted her hands, palms facing out. "Okay. It's your place, your decision." Again, her tone suggested the opposite, that she didn't think much of MaryLou's choice.

MaryLou smiled, either blind to Sondra's attitude or ignoring it. "We'd better get going," she said. "See you Sunday?"

We got back in the SUV and headed south, down the boulevard. "Sondra means well," MaryLou said, as we moved through rush hour traffic. "I feel sorry for her." She maneuvered the SUV into the right lane. "Her son Dustin was about Lyman's age when he died." She cleared her throat.

"How sad."

MaryLou flipped the blinkers and turned right, onto a narrow road that wound its way up a hill. "Drugs. Nobody knows what happened exactly, except he was high. He stole a motorcycle, took it on the highway and drove head-on into a truck."

No wonder Sondra was difficult. How heartbreaking to lose a child. I wondered about Dustin's story: Bad Seed? Or bad choices combined with bad luck? Whenever I'd misbehave, Aunt Elaine would say I was born to be bad, cursed by the genes of my wayward parents. Maybe that's the reason I never had children. Too late now, despite those tabloid headlines about post-menopausal women giving birth.

MaryLou and I were silent the rest of the trip. When the SUV pulled into the driveway by the cabin, our goodbyes were subdued. I took my bag of groceries and watched the SUV drive away. Suddenly it skidded to a stop. The driver's side window rolled open. MaryLou's head poked out. "Don't forget," she shouted. "Dinner with us on Sunday." The window closed and the SUV headed down the road. Trudging up the path, I puzzled over my day. Being in a new situation was like watching a play unfold, line by line, scene by scene, until the full story finally emerged. Did I dare hope for a happy ending this time?

Midway up the path, I lifted my head to look at the cabin. Yikes! I almost dropped the grocery bag. A man. He was crossing the cabin porch. He was reaching for the doorknob. My heart pounded in panic. "Who're you?" I yelled.

The man swiveled to look at me. "Well, hello, darlin'." He offered me a Texas-sized smile. "Cowboy. Who're you?"

As soon as he introduced himself, I recognized him from the Alice XXOO photograph in the bedroom. I went up the path, climbed the steps and stood across from him. He had Paul Newman eyes, blue and brave and sexy, and his sun-bleached hair was pure Robert Redford. I couldn't help the tickle of interest I felt, looking at him.

"Ruby," I told him. I met his gaze straight on, giving him a pleasant smile but nothing too friendly. He might be sexy but he might also want to reclaim residency in the cabin. "You must've come to get your things."

He frowned. "Get my things?"

As usual when I'm nervous, words tumbled from my mouth. "MaryLou said I could be the caretaker because you were moving out. And you're getting married."

"Nope. Didn't work out." The scowl on his face warned me not to say anything more. After a moment of silence between us, he rubbed his chin thoughtfully. "Looks like you and me got a problem."

Clarence chose that moment to start barking loudly. Probably he'd awakened and remembered he was supposed to be guarding the place. From the other side of the thick wall, he sounded mean as a junkyard Doberman.

Cowboy had been reaching to open the door but he yanked his hand back as if the knob was burning hot. "What kinda' monster you got inside?"

"Clarence, it's okay, boy. It's okay." Gingerly, I pushed the door open. When he saw me, Clarence stopped. He gave a token growl at the man behind me and then sat, tongue lolling from his mouth. "What a good boy," I told him. I set the bag of groceries down and knelt to pet Clarence, holding onto his collar just in case. "You can come in now," I called to Cowboy.

He walked in, ducking his head automatically as he came through the door. "Well, shoot," he said. "It's Snoopy."

I let go of the collar and stood. Clarence got up, walked over to Cowboy and sniffed loudly at his boots. "His name is Clarence now," I said.

Crouching in front of Clarence, Cowboy rested one big hand on the dog's head. "Seems to like his new name better. Don' cha' big boy?" Cowboy's long fingers began to scratch Clarence between the ears, the way you do with most dogs. Not bulldogs named Clarence. Clarence Two turned in a half-circle, finishing with his back to Cowboy.

"He wants you to scratch him on his favorite spot, right above the tail," I said.

Cowboy applied his fingers to the task. After a bit, he looked up at me, blue eyes glittering. A smile lurked at the corner of his mouth. "You can be next, if you want."

"I don't think so," I said, not friendly, not hostile.

"No," he said. "Not funny. Sorry." Cowboy stood up.

Clarence sat down.

"Sorry, ol' boy," Cowboy said. "I guess I'm just a sorry kinda guy. I'm thinkin' it ain't fair for me to show up and kick you out when I tol' MaryLou I was leavin' for good." He looked at me with those sexy eyes. "If you don't mind, I'll just grab a few things for tonight. I can get the rest of my gear later."

A sigh of relief escaped my lips. "Thank you. I love being here." Not to mention I had nowhere else to go.

He gave me a sideways look that might have meant "How could you not?" but he didn't say it aloud.

"Look," I said. "Would you like some coffee?" I picked up the bag and waved it in the air like a little flag of surrender. I knew I had to watch myself or I'd end up doing something stupid, like offering him the cabin back.

"How 'bout something better 'n coffee? I got some good red stashed in the bedroom closet." He was already moving in that direction, his long legs carrying him across the living room in a few strides. I followed after and found him on his hands and knees, rummaging on the floor of the closet, his rather nice, tight butt facing in my direction.

I leaned against the doorjamb, wondering about a cowboy who liked wine. A few seconds later a muffled but triumphant cry came from the closet and then Cowboy himself emerged and stood up, holding a bottle of wine in each hand. "A California syrah," he said, "and a Willamette Valley pinot noir. Your pick."

We ended up emptying both bottles, starting with the pinot. For supper, we shared the syrah, peanut butter on saltine crackers and a lot of laughs. It was 9:00 PM when Cowboy finally pushed his chair from the table and stood up, saying he'd better be going and would come back the next day with his truck.

I felt a guilty panic. Thanks to me, Cowboy was temporarily homeless, and I knew from my recent experience that being homeless was the worst.

"Don' worry, darlin'," he assured me, as if he'd channeled my thoughts. "Devin and me are ol' buddies. I'll just crash on his living room couch." We walked out on the porch. It was a crisp night with a clear sky and plenty of moonlight. I offered him a flashlight. He said he'd walked the path to the Hunter house at night plenty of times. Even so, I almost invited him to spend the night when he leaned down to brush my mouth softly with his lips. "G'night darlin'," he whispered.

Despite Clarence's comforting snores, I tossed and turned in the big bed for a long while, thinking about Cowboy, replaying the evening. I alternated between horny fantasies and nervous worries. Towards morning, I became

41

convinced Devin would convince MaryLou to change her mind so that Cowboy could be caretaker again. The faint light of morning showed through the window. I wished time would stop. It didn't and neither did the pressure in my bladder. I threw back the covers and swung my legs to the floor.

CHAPTER 6

After several cups of coffee and a slice of toast smeared with chunky peanut butter, I decided to go for a long walk with Clarence. Despite the foggy morning, I was eager to explore the property and reluctant to be in the cabin when Cowboy showed up. I launched a frenzied search for Clarence's leash, scouting through the rooms, digging through couch pillows, peering under the bed, until I remembered stuffing the leather strap in my purse. It was like the forgetfulness of childhood, when I searched endlessly for toys that vanished and magically reappeared.

Clarence tolerated my fumbling while I figured out how to clip the leash to his collar. He'd been well-trained by someone. I wondered if one of the Hunters had been patient enough to teach him. He heeled without being told as we headed around the back of the cabin and followed a narrow deer path through a dense stand of trees. I had the eerie feeling I had stepped into an enchanted forest. Wisps of fog flitted between the trees like vague ghosts. More than once, I had to dodge low-hanging branches that grabbed at my hair. It was cold and creepy and I almost turned back.

The path climbed higher and higher and suddenly there was blue sky and sunshine. Up here the air was crisp and smelled of mud and composted leaves. I knew that underneath the goop, pale green shoots were starting their reach for the surface. The thought made me smile. As we walked along, I listened to my steady breathing and Clarence's asthmatic huffing. Somewhere above us a woodpecker cackled triumphantly.

After a time, the path's jigs and jogs led us back to the paved road, maybe a mile or so above the cabin. The road dead-ended here, in a flat, wide circle almost on the crest of the hill. Clarence and I paused to catch our breath and admire the view. Above us, there was the large blue sky and a few ragged clouds. A small plane buzzed in the distance, heading for the Salem airport. The fog had lifted from the valley floor and I could see a checkerboard of brown and green

43

fields encircled by the wide, meandering channel of the Willamette River. I couldn't remember the last time I'd felt so healthy and at peace with myself.

The walk back to the cabin along the paved road was steep and made my knees ache. At the driveway, I tightened my hold on Clarence's leash, wanting to approach cautiously. There was no sign of Cowboy until I went up on the porch and saw the note scotch-taped to the front door. I read it aloud to Clarence. "Thanks Ruby. See you at the Hunters for Sunday dinner." *Damn.* I'd forgotten about the dinner invitation from MaryLou. Sticking the note in my pocket, I went inside.

At first glance, everything was in place, nothing had changed. A more careful search revealed that Cowboy had removed all his stuff from the drawers and the closet. He hadn't forgotten the wine either, or the photo from beside the bed. The bathroom medicine chest was emptied but he'd left a robe hanging from the door hook. To my surprise, he'd added a few things. On the kitchen table, there was a bouquet of carnations wrapped in plastic, the kind you buy at a supermarket. Next to the flowers, there was a folded newspaper and a twenty-four ounce cup of latte from a local designer-bean coffee shack.

My heart made a little blip. He likes me, I thought, and immediately scolded myself. Getting involved with someone would only complicate my attempt at a new life. Besides, a history of wrong men had me leery of starting up with anyone, let alone falling in love.

Donnie was my first big heartbreak. We got married a year after I came to work in his waterbed store on East Burnside in Portland. Two years later we split up when I found out he was shtupping all the new saleswomen he kept hiring. Of course, that was how he and I first hooked up, so I don't know what I expected.

I was twenty-eight when I moved to Seattle, found an office job and met Bob. We stayed married almost seventeen years, our relationship drifting from obsessive togetherness to compatible boredom, until he left a message on our home phone to say he was going to Mexico and never coming back. My tears dried fast when I discovered that Bob had cleaned out our bank account, leaving me only a load of unpaid bills and a second mortgage on the house. I hung on as long as I could, but when I lost my job at ARF, it was a quick slide to down and out.

I finished arranging the carnations in a mason jar filled with water and took a sip of the latte. It was still hot and delivered a strong jolt of espresso, the way I like it. Oh well, I thought. Flirtation is good for the ego. Just keep it simple and don't get tangled up with another Nowhere Man.

Underneath the table, Clarence snored contentedly, his head resting on my feet. I settled back in the kitchen chair and picked up the *Statesman-Journal*. The front page of the newspaper was all sadness and horror: murders, robberies, train wrecks, little wars here and there around the globe. I scanned several articles: "Local School VP Arrested for Bilking District in Computer Scandal," "More Bodies Found in Apartment Building," "Earthquake Toll at 51." Sighing, I spread the *Statesman* on the table, smoothing the newspaper so it was flat as a tablecloth. The inside page was headlined "Good News to Start Your Day." Fortified with a sip of frothy latte, I bent closer to study the stories. One article was about a five-year old boy finding a diamond ring in his sandbox. Another was about a neighborhood work group building a playground at a local park. Next to it was a photo and story about the newly named Man of the Year.

I gaped at the grainy picture. After all those years, Uncle Mike was smiling up at me. I'd found Uncle Mike in the morning news.

In the photograph, Uncle Mike was older, grayer, and somehow kinder-looking than I remembered. Maybe it was the grin spread across his face that softened his features from the stern countenance of my memories. I scanned the article: Governor's award, founded Kid's Place, hundreds of youth turned their lives around, storefront school for homeless youth, civic leaders praise, kids adore. The photo caption quoted the hero: "Every kid matters. Giving up on a kid is giving up on tomorrow."

I had the dizzying sense I'd been dropped into an alternate reality where up was down and down was sideways, where Uncle Mike, ogre of my youth, was Uncle Mike, Hero of the Year.

Impulsively, I jumped up to get the phone book I'd seen on a kitchen counter shelf near the phone. Salem isn't populated like Los Angeles or New York or even Portland, so the book was only a couple inches thick. There was a column full of Lewises, from Albert to William. Three of the listings were Michaels but two of them were for Michael D. Lewis, D.D.S. with one listing for home and the other for his office. I stared at the line for Michael M. Lewis, at 33145 Hopewell Road. Uncle Mike.

I jotted the address and telephone number on a small slip of paper and tucked it in my jeans pocket. If he was the man I remembered, I wasn't sure I wanted to see my uncle. My uncle, with his questioning eyebrows, his frown of disapproval. My aunt had been over-protective, almost smothering. When she died, I caught the scent of what I thought was freedom. I resented Uncle Mike's attempts to rein me in. I was a captured princess. He was the monster who held me.

But people change. I wasn't that silly girl anymore. If Uncle Mike was Man of the Year, apparently he'd turned into a great guy. Or maybe he was that way all along and I'd been the monster. The very idea made the coffee turn to acid in my gut. I set the cup on the table and saw that my hand was trembling.

I spent the rest of the day and most of Sunday cleaning the cabin, making it my own. I started a list of things to do and stuff to buy, like something to get rid of the mold ringing the bathtub and more food than just peanut butter and bread. By the time the winter dusk fell, I was ready for my pajamas. Instead of bed, though, I had a dinner invitation. I took a quick shower and got dressed in my last semi-clean sweater from the suitcase. I wasn't brave enough to try the path over the creek at night so I drove down the hill. I left Clarence behind, figuring he wouldn't be enthusiastic about a reunion with the Hunters.

I wasn't looking forward to the experience either. I would have to dance carefully through the evening. I'd waltz around Devin's unpleasantness and side-step Cowboy. With MaryLou, I would dance a traditional folk dance - lean in, circle, pull away – because I was charmed by her and suspicious at the same time.

The driveway was empty. In spite of myself, I was disappointed that Cowboy's truck wasn't there. I parked and followed the flagstone path to the house and the covered porch that sheltered the entry. A dim light over the door revealed a small area littered with tennis shoes of all sizes. I picked my way through them and rapped my knuckles on the door, twice. Before I could deliver the third knock, I heard the rattle and snap of the lock being unbolted. The door opened a few inches. Devinda's pale face appeared in the slit.

"You can't come in," she said, her little-girl voice sour as spoiled milk. "Mommy went to the store. And you can't come in."

I glanced around, searching for a place to sit or something to lean against, pretending not to notice the meanness in her voice. "I'll wait out here."

"No. You can't stay here."

I shrugged. "Okay. I'll go sit in my car." I took a few steps and then turned, thinking I heard the little girl's voice. "What?"

"Jesus hates you," she hissed. "Jesus hates you and you're going to hell." The door clicked shut.

The brat had cursed and condemned me. I kicked at one of the small tennis shoes near my feet and fantasized revenge. I imagined forcing my way into the house to tell her off. Somehow, my words would transform Devinda into a sweet, cooperative, angel-faced child. Then I pictured the little girl's pinched face and the way she stood waiting for MaryLou after school, quiet and alone amidst the shrill energy of the other children. My anger faded. I picked up the shoe and dropped it near its mate.

I'd been back at the cabin a full hour before MaryLou called, wanting to know when I was coming.

"Didn't Devinda tell you I was there earlier?"

"No, no she didn't." My ear filled with MaryLou's shrill call for Devinda to come to the kitchen. After a moment or so, MaryLou sighed. "I don't know where she's gone to. Probably upstairs with her brother." MaryLou sighed. "She can be a bit difficult sometimes."

I murmured something sympathetic. All the while, Devinda's sad face shimmered in my mind's eye.

"Listen," MaryLou said. "Devin just called to say he and Cowboy were running late and they'd get dinner out. And Sondra can't make it either. Would you mind if I came up to the cabin for a while? I've got Thai take-out and a bottle of wine. The kids will be happy with a frozen pizza in front of the TV."

A few minutes later, MaryLou's new Chevy Suburban roared up the road and into the driveway. When she came into the cabin, the normally lethargic Clarence rose from his spot on the carpet and trotted into the bedroom. I figured Clarence was using the avoidance technique. No point in tempting MaryLou to take him back home. He stayed out of sight until she left, sometime after 11:00 PM. As soon as the door clicked shut, he ambled into the front room to snuffle at my shoes and pants, the dog version of finding out what's been going on. Apparently he was satisfied. He collapsed to the floor, heaved a great sigh and began snoring softly.

Maneuvering around Clarence, I cleared away cartons of Thai food, wine glasses and dirty plates, all the while thinking about the evening. It had been way too long since I'd enjoyed the give and take of conversation between girlfriends. We'd discovered our likenesses and our differences. Like me, she was an orphan. As a baby, she'd been adopted by the Mayfields, who were both descendents of West Yamhill's founding families. As a result, we couldn't have been more different in our backgrounds. MaryLou grew up rural and rich and I was raised in one of Portland's working class neighborhoods. Maybe that's why we seemed to be totally opposite in our views about everything from the use of astrology to the music of ZZ Top.

I smiled, remembering our exchange about music. I'd discovered some cassette tapes and an old player mothballed on a shelf in the linen closet. I didn't care much for the Country & Western selections except for a remixed Hank Williams album but I was thrilled to find a huge selection of rerecorded Rock n' Roll, an array of CD's that included the Beatles, Bruce Springsteen and Janis Joplin. Before MaryLou showed up, I put a tape in the player with the volume turned low. It was when we started to munch on the pad Thai, curry beef and some especially yummy garlic shrimp that our conversation quieted and the music flowed into the silence.

MaryLou made a face. "How can you listen to that stuff?"

I swallowed a mouthful of noodles. "ZZ Top? They're great. Cowboy left a bunch of good music."

"Those aren't Cowboy's. They're Devin's."

"Oh. I didn't realize he was into music."

MaryLou nodded. "He was in a band when we met. But they only played on weekends, so he gave it up when we started dating."

"What about all these tapes? Will he mind if I listen to them?"

"Don't be silly. Of course not."

"It's just hard to believe someone with such a great collection wouldn't want to listen to it."

"It's my fault." MaryLou shrugged. "I just don't like listening to that noise. I made him bring them up here."

"You're kidding. How could you not like Springsteen? And the Beatles? Come on."

MaryLou laughed. "I used to love the Beatles when I was younger. Especially Paul. My friends and I used to scream ourselves silly whenever we saw his picture or heard his voice."

Another difference. My favorite Beatle was John Lennon. I never screamed for him but I cried when I heard the news he was killed.

Over the next few weeks, MaryLou's visits became routine. I began to think the caretaking job was less about the property and more about being there at the cabin for MaryLou. She'd show up in the early evening, after work and soccer, bringing wine and feasts of Thai takeout or something from the Greek Deli on State Street. Clarence continued to avoid MaryLou, disappearing into the bedroom as soon as he heard her steps on the porch. As for me, I looked forward to those intimate evenings. We told each other stories from our lives, like the first time we got our period, and silly things like the best pair of shoes we'd ever owned. Mine were red Capezios Aunt Elaine bought on sale for my seventh birthday. When I wore them, I was graceful and delicate, like a real ballerina. For MaryLou, the shoes were a pair of $500 dollar black leather boots with three inch heels she bought in New York City.

"I was honeymooning with my first husband and he took me to Saks." Wine splashed dangerously up the sides of MaryLou's wine glass as she leaned back in the chair. "He told me I could buy whatever I wanted as a souvenir. We walked around the store for hours, looking at clothes and jewelry. I couldn't make up my mind until I saw those boots on display. I knew instantly I had to have them." She sighed dramatically. "That was long ago, when I wore a size seven dress."

"You were married before?"

MaryLou nodded. "Couple of times. Devin's my third. What about you? Ever been married."

"Twice. Never again."

"You can't mean that, Ruby. You're pretty, you're smart and you're a wonderful person. I know you'll meet the right guy someday."

Maybe it was one glass too many of lukewarm, cheap Chablis. Maybe it was bitter residue from my failed marriages. That and a resulting case of hard-bitten cynicism. "It's all a bunch of crap," I sneered. "Believing there's a perfect love somewhere in the universe, waiting for some Prince Charming who'll fall in love with me at the drop of a glass slipper." I set the wine glass down hard on the table.

In the dimly lit room, MaryLou's face shimmered like a pale moon. "You have to have hope, Ruby. You have to believe. Believing really can make good things come true."

"Ha!"

She leaned forward and there was an earnest tone in her voice. "It happens. Look at me and Devin."

"Come on, MaryLou. You and Devin are hardly Mr. and Mrs. Perfect Marriage. He treats you like shit sometimes."

MaryLou's head jerked back, as if I'd slapped her. "How could you say that," she gasped. Her face was pale and pinched and in that moment I saw Devinda's resemblance to her mother.

We sat staring at each other. The tick, tick, tick of the clock measured our silence. Finally, I stuttered an apology. "Sorry. I didn't mean to hurt your feelings."

MaryLou stood abruptly and began gathering her things. "Devin and I have a wonderful relationship," she said, going to the door. "You don't know. You have no idea what a good relationship is." Neither one of us said good-bye.

After she was gone, Clarence joined me in the living room. I sat in the overstuffed chair, methodically scratching Clarence's back, trying to work out which one of us was kidding herself. Could it be true the Hunters had a wonderful marriage? Was it my own sad history that made me view all relationships with a negative eye? The questions floated unanswered in my mind.

One thing I did know: I should have kept my mouth shut. Think first, talk second. I got that bit of advice from my second ex, Bob, after I got into a heated debate with his boss, about whether the Viet Nam war had been wrong or right.

We were at an office party. I was standing next to Bob, balancing a paper plate and a plastic glass of cheap wine, smiling politely at the boring chatter, when a loud voice turned our heads.

"We should've just bombed the shit out of those fucking Gooks, killed them all," Mr. Baker, the boss man, loudly proclaimed to the small, admiring crowd gathered around him.

"Excuse me," I called out. Heads swiveled my way. I set my plate and glass on the nearest table and started talking about how we weren't playing video games, we were talking about the murder of real people, innocent women and children.

Mr. Baker glowered at me and shook his head. I heard that after Bob and I left, Mr. Baker called me a liberal and a bitch. Still, as Bob ushered me from the room, a few people made eye contact and gave me small, approving nods of agreement. The others kept quiet. I hoped they were at least thinking about what I'd said. Despite Bob and despite all the Mr. Bakers in the world, I've always believed there are times you have to speak up. Otherwise we'll turn into Night of the Living Zombies.

Still, there's a fine line between speaking your mind and being nasty. I awakened the next morning, still in the chair. I was cold and stiff and I regretted what I'd said about the Hunter marriage. When MaryLou didn't visit three nights in a row, I dithered about how to approach her. On the fourth day, before I figured out what to do, MaryLou showed up. I opened the door to her knock. She held a bag of Thai takeout in one hand, a bottle of red in the other. Words of apology tumbled out of my mouth and MaryLou's mouth all at the same time so that neither of us heard exactly what the other one said. It didn't seem to matter.

Our reunion was as joyful as our impromptu celebration dance after we'd finally pushed the van across the road the night we met. MaryLou resumed her visits to the cabin. She showed up three or four times a week, bringing food and wine but something about the flavor of our friendship had changed. Our conversations were gourmet French vanilla, all about Big Ideas, like the existence of God and the meaning of life. We stayed away from gritty chocolate chip mint talk about daily events and avoided any emotional double chocolate fudge.

Unlike most people, we didn't avoid religion and we argued about politics. She'd been raised a Republican, admired Reagan, hated paying taxes. She didn't approve of President Clinton and his sexual exploits. When I accused her of believing Hilary Clinton deserved it because she was too pushy, MaryLou's denial was half-hearted. Luckily, MaryLou wasn't a registered voter.

Even though I'm a slightly paranoid, anti-establishment drop-out, I've voted in every national election and most local ones since I came of age. I'll admit a time or two I lied about my permanent address. It's almost a compulsion with me to vote. I owe it all to Mrs. Bennington, one of the few high school teachers who got through my teenage wall of resistance. She used to tell us that you don't get to complain about the government if you don't make an effort to vote. Nobody I vote for ever wins, so I have plenty of complaints.

One night, our subject was synchronicity. MaryLou said the word was about how things appear just when you need them. She said only synchronicity could explain how Howard Sykes showed up just when she'd been thinking about how to bring her message to TV.

"That happened to me too," I said, explaining how I'd been thinking about my uncle for a few days before seeing his photograph in the newspaper.

"You've got to get in touch with him." MaryLou's eyes sparked with intensity. "Family is important." MaryLou's adoptive family had died out, except for a great-aunt. "Every year on my birthday, she sends me a generous check. Usually, it pays for the family vacation. This year," MaryLou grumbled, "we may have to use the money to keep Devin's business afloat."

I recalled my visit to the SETII offices, a month ago. "Capitol Investment Enterprises," I said. "Capitol's short on capital."

MaryLou smiled and flapped her hands in the air, a gesture she often used to indicate something too complicated to be bothered with.

That night, as I climbed into the wonderful bed, I thought some more about Devin's business. If he was going bust, he had reason to be short-tempered and cranky. No doubt I was seeing him at his worst. The new me ought to be more tolerant and cut the guy some slack.

And the same for Uncle Mike. Tomorrow morning, I would call him.

CHAPTER 7

The next morning I performed the chores that had become my usual routine - building a fire in the woodstove, fixing breakfast for Clarence and coffee for me, tidying the cabin, hauling a load of wood from the shed to the house, sweeping the deck - all the while, rehearsing possible conversations with my uncle. It was Saturday and I didn't want to call too early. On the other hand, I remembered Uncle Mike as an early riser. By 10:30 AM, I couldn't put the call off any longer. My hand trembled as I dialed the number.

"Lewis Residence." The man's voice was a rumbling baritone.

"Uncle Mike?"

"Who?"

"Mike Lewis. Is he in?"

"No. Mike isn't here right now."

"Would you please tell him Ruby called? His niece Ruby. And tell him I'm doing okay and I'd like to see him."

"Ruby?"

"That's right. Ruby Dubin."

"Ruby, it's me. Barry. From SETII."

Now I recognized the voice. "Barry? What are you doing there?"

"Oh. Well, Mike's a good friend and I like to hang out here. But holy shit, Ruby. Are you saying Mike's your uncle?"

"Maybe. Did your Mike Lewis have his picture in the newspaper a while back for being Hero of the Year?"

"He did." Barry's delighted shriek blasted my ear. "I can't believe it. This is so exciting. Where are you? You've got to come here right now. We'll surprise Mike when he gets home. It'll be fabulous."

"I don't know." My uncle had to be in his 70's. For all I knew, he could have a heart attack from the shock of finding me in his living room after all the years of angry silence. And there was a distinct possibility he wouldn't want to see me at all.

"Hold on. I think Mike's home. Don't go away."

I switched the receiver to my right ear, thinking I should probably hang up before I got my feelings hurt.

"Ruby? I can't believe it." He was breathless but I knew Uncle Mike's voice as soon as he said my name.

My mouth was so parched I thought my tongue would shrivel and crack. "It's really me."

"Ruby. My god. After all this time." He heaved a deep sigh. "I'm so glad to hear from you."

I suddenly felt sixteen again, making excuses for myself. "I guess I could've tried to contact you before but I figured you wouldn't want to hear from me. But when I read about the Governor giving you that award, I started thinking about calling you. It just took me a while to build up the courage."

"Is everything okay?" There was a tremble of doubt in his voice. "Are you . . . ?" He didn't finish the sentence. Maybe he was afraid to. The last time he saw me, I was a reckless twenty-year old college drop-out. I was unemployed, unambitious and unforgiving. Twenty-five years later, he had to figure there was a good probability I'd continued my journey into loserdom. I had to admit there were times I'd come close to crossing the border into that sad state.

"I'm doing okay," I said. "Better than okay. The thing is, for a while now I've been thinking I owe you an apology. Or maybe two or three." I took a deep breath and let it out. "I'd like very much to see you. If you're willing, that is."

There was only silence, except for a faint crackling on the empty telephone line. My heart beat a nervous pace. I could hardly breathe until I heard his voice again.

"Ruby. You don't know how happy this makes me." He didn't sound happy the way he kept harrumphing and clearing his throat. "Can we meet now? Do you want to come here? Or I could come to you. Where are you?" A deep rumble-bumble voice on Uncle Mike's side of the line became more and more insistent. Probably Barry.

"Ruby," Uncle Mike said. "Excuse me." I heard a muffled conversation in urgent tones but I couldn't make out a single word. "Sorry for that." Uncle

Mike was back. "Now. Why don't you come here? Could you make it this afternoon? Say 3:00 o'clock?"

"I guess I could." My heart was playing bongo drums again. I scribbled Uncle Mike's directions on a scrap of paper, my handwriting shaky and barely readable. As soon as we hung up, I raced into the bedroom and started trying on clothes. The bed was soon littered with my entire wardrobe: a black velvet blouse, three tee-shirts (one long-sleeved and two short-sleeved and all of them black), a black and red checked jacket and a charcoal gray cardigan, two pairs of jeans and one pair of black and white striped cotton pants. I could fit all that, plus underwear and an extra pair of shoes, into my battered green suitcase. A portable life is an independent life, I tried to reassure myself, although sometimes the scantiness of my worldly goods made me feel hopeless.

I hadn't lied to Uncle Mike, though. Lately, I'd been doing all right. I'd discovered a peacefulness I'd never experienced before. Aside from MaryLou, I didn't see many people. A couple of times, Cowboy hiked up to the cabin when he was visiting the Hunters, but he came no further than the porch and stayed only a short while. The solitary spell was good, giving me time to mull over my past and contemplate my future. I spent my days reading and thinking. Once a day, the dog and I walked the perimeter of the property to make sure all the gates were closed, all the fences standing unbroken. I figured it was the least a caretaker should do. Except on really cold days, Clarence set the pace, a leisurely stroll that halted frequently while he circled trees and followed odd digressions off the path, snuffling after whatever his pushed-in nose could detect.

As if he knew I was thinking about him at that moment, Clarence galumphed into the room. He plopped at my feet, panting heavily, and farted.

"Geez, Clarence," I started to complain. "You're worse than your namesake ever was." I stopped, suddenly inspired. Clarence would be my ambassador. I felt certain Uncle Mike would easily succumb to the charms of the second Clarence. "Young man," I told him. "You're coming with me."

He wiggled his butt and shook that stub of a tail, showing his approval of my idea. I didn't accomplish much that morning except for trying on all my clothes. I wanted to look right, but I had no idea what right was. In the end, I got dressed in my newest pair of jeans and the black velvet shirt, grabbed my jacket, purse and Clarence's leash and tucked the piece of paper with the directions in my pants pocket.

With Clarence in the back seat, I headed out a narrow road that led through the rolling countryside, past emerald fields dotted with cows and horses and the occasional farmhouse. This was a different route to Salem that would bring me into the west part of town, instead of the downtown area. As I approached the city limits, the road widened and the landscape changed to subdivisions and sprawling mobile home parks and clusters of small commercial operations. By the time I got to the south part of town, I was clammy with perspiration and feverishly warm, as if it were August instead of the end of February.

The entire drive from West Yamhill to Salem, I'd tried to remember Uncle Mike's photo from the newspaper, but the image of a younger man kept superimposing itself. I pictured him the way he looked the last time I saw him. We'd arranged to meet in a small Chinese restaurant on Broadway. I was out of work and close to penniless. Over the hot and sour soup, I asked Uncle Mike for the money my aunt had left for me. Uncle Mike slurped a spoonful of soup and shook his head. "Only if you go back to college."

Our conversation ended abruptly. I pounded my fist on the table, scattering silverware and overturning my water glass. I was convinced he'd stolen my inheritance.

"You're a thief," I screamed. "Fuck you."

The crowded room hushed, plates of sweet and sour pork and moo goo gai pan forgotten while the diners stared at the drama unfolding at our table. I shoved my chair away from the table and stood, and without further acknowledging my uncle, I stormed through the restaurant and out the door.

When I'd shared this guilty memory with MaryLou, she urged me to contact Uncle Mike, and to apologize. "Cleanse yourself of the guilt," was how she put it. I was realizing I wanted a lot more from this meeting than to merely rid myself of remorse for that youthful stupidity.

Mike's directions led me right to his address. I parked the car in front of the modern-looking house, its straight, clean lines a stark contrast to the Queen Anne-style house Uncle Mike had lived in with Aunt Elaine. I snapped Clarence's leash onto his collar and we got out of the car.

Slowly, in deference to Clarence's short legs, we climbed a flight of wide, wooden steps. The oversized steps led up to an overhang and immense double doors, painted fire engine red. Just as we reached the top landing, one of the doors swung open, revealing a sturdy-looking man with short gray hair. He was dressed in khaki pants and a sporty, navy blue shirt. Grinning widely, he stepped forward and gathered me into his arms. I was flooded with memories of my childhood, memories of love and comfort and warmth. I tucked that surprise away to consider later, in private. When we finally pulled from the embrace, I saw that Uncle Mike's cheeks were shiny with tears. His polo shirt was wet on the shoulder, where my cheek had pressed against it. It took a moment to realize it was damp from my tears.

And yet, we stood staring at each other, paralyzed by all the years and all the things there were to say.

Clarence saved the day. He nudged Uncle Mike's leg with his snout.

Uncle Mike looked down at Clarence. "Well, well. Look who's here." He bent to give Clarence a rub in just the right place. The dog melted into a puddle of fur. Uncle Mike laughed and crouched lower so he could keep scratching.

"I named him Clarence the Second," I said. "I hope you don't mind."

Uncle Mike looked up at me. His blue eyes wrinkled with laugh lines. "Heck, no. Clarence is a great name." He gave Clarence a few more pets and then stood, facing me, eye-to-eye. "Look at you. You turned into a beautiful woman."

I snorted good-humoredly. Mentally, I was shaking my head at the realization that Uncle Mike was only 5'6" or so, not very much taller than me. The uncle of my memory towered over me, even after I grew from youth into young adulthood. What else had I gotten wrong?

"I'm so happy to see you," he said, putting his arm around me. "You too, boy, you too," he added, reaching to pet the insistent Clarence. "You know, I thought maybe you were. . . ." He paused, swallowing hard, his Adam's apple bobbing. "I thought you might have died."

"You know what they say. Only the good die young."

Chuckling, Uncle Mike shook his head. "Anyone with a bulldog can't be all bad. Right, Clarence?" The dog barked softly at the sound of his name and wiggled his butt excitedly, making us laugh.

Uncle Mike guided us inside, shutting the door behind us. The house was like something Frank Lloyd Wright might have built, blending wood and stone and glass with dramatic effect. The view from the floor-to-ceiling windows on two sides of the house gave me a sensation of hovering over the treetops. We took a quick tour. The furnishings were big and sturdy, with lots of rich leather and polished wood. The large living room had an extra-wide couch, upholstered in a nubby chestnut brown, and an oversized leather chair that would easily have seated Hoss from the TV show *Bonanza*. In the kitchen, like the rest of the house, everything was tucked away and tidy. Only the den was messy, with stacks of folders and envelopes on the desk and even a few piles of paper on the floor. Mounted on the wall over the mahogany desk was the plaque Uncle Mike held in the newspaper photo.

"There's your award. That's so cool." As soon as the words slipped out, I silently berated myself. Cool? Why didn't I tell him it was groovy and far out? He would think I never grew up.

Uncle Mike tapped his finger on a group photo hanging next to the plaque. "I was proud of the award, sure, but I'm more proud to say that every one of these kids finished high school and turned out okay." His blue eyes sparking with passion, he described how he had the idea of founding an after-school program when a neighborhood kid died from a drive-by shooting. His story surprised me as much as the easy way he acted the host. When we returned to the living room he poured two glasses of a crisp Willamette Valley pinot gris and urged me to consume countless crackers slathered with goat cheese spread. None of this fit with my memory of Uncle Mike as a cold and distant person who'd been mean to everyone but his dog.

I gave him a brief-as-possible update of my life, quickly glossing over the two failed marriages, and the series of low-paying jobs. He didn't react one way or the other. The only uncomfortable moment came when he asked where I was living.

"I'm out in West Yamhill, caretaking a place up in the hills."

"Oh, yes. For the SETII person, as I understand."

"You sound as if you don't like MaryLou very much." I set my wine glass down and watched him curiously, wondering at the sudden nervousness he betrayed in the way he fidgeted with the wine bottle, moving it slightly to the left and moments later moving it back again.

"I've never met the woman. But I have heard some of her broadcasts. Have you ever listened to her?"

"Actually, no. I don't have a radio, except in my car."

He shook his head. "I think she's full of crap, but Barry adores her."

"Barry," I said, shocked that I'd forgotten him all afternoon. "What about him?"

I shrugged. "Nothing, really. Just that it's weird I would meet him and you would know him too. I guess you guys must be really good friends, huh?"

Uncle Mike inhaled deeply and blew the air out with a long whoosh. MaryLou would have called it a cleansing breath. She'd tried to teach me how to do it one night when we'd had too much wine. Every time I breathed in, I hiccupped, causing both of us to collapse with giggles. Uncle Mike, on the other hand, looked ready to have that heart attack I'd worried about. His face was pale. Sweat was beaded on his forehead.

I leaned toward him and lightly touched his shoulder. "You okay?"

"Asthma," he gasped. He stood quickly, banging into the coffee table in his haste. "Excuse me. I'll get my inhaler."

When he returned, we were awkward and uneasy with each other. The charm had worn off and we'd both turned back into frogs. I was sure I knew the reason for my uncle's little seizure. I'd been thinking about it myself, but didn't know how to talk about it.

"Look," I finally blurted. "The inheritance? I'm sorry I said you took it. And I don't want it. You don't have to worry about it. I know it isn't very much money but you deserve it, for raising me after Aunt Elaine died and for putting up with me."

"The money?"

"I don't want anything. Really."

A half-smile appeared on his lips. "I've never touched that money, Ruby. It was your aunt's gift to you. I kept hoping you'd show up. And you're right, it's not much, but it's a good nest egg for you." Once again, he hustled from the room, calling out that he was going to write me a check.

"I never did graduate college," I said, when he came back.

"I think we can waive that requirement now. You seem pretty level-headed. I can suggest a bank if you want me to," he said, handing me a check. "Just don't cash that until I can transfer the money." He smiled. "Should only take a couple of days. I'll call and let you know."

"Sure. Thank you." I took the check, and without looking, folded it and stuck it in the same pocket that held the directions. I was embarrassed. I wanted to leave. Dusk was turning to dark, time for Clarence and me to head back to West Yamhill.

Uncle Mike didn't seem sorry to see me go. He stood at the door, arms at his side, watching me follow Clarence's careful pace down the stairs. When we got to the bottom he called to me. "Ruby."

"Yes?" I stopped and looked up to where he was standing by the door. The porch light cast a golden halo around his head.

"Let's not lose touch again. Please."

I waved my hand and gave him a smile of agreement, even though he probably couldn't see it.

When I got home, I couldn't hold my curiosity anymore. Before I even shed my jacket or unsnapped Clarence's leash, I pulled out the check. One hundred thousand, forty-two dollars and thirty-seven cents. Not a fortune but more than I'd ever had all at once. My hand shook slightly as I carefully refolded the check and put it in the secret pocket of my wallet. Maybe my life really was turning around. Or maybe Uncle Mike would have second thoughts and this small rectangle of paper would be worth nothing at all.

CHAPTER 8

For a week or so, I took the check out almost every day, to reassure myself it was real. Time went by. Uncle Mike didn't call. When I finally got the courage to call him, there was no answer. I left a message but he didn't return the call. I didn't try again. I was disappointed by his rejection. I stopped looking at the check. It was in my wallet and there it remained. I knew I'd have to deal with it sooner or later, and I opted for later.

I wasn't desperate anymore. I was, in fact, quite happy. Although I'd always been a city dweller, my new rural life felt comfortable and familiar, like a faded pair of jeans I'd worn so long they'd form-fitted to my body. It was as if I had always awakened at sunrise in the big bed, watching the dawn slowly light the east-facing window. As if I had always gone to bed by 10:00 PM, snuggled under the comforter, falling asleep to the lullaby of Clarence's snores and the rhythm of rain dripping from the eaves of the cabin.

Wet weather had started the day after my reunion with Uncle Mike and continued through March and April, each day as gray and soggy as the one before. As daytime temperatures warmed, melting snow mixed with too many inches of rain. All over the state, rivers and creeks and drainage ditches were flowing at flood stage. May Day came and went without a word from Uncle Mike. My disappointment curdled into the sourness of a bruised ego.

It was the Sunday after Mother's Day when MaryLou phoned and invited me for dinner, mentioning something gourmet to be prepared by Devin and the kids. MaryLou was a constant visitor to the cabin but I hadn't been down to the Hunter house since the day Devinda refused me entry and said Jesus hated me. I accepted the invitation but I was nervous about my reception. I left Clarence home.

This time, the door stood open. I was greeted by the raucous noise of music, heavy on the base. Lyman was in the living room, flopped on the couch and transfixed by the music video flickering on the TV screen. A bevy of near-naked women writhed and wriggled around a man who ignored their enticements as he strutted down a stage-set street. The man wore baggy pants and a hooded sweatshirt that was unzipped to display his tattooed chest. Multiple gold chains hung from his neck. Diamond studs flashed on both earlobes.

I gaped at the video, feeling old and grumpy. Times change and so does music, from ragtime to rock-and-roll to rap, but girls and boys still get the same screwed-up message about sexual behavior.

"Ruby." MaryLou was standing in the doorway between the living room and the hall leading to the kitchen.

"Hey, MaryLou," I greeted her.

"Did you just get here?" Without waiting for my response, she turned her head in the direction of the couch. "Lyman, did you say hello to Ruby?"

"Hello Ruby." He looked up and flashed a smile that faded as soon as he returned his gaze to the TV screen.

I told him hello, although I'm sure he didn't hear me, and followed MaryLou down the hallway and into the kitchen. "Are you hiding back here?"

She splashed a generous serving of red wine into a long-stemmed wine glass and handed it to me. "It's the quietest place in the house. Devin's in the garage and Devinda's in her bedroom, playing with her new Barbie."

My mind conjured an unpleasant picture of the girl's small fingers wrapped around Barbie's neck. MaryLou's next words erased the image from my mind.

"I need you to work at SETII for me," she announced.

"What?" My fingers tightened around the glass stem. "Are you serious?"

"Sondra needs to take some time off to go to this weight-loss place in Arizona. I've got to have someone I trust to take her place." She smiled. "It's just for a few weeks. Please?"

I stared at the floor, thinking about what to say. I didn't want to give up my time at the cabin. I'd started weeding the flower beds and I'd already cleared out the vegetable garden and planted some early starts. The physical labor had me feeling fit and strong. Furthermore, there was nothing as therapeutic as taking a walk in the woods with Clarence. He heeled. I healed. I was starting to recover from my chronic case of self-pity. Giving that up could cause a relapse. Plus, I would get behind in all the weeding.

"What about caretaking the property?" I said. "When would I do that?"

"Caretaking?" MaryLou waved an arm. "We both know there's not much to do. Besides, if you do this for me, I think we could talk about you being able to live at the cabin for as long as you want." She leaned forward and put her hand on my arm. "I know how you feel about the place. Just do this for me and the cabin is yours. I'll even put it in writing."

"Really?"

"Ruby." MaryLou's eyes widened. "I wouldn't lie to you. The cabin is yours."

My heart beat fast. This was another piece of good luck that might turn out to be an empty promise. Good luck brings bad, my aunt used to say, as a warning not to gamble. But what's life if you don't?

"Okay," I agreed. "What do you want me to do?"

"It's easy. Just the phones. Reception. A few letters to word process."

"MaryLou, I don't know how to do any of that stuff."

"Don't worry." She waved a hand in the air as if anyone could perform these simple tasks. "You'll learn."

I'll learn, I kept reassuring myself over dinner, which turned out to be a super-size pepperoni pizza from Mama Mia's and salad-in-a-bag from the West Yamhill Market. Not my idea of gourmet. At least I was spared Devin's brooding presence, since he chose to eat in the garage so he could continue working on his old car. The kids ate in front of the TV.

The following Monday morning was my first day of work. I drove down the road, took the winding curves of Ridge Road to Seven Hills Road, and then the ten miles to South River Road and into Salem. After a few days, the ride was routine and by the end of the first week, the server at Java-To-Go recognized me with a smile when I pulled in for my daily sixteen-ounce skinny latte.

At the SETII office, I saw MaryLou only briefly each day. I saw her crew even less. They spent hours behind the closed door of MaryLou's office, the buzz of their conversation like bees in the wall behind me. Upstairs, Devin made the floor boards creak with his prowling but I hardly ever saw him.

It wasn't long before I mastered some computer basics, surprising myself by enjoying the technology I'd sneered at before. Another of life's ironies, I guess. By the end of the first week, I was a champion at punching buttons on the telephone, like some kind of pinball wizard. When I got home I rushed outside to weed and garden, to take advantage of every last bit of light. My busy days didn't give me the time or headspace to obsess about Uncle Mike's silence.

At SETII, every day there were more and more calls about the upcoming television show. Mostly, the calls were from fans of MaryLou's old radio show, wanting to know what channel to tune in and at what time. Others had a different agenda. "You remind MaryLou how good I sung the time we went to the retirement home and did Christmas Carols," instructed a man calling himself Charles Ray. I wondered if he made that name up. Some people offered advice, like the shaky-voiced old woman who instructed me, "You tell MaryLou to stand kind of sideways and suck in her cheeks to look thinner. And wear navy blue."

In between phone calls, I dealt with the people who came to the door hawking cosmetics, clothes, laser surgery, real estate and at least ten or twelve deals-of-the-century. MaryLou said she was amazed how I sorted the important, message-taking calls from the ones requiring a "thank-you-but-no." I couldn't help feeling proud of her praise but really, it was just common sense.

I was less sure how to deal with the SETII Betties, the group of women who haunted the office. To me, their uncomplaining niceness was unsettling. They were breathless over MaryLou, endlessly praising her, and they were willing to do any task, no matter how humble. If there wasn't a SETII Betty at the copy machine, there was one cleaning toilets or vacuuming floors. Jaqi, the gray-haired woman I'd seen in the kitchen on my first visit, told me they called themselves SETII Betties because the first two women who dedicated their service to MaryLou were both named Betty. When I asked MaryLou, though, she shrugged and shook her head. "I don't know. I have a hard time remembering who they are, so I just call them all Betty."

No one else seemed to care, even the women themselves, but I was bothered that they were so anonymous, so taken for granted. This complicated and confused my feelings about MaryLou. On one hand, there was an undeniable connection between us because of the strange way we'd crossed paths. Even more, she'd offered me the chance to start a new life. She'd offered me the cabin. Because of this, she had my gratitude, my loyalty.

And yet, unlike the SETII Betties or Barry, Laura and Janet, I didn't get goo-goo eyed when MaryLou spoke, didn't think her words were pearls of cosmic wisdom. I couldn't ignore the contradictions between MaryLou's SETIIisms and her personal life. The night we met, I'd judged her as ditzy but kind and sensitive. Inside the Hunter home, I saw an unhappy woman with a self-centered husband and two spoiled-brat kids. At SETII, she was usually self-assured and in charge. And some nights, when she visited the cabin, she was funny and smart and the best friend I'd never had. Other nights she drank so much wine I had to escort her down the hill.

As late spring blossomed into early summer, MaryLou seldom had time to come up to the cabin. She spent long hours at work. The SETII crew was immersed in preparing for the show, due to air in mid-September. They didn't have time to wonder about O.J. Simpson's innocence or guilt. Like most Americans. I followed the drama, from the tragedy of murder and the two motherless children to the high comedy of the SUV chase on the freeway. It was a soap opera of love, jealousy, power, the fallen hero, the beautiful, doomed woman, and the over-riding sadness and frustration of race relations in America.

Early July, Sondra returned to work part-time. She'd shed fifty pounds, had her stringy gray hair stylishly cut and colored an auburn-brown and wore a new wardrobe selected with the help of a Nordstrom's saleswoman. Apparently, she'd avoided the Arizona sun, maintaining her usual ghoulish pallor. Everyone else gushed over her new look, but I thought the weight loss enhanced her wrinkles, so she looked like an albino prune. Now that she was thinner, Sondra's resemblance to her brother Devin was unmistakable. That wasn't an endearing quality, as far as I was concerned.

MaryLou asked me to keep working a few more weeks until Sondra got back to full strength. Until then, Sondra would work part-time, redecorating the office. Reluctantly, I agreed, wondering why someone who'd been at a spa for a month-and-a-half needed more rest. After the first half-hour of the first day Sondra came back to work at SETII, I knew I didn't like her. Her treatment of me and the other SETII staff was rude and sometimes it was downright mean.

Sondra took on her new assignment with a passion, as if she needed to transform not only her looks but also her surroundings. She showed up every morning at eleven o'clock and worked until Devin was ready to get lunch. The two of them would often disappear for several hours. When she was there,

Sondra papered the walls with posters, the kind with cheery sayings like "Up, up and away," and a background of multicolored balloons floating in a royal blue sky.

The worst poster, prominently displayed over the coffee pot in the break room, featured a cartoon skunk with long eyelashes and a pink rose tucked behind a perky ear. Above the skunk, in lettering made out of little cloud puffs, the platitude read "Even little stinkers need love." Better an Elvis on black velvet than the inanity of Sondra's posters. That was my unvoiced opinion. Luckily, Sondra said she'd wait to fix up her office - the room I worked in - until I was gone and she'd been forbidden to touch MaryLou's office.

I stared at the stinky skunk poster almost every morning. It had become my job to start the coffee pot, since I usually got to the office earliest. The others wandered in later, especially when they'd worked long hours the night before. That's why I was surprised to find Janet, Laura and Barry, AKA The Crew, sitting at one of the round tables in the break room one morning, the coffee pot already half-empty. Yawning, I slid into the chair Barry pulled out.

"Good morning, sleepyhead," Barry teased.

"What's going on?"

"Haven't you heard?" Laura's round cheeks were pink with excitement.

"MaryLou's on TV," Janet said, gesturing at the television on the counter next to the refrigerator. "On the *'People and Places'* show."

"How come I didn't know about this?" I said.

"Shh," Laura said. "It's started."

On the screen, images flashed in quick succession: snowy mountains, pine trees, the whitewater rapids of a river.

"And now," a baritone voice intoned. "It's the *People and Places* show, with your hostesses Misty and Joni. Good morning, girls."

The camera switched to a studio set. Two look-alike women, one blonde, the other brunette, were perched on swivel armchairs, showing lots of leg and white teeth to the camera. The two women waved at the announcer, now visible on camera, a white-haired man with a clownishly large nose.

"Don't forget, folks," the announcer said, shaking his finger at the screen. "This program is brought to you through the generosity of our sponsors. So you need to do your part and buy these wonderful products." I turned away as the image shifted to an ad for laundry soap featuring four animated bubbles singing about clean clothes to the tune of the old Beatles song *Help*.

I snorted. "Girls. They must be thirty, thirty-five years old. And since when is advertising considered generosity?" No one answered me. I got up and poured myself a cup of coffee. As I headed back to the table, MaryLou came down the hallway and into the room. She was wearing black pants and a white shirt with swirls of silver glitter that sparkled when she moved. Sondra was at MaryLou's side, looking dull in comparison, even though the rust brown pantsuit she had on was probably hand-picked by the Nordstrom shopping consultant she'd bragged about.

Laura hissed at me to sit down. The show was starting. Once again we were intent on the screen, watching for the image of MaryLou, although the actual woman was standing only a few feet away.

"There she is," Laura said, as if the rest of us couldn't see for ourselves. A two-dimensional MaryLou appeared from behind a curtain, walking slowly towards the grouping of armchairs where Misty and Joni waited with perky smiles pasted on their lips. The television version of MaryLou was wearing a loose-fitting, floor-length navy blue dress. It reminded me of a one-size-fits-all graduation gown. Or maybe a minister's robe.

In the room, Janet and Laura applauded.

"Welcome, welcome," said the brunette, Misty, in a little-girl voice. "This is such a great honor. Thank you so much for being on *People and Places* with us."

"I'm just thrilled," Joni squealed.

Settling herself into the armchair between the two women, MaryLou nodded. A small smile touched her lips.

Joni leaned forward, speaking to the camera. She was dressed in a baby blue miniskirt with a white blouse. "I'm pleased to introduce MaryLou Hunter. Starting fall season, she'll be part of the evening line-up on TV 12, your local window on the world." I wondered if she got a bonus for mentioning the station's call letters and motto. It was probably just part of the job description. "Today, MaryLou is visiting to talk with us about her new show. Tell us more, Misty."

"They should let MaryLou talk," Barry complained in a low voice.

"Shush," Laura hissed.

Misty had on a peach blouse with a brown slit skirt. Apparently she and Joni ignored the rule about wearing navy blue. It was obvious they'd made the right choice.

"Thank you, Joni." Misty tossed her blonde tresses like a model in a shampoo ad "We'll talk with MaryLou in a few moments. But first, let me tell you about her."

A photo of SETII's Victorian house filled the screen, followed by shots of the cabin and then a panoramic view of the enchanted woods and the hills at the top end of the property.

"MaryLou Hunter is a local gal," Misty said. She squinted ever so slightly at the white card she held in her hand and started to read. "Her family came to West Yamhill during the depression. The cabin was built by MaryLou's grandparents, John and Alma Krauss, and their family of three sons. They struggled to survive until a simple invention by John Krauss turned into a family fortune." Misty looked up at the camera, tilting her head flirtatiously. "I don't really get what he invented," she giggled. "But I guess what's important is the money, honey. Anyway, our gal MaryLou is so All-American, she still lives in the cabin her grandparents built."

Misty's story didn't fit with what I remembered of MaryLou's account. And surely MaryLou hadn't told them she occupied the cabin. While I was pondering this, the picture changed to an aerial photo of Salem. "But this is where MaryLou's story really begins," Misty's voice pronounced.

"They're going to let her talk now," Laura squealed.

"Stay tuned folks," commanded the deep voice of the announcer. "You'll be hearing some genuinely real pearls of wisdom from this very, very special lady." The camera drew back for a long shot of the set with MaryLou, large and blue in the center of the screen. "And now this." It was the soap commercial again.

"This is so exciting," Laura said, speaking over the TV noise. "Isn't it great?"

That wasn't my reaction. I wondered why anyone would watch this program if they didn't have to. I looked at MaryLou. She was in a huddle with Sondra and Devin. I couldn't tell whether they agreed with Laura or with me about the show. Maybe they were talking about something else altogether. I gave a mental shrug and poured myself another cup of coffee, even though my bladder was already sloshing.

"They're back," announced Laura.

"We're back," Misty brightly reassured us. "And now, the moment you've been waiting for. MaryLou Hunter's wise words of advice." She turned sideways, her short skirt hiking further up her long, well-formed thighs. "Okay, MaryLou. Let's start with the most important question first." Misty giggled. "Tell us how to get rich."

The camera panned MaryLou's face. Up close, I could see she was wearing makeup. The red lips and rouged cheeks made her seem a different person, MaryLou but not MaryLou.

"Thank you for this opportunity. I'm humbled and grateful for this chance to connect with so many people at once. I'd love to share what I know about how to make money. I want everybody to know how to be rich and happy." Unlike Misty and Joni with their constant smiles, MaryLou's face wore a serious expression.

Misty and Joni looked out at the television audience with fake, wide-eyed surprise and laughed. "Okay," Misty said. "Get your pencils ready. The big secret is about to be revealed."

MaryLou frowned. "It's no secret. There are a few people who'd like the rest of us to believe that getting rich is beyond our reach but I believe anyone can do it. I know we all have the power to manifest what we want in this life. All you need to do is believe. It's as simple and as difficult as that."

Joni interrupted. "Believe in what?" She sounded as if she really wanted to know.

"Believe in yourself," MaryLou said. "Believe you deserve it."

"That sounds too easy," said Misty. Her thinly plucked eyebrows arched skeptically.

MaryLou shook her head. "It's not easy. And it's especially not easy for people who've been told they aren't good enough or smart enough or deserving enough."

Misty sat back in her chair. "Whoa," she said. "You sound serious." She looked into the camera and winked, inviting us to laugh.

"I feel strongly about this," MaryLou said. Her right hand reached up to comb through her tight curls.

"Well," Misty exhaled. "I wish we could hear more, but it's time to go."

Joni leaned over and grabbed MaryLou's hand. "Thank you," Joni said in a voice barely above a whisper. "Thank you."

"We all want to thank you, MaryLou," Misty said. "And for those of you who want to know more, starting mid-September, you'll be able to see MaryLou at 7:30 PM, right after *Wheel of Fortune*."

The screen filled with another shot of Joni and Misty and MaryLou. Joni was talking intently with MaryLou but Misty was busy waving and yelling, "Goodbye, goodbye. Join us tomorrow when we show up at the base of Mount St. Helens, the volcano that blew its stack. We'll meet a couple of local characters, including a man who claims to channel the ghost of Harry Truman, the old hermit who refused to leave the mountain when it erupted. See you then."

Barry got up and turned off the TV. "I've seen worse," he said. His discouraged tone of voice gave his lie away.

"It was fine," Laura said, pushing her chair from the table and standing up. She looked at Janet and then at me, hoping for confirmation.

"They didn't even mention SETII," Janet said.

"Hey, people." MaryLou's voice overrode our conversation. She strode purposefully to where we stood, put an arm around Barry, the other around Laura.

"C'mon. Cheer up. I bet we got some people intrigued, people who'll turn on the TV just out of curiosity to see what I'm all about."

Out of the corner of my eye I saw Sondra move closer until she was standing to the left and just behind me. I turned sideways, uneasy, protecting my back. I could see Sondra's lips puckering and trembling, as if she could hardly hold back the words filling her mouth.

"We've got to do better," she said. "We have a backer who likes MaryLou and SETII a lot, but he's still a businessman and he still pays attention to the bottom line. We need everybody to put their energy behind this. Do you think it will happen all by itself?" Sondra started forward, bumping against my shoulder as she passed. I wondered if she'd done it on purpose. With her next words, I knew.

"There are people right here in this room," Sondra said loudly, "who don't even listen to MaryLou's radio broadcast. Aren't there, Ruby?"

The room got so quiet I actually heard several people gasping in shock. I was one of them.

Sondra pushed on. "There are people who pretend to love MaryLou and honor her gifts. But behind her back, they laugh at her and belittle her. They pretend to believe in what SETII is all about. But they don't. Isn't that right, Ruby? " A smirk of satisfaction lifted Sondra's lips. She was sure she'd just dropped a bomb and she was gleefully waiting for the explosion.

"That's not true," I protested, scrambling to defend myself. "Not exactly."

MaryLou's calm voice interrupted me. "Thanks for your concern, Sondra." Her velvet brown eyes held Sondra in their gaze. "You don't need to worry about Ruby. She's as much a part of SETII as any of us." With a sweep of her arm, MaryLou indicated everyone in the room. There was something queenly in the gesture and it fixed our attention on her. Like a skilled actress, she waited. And then she spoke again.

"You seem to have forgotten there's no radio reception up at the cabin. How could Ruby listen to the show? Now, let's get to work, everybody." Without another word, she turned and walked out of the room.

I turned, intending to follow MaryLou, but Sondra was quicker. She moved to block my way. "I don't care if you have to leave that stupid cabin. You should listen to the show. Where's your loyalty?"

"What's this got to do with loyalty?"

"Everything. It's got everything to do with it." Her voice quivered with intensity.

I looked at the skunk poster she'd hung on the break room wall reminding us to be charitable. Even to stinkers. "You're right," I said. "I'll listen tonight."

"It's too late," she hissed. "You've already proved you're a traitor."

"Traitor? Isn't that a little harsh?"

Sondra leaned forward. Her eyes narrowed into slits. "You're the snake in our garden. You wait. I'll get you out." The others in the room, even Devin, stood wide-eyed and open-mouthed, like onlookers at a traffic accident.

My first impulse was to unleash the killer-dog attitude snarling in my gut. I wanted to scratch her face, tear her hair and bark insults at her. Luckily, my brain took command. I moved to make my escape. This time, Sondra didn't stop me. The hard look she gave me was enough.

CHAPTER 9

I scurried away to the shelter of my office, but I couldn't escape the guilty knowledge that Sondra was partially right, even if she was crazy and mean. If I'd wanted to hear MaryLou's broadcast, I could have driven up the road to catch reception on my car radio. My excuse - that I was usually asleep when the show aired in its late-night slot - was also a sham. The truth? I liked MaryLou but the SETII message left me lukewarm. I was so sure I wouldn't be much interested, I'd avoided tuning in.

I vowed to remedy my failure. I owed that much to MaryLou. If the show was taped I would get a copy. If not, I'd drive to the top of the road and listen that very night. Satisfied I'd solved my problem, I plopped into the office chair and swiveled to face the desk. The message light on the phone blinked impatiently. There was work to be done. I grabbed a notepad and pen and put the telephone headset on, settling it over my ears like earmuffs.

"Ruby?" Barry stood in the doorway.

I gestured him in. "Give me a minute, okay? I've got to finish getting the phone messages."

Barry nodded. He walked to the window, paced back again, then stood in front of the desk, nervously shifting his weight from foot to foot.

I scribbled the last of twenty-four messages and pulled off the headset. "What's happening?"

"Nothing much. It's just we haven't spoken in forever." He smiled. "Not since the day you discovered your long lost uncle."

"You're right. We've all been so busy. Uncle Mike too. He's been out of town, I guess."

"Uh uh. He's been back . . . ." Barry's eyes widened. "Holy shit. I think I just goofed."

"It's okay," I reassured him. "I'm not surprised he doesn't want anything to do with me. He thinks I'm worthless."

"No way." Barry shook his head. "It's because he's afraid. Afraid of your judgment."

"My judgment? You mean about the money?"

"Money?" Barry frowned and cocked his head.

"See, I realize now that he did the right thing. I mean about not giving me the money before. I don't judge him for that. I used to but not anymore."

Barry blew a long puff of air through his lips, as if he'd been holding his breath. He put his arms out, palms up, and started backing out of the room. "Look Ruby," he said, shaking his head. "I don't want to get in the middle of this. Why don't you call Mike, okay?" With that, he turned and scooted away.

"Maybe I will," I said, although Barry had already disappeared. I turned my attention to the scribbled sticky-notes MaryLou had put on the desk, her version of a to-do list for me. My day would be full, I could see that. On the top note MaryLou had scrawled "urgent - coffee, stamps, toilet paper," which I liked because running errands to the store and post office meant I'd get out of the office for awhile. Midway through the stack of notes, I found one that had a cryptic command. "R – Need to talk. See me ASAP."

Arching my back to stretch the sudden tightness in my muscles, I reread the message. Was MaryLou angry, even though she'd defended me? Why else would she leave this kind of note? Like vicious yellowjackets, the questions swarmed in my mind.

Through the wall, I heard the indistinct but familiar voices of MaryLou and The Gang, deep into script-writing. Despite the ASAP, I knew better than to interrupt them. I stared at the note as if it might reveal something new. One thing was sure. After Sondra's attack, followed by Barry's revelation about Uncle Mike and then this strange note from MaryLou, I knew it was not my lucky day.

"Well, well, well. Miss Ruby Doobie Do." Cowboy slouched into the room, thumbs hooked in the belt loops of a tight pair of jeans. The sleeves of his plaid snap-button shirt were rolled up, showing tanned, muscled arms. With his weather-beaten face and squinty, sexy eyes, he looked like the Marlboro cowboy before he got lung cancer. "How are ya', darlin'?"

Skitching the chair forward, I stuffed MaryLou's message in the pocket of my corduroy jacket and gave Cowboy a neutral smile. "Are you here to see Devin?" I asked, in my best receptionist voice.

He looked down at me with sleepy eyes. "I came to see you, darlin'," Cowboy said, balancing his butt on the edge of my desk. "I came here special to ask if you'll have dinner with me tonight."

I shook my head. "I can't. I need to go home to feed Clarence." I admit I was gratified when Cowboy's expression reflected his disappointment. I'd always assumed Cowboy's flirtation with me was nothing more than reflex on his part, that it was just the way he related to females. I was okay flirting with him but I wasn't heavily invested in Cowboy stock.

"Here's an idea." Cowboy's face lifted with hope. "I know a great little place not far from West Yamhill. I'll just follow you home. That way, you can feed that ol' hound of yours and then we'll go to dinner. Pretty please?"

I didn't answer right away, tongue-tied by conflicting urges. I was thinking I shouldn't start something I didn't want to finish. At the same time I was convincing myself it was no big deal to go to dinner one time.

"Okay," I said. "I'll go to dinner with you if you quit insulting my dog. Clarence isn't a hound and he's only a year old."

Cowboy grinned. "Deal. I'll meet you back here about 5:00, okay?"

I glanced at the papers piled to the side of the keyboard and thought about my hunt-and-peck typing skills. "Make it 5:30, just to be sure."

As soon as Cowboy was out the door, I eyed the clock. My best opportunity to catch MaryLou was at noon, when the crew usually took a short break. I worked a while longer, cleared the desk and went into the reception area. I could hear Barry, Laura and Janet on the other side of the wall, in the foyer, talking and laughing noisily as they went out the front door. Quickly, I slipped down the hallway and tapped on the door of the big office. "It's me." When I heard a muffled response, I took it as invitation to enter.

MaryLou was sitting in one of the comfortable chairs, her lap filled with the mail I'd stacked on her desk yesterday afternoon. She gestured at the other chair, inviting me to sit, the silver glitter on her shirt sparkling like a million mirrors when she moved her arm.

I perched on the edge of the chair, my nervous hands clasped almost prayerfully. "You wanted to see me?"

She nodded. "Listen, Ruby. I hope you weren't offended by Sondra. You know she means well. She just gets a little overzealous sometimes."

"I guess."

"I'll speak with her of course. But I'm hoping you'll go the extra mile to be understanding. She's . . . how shall I say this? She's had some challenges in her life and sometimes it's hard for her to turn her negative energy into something positive." MaryLou smiled. "You understand."

"I guess." I was repeating myself. There was that worm of doubt, nibbling, nibbling.

"I knew you would." MaryLou brushed the pile of letters from her lap, careless of how they dropped onto the floor. She stood, took a few quick steps across the room and pushed the door shut. "Listen," she said, turning to face me. "There's something else."

She moved slowly this time, and dropped heavily into the chair next to mine. I watched her expectantly as she closed her eyes and took a few deep breaths. Finally, MaryLou leaned forward, laid her hands on my knees and looked into my eyes. Her gaze held me in place as effectively as did her hands.

"Ruby," she said. There was a breathless quality to her voice. "Ruby, I need your promise of silence."

"Silence?"

"Howard Sykes," she said, still staring intently at me.

"Sykes? What about him?" There was a subtle tightening of her hand on my knee.

"I need to keep it quiet that he's helping SETII."

"Why? What is he? A gangster?"

MaryLou blinked rapidly. She pulled her hands away and sat back in the chair. "Of course not," she said. Her voice was thin and tight. "How could you think that? Mr. Sykes is an honest businessman. It's just that he's involved in a political campaign right now, so we want to downplay his involvement, okay? It's no big deal. Just until the election is over." Waving her arm airily, she gave me a reassuring smile. Her blouse glittered crazily as she moved. "Tell me you'll keep it to yourself."

My stomach gurgled, a sure sign I felt uneasy. I pulled my spine straight, folded my arms across my chest and narrowed my eyes at MaryLou. With her back to the window, her face was half-shadowed but I could see that a strained smile lingered on her lips. There was nothing happy in her eyes. Behind her, framed by the window, a gardener pushed a lawnmower back and forth across the patch of front lawn. The muted growl of the mower engine through the closed window and the steady hum of the old building's heating and cooling system were the only sounds in the room.

MaryLou leaned forward. "Ruby," she said. "Why're you making such a big deal out of this?"

"I'm sorry. I can't say yes to something I don't understand," I said, trying to explain my reluctance to both of us. "I'm just not sure exactly what you're asking of me."

MaryLou sat back in her chair, as if my words had shoved her away.

Just then, the door banged open. Devinda ran into the room, heading for MaryLou. The little girl had on a sleeveless pink leotard, white leggings and black ballet slippers. The clingy material of the leotard outlined every bone in her ribcage. She looked so underfed and frail, she could have posed for a "Save the Children" ad.

"Mommy," Devinda yelled, as she climbed onto MaryLou's lap. "Mommy. I have to tell you something."

"Shh. Calm down." Mary Lou wrapped her arms around the little girl and began to rock her. "I'll listen to you but you have to calm down first. You have to use your inside voice."

"No. I don't have to." Devinda struggled out of her mother's hold and stood facing her, skinny arms bent and fists planted on non-existent hips. The child's eyes darted sideways, in the direction of the door. Moments later, Devin appeared.

Devinda turned to him. "Daddy." Lifting an arm to her eyes like a bad actress, Devinda made crying noises and heaved her shoulders up and down. "Mommy hurt me."

"That's not so," I blurted, before my mind caught up with my mouth. Immediately, I apologized. "Sorry. I shouldn't have said anything."

"Oh, Ruby," MaryLou said. "Thank you. That was a pure expression of your loyalty and I treasure it." She clasped her hands over her heart. "Thank you," she repeated.

Her response took me by surprise. I knew perfectly well I'd reverted to the emotional age of seven, instead of behaving like someone who had celebrated enough birthdays to be called ma'am by grocery clerks. My outburst was sparked by dislike of the little girl who had invoked Jesus against me, rather than by loyalty to her mother. MaryLou had assumed the best about my motive. Maybe I should return the favor.

Meanwhile, ignoring me as well as his wife, Devin bent his long frame until he was eye-level with his daughter. "Devinda," he said. "Tell me what really happened."

The little girl brought her arm down and looked at him with hot, dry eyes. Her lower lip began to tremble. "But I did get hurt, Daddy," she burst out, real tears running down her cheeks. "Honest I did."

"Did Mommy do it?"

"No." Devinda bowed her head. "It happened at school."

"Tell Mommy you're sorry."

I could barely hear Davinda's whispered apology.

MaryLou rose from her chair and went to stand by her husband and child. "Devinda," she said, cupping a hand under the girl's chin to raise her head. "You know Mommy would never hurt you on purpose."

"I know." Snuffling loudly, Devinda wiped the back of her hand under her nose.

Devin straightened, standing to his full height, almost a foot taller than MaryLou. "Let's do a start-over," he said. "We'll pretend nothing ever happened. Okay?"

"Okay." MaryLou smiled encouragingly, first at Devin and then the little girl.

"Okay," echoed Devinda. "And I'm going to make my hurt go away too." She squeezed her eyes shut and wrinkled her face, concentrating hard. After a moment, she blinked. "It's gone."

"Now tell Mommy the surprise," Devin instructed.

"Mommy, guess what? There's going to be this show at gymnastics and I'm going to be the star and Daddy's going to take pictures of me." Eyes wide, she looked up at MaryLou expectantly. "Isn't that great?"

"It's fantastic," Mary Lou said, dropping to her knees and enveloping Devinda in a hug. The little girl endured the embrace this time, but she kept her arms at her sides and didn't hug back.

"I've got to get some photos of her so they can make posters," Devin said. "Do you remember where we put the camera?"

"Lyman broke it," Devinda shrilled, turning to look at her father. "He broke it and threw it away. I saw him"

"What?" Devin's face darkened.

MaryLou let go of Devinda and stood, struggling slightly to pull herself upright. "Lyman threw the camera away but he did it for me. I was the one who broke it."

Devin started to speak but MaryLou kept talking louder and faster, silencing him. "It was old and wasn't working right. I've been thinking we should get a good digital camera. It'll be great for taking those pictures of Devinda. I'll get the checkbook."

Moving quickly to her desk, she yanked open the big bottom drawer, lifted her leather bag by the straps and set it onto the desktop. The three of us looked on, a captive audience. Even Devinda was silenced by MaryLou's activity. Plunging her arm into the purse, MaryLou rummaged around. She began pulling items out of the bag - a few crumpled tissues, a bulging wallet and a baggie filled with broken graham crackers - until her face lit with success and her shirt sparkled happily. She yanked a green plastic checkbook out of the purse and held it in the air, a magician displaying a rabbit.

"Here you go," she said, offering the checkbook to Devin. "Get whatever camera you think is best."

Devin took the checkbook and slipped it into his back pocket. "Thanks." A belated smile lifted his lips. "Devinda. Let's go." The little girl scurried to follow him from the room.

"You've been quiet," MaryLou said, as soon as her husband and daughter disappeared. She came around the desk and leaned an arm on the back of the chair, looking down at me. "What're you thinking?"

I lifted my eyebrows into my forehead and held my hands out, palms up. "Nothing."

With a sigh, MaryLou turned away. She walked to the desk and plopped into the black executive chair. "I know you don't like her," she said, waving away my weak sputters of protest. "She's a difficult child to like. We're so lucky that she bonded with Devin. She's adopted, just like you. Her birth mother was a drug addict. Devinda actually went through withdrawal when she was born. It was horrible."

Maybe that explained Devinda's scrawny figure and pinched face. I'd assumed these were physical manifestations of her Inner Spoiled Brat. Now I knew the kid had plenty of reasons to be a monster. The sour taste of guilt filled my mouth.

MaryLou plucked a tissue from the holder on her desk and dabbed at her eyes. "Devinda's mother was my sister. My sister Sally."

"That's tough. I'm sorry."

MaryLou nodded. "Thanks." She raised her arm to check her watch. "Oh, dear. I've got to get busy."

I stood. "Sure. Me too."

"Just one thing." MaryLou clasped her hands and rested them on the edge of the desk. "We didn't finish our conversation before. Can I count on you not to say anything about Mr. Sykes?"

I shrugged. "Sure. Whatever. I won't breathe a word." I still didn't understand why, but it seemed less important.

MaryLou unclasped her hands and stood. "Let me give you a big hug," she said, stepping around the desk and gathering me in her arms. "You are such a good friend."

If it wasn't for the extra padding the years have added to my frame, she would have squeezed the breath right out of me. I didn't mind though. Given the rebuff from my uncle, I was grateful someone cared.

Not until later, driving up Seven Hills Road with Cowboy's truck in my rearview mirror, did I realize I hadn't asked for a tape of the show. That meant I'd have to go somewhere with radio reception to hear it. I was obligated now.

CHAPTER 10

"That's new," Cowboy commented as we approached the cabin. "You planted a bunch of flowers by the porch."

I shook my head. "They were here. Just hiding behind a bunch of weeds."

"Never noticed them. Guess I'm not much for gardening." He halted and turned to survey the yard. "You've sure done a nice job here, better'n I ever did."

I managed a polite denial and a restrained thank you, although personally, I thought so too. After planting a small vegetable garden, I'd dedicated myself to liberating the flower beds from their imprisonment under layers of mulched leaves and the unchecked growth of weeds and blackberry vines. It was some of the hardest work I ever did and I felt smug satisfaction at Cowboy's compliment as I led him inside.

Clarence was stretched out in his usual spot, snoring loudly. Twice I called his name before he stretched, languid as a cat, slowly rose up on all fours and ambled over to greet us. He gave Cowboy's boots a few curious sniffs before moving to my side. I bent to scratch his neck and the soft place by his ears, where his fur was all white. He panted a thank you, long tongue lolling out the side of his mouth.

"Okay, Clarence. Dinner time." I straightened and turned to Cowboy. "Just give me a few minutes. I'll feed Clarence and change into some dry clothes." I fanned my hands by my armpits, pantomiming sweat. This was one of the first really warm days of the season and the long-sleeved black shirt I'd picked that morning had been a bad choice.

Cowboy laughed. "No problem." He sat down on the couch and leaned back. Almost immediately, he leapt to his feet again. He turned and glared at the cushion as if it had bitten him on the butt. "You moved the couch," he said.

"Yup. Guilty as charged."

81

"Sorry." His face colored an embarrassed pink. "I didn't mean that the way it sounded. It's just, I don't know, confusing. I mean, here I am in this familiar room, a place I've lived in for years, and then suddenly it's not familiar, it's not the same room. Except it is. It makes a person dizzy, you know?"

I nodded sympathetically, thinking of my own dizzied reaction to meeting Uncle Mike again. I'd felt completely topsy-turvy when I realized how different he was from my past experience of him. Personally, this still had me shook up. I wasn't sure anymore he'd ever been the stern and forbidding man I remembered.

Cowboy folded himself back onto the couch. For a minute or so, he looked around the room, nodding thoughtfully. "The place looks nice. It really does. You're a better caretaker than I ever was." He shifted his weight on the couch and cleared his throat. "I guess what I'm trying to say is, you belong here now."

"Thanks. I appreciate you telling me that." The grin was still on my face when I turned and went into the kitchen. I got the dog food from the cabinet and scooped a cupful into Clarence's bowl. As soon as I set it down in front of him, he commenced gobbling. In seconds, he'd licked the bowl clean. Clarence moved fast when food was involved.

I went into the bedroom, yanking off my sweaty shirt as I crossed to the chest of drawers. I intended to pick something more appropriate for a warm evening but I had a hard time focusing. My mind kept returning to Cowboy's comment: "You belong here now." It was true. Never had I felt so comfortable, so secure, so nestled into a place. The cabin and the garden were my personal paradise and I wanted to dwell in this idyllic spot for the rest of my life.

I had some lofty thoughts about my future, but it wasn't long before my mind descended to the mundane. Paradise made me think of Eden. Eden suggested apples. Apples made me choose the red blouse and change into my red sandals too. I gave myself a spritz of *Wanna Play?* - the drugstore version of a pricier cologne - and hurried out of the bedroom, anxious to get to dinner. I was hungry.

Clarence had made friends with Cowboy and was getting his back scratched.

"We'd best get going," Cowboy said, when I walked in the room. He gave Clarence a pat and stood. "Sorry, old boy."

Clarence walked away, paws dragging on the floor – scritch, scratch, scritch – as if it took great effort to get to the center of the living room. Once he accomplished the distance of three or four feet, he heaved a Shakespearean sigh of disgust and flopped to the floor.

"Don't be so cranky," I told him, bending to scratch behind his ears. "Maybe I'll bring you home a treat."

Outside, the air smelled of dust and hay, like an old barn. We walked to the truck without saying anything. I felt self-conscious, as if I'd reverted to my awkward teenage self.

"We're going to my favorite restaurant," Cowboy said, ushering me into the truck's passenger seat. "It's down by the Yamhill River. I reserved seats overlooking the water."

"Sounds great."

"This place is better'n great. Last summer I went there so often, I got to try everything on the menu."

Cowboy guided the truck along the twists and turns of the back roads, heading towards West Yamhill. All the way, he described his favorites on the menu: hazelnut-breaded halibut, blackened salmon, pork loins with cranberry glaze. Dessert was a toss-up between a double chocolate cake and crème broule with caramel. I listened, salivating like Pavlov's dog.

"Here it is," Cowboy said, hanging a hard right into the graveled area fronting a wooden building. "The Homestead. You're in for a treat."

The small parking area was almost empty. Cowboy guided the big truck into a parking slot and turned off the ignition. The diesel engine clanked and shuddered. We got out of the truck and walked along a wooden sidewalk to the front door. My rubber-soled sandals didn't make the same satisfying thunk on the wood planks as Cowboy's cowboy boots. Up close, I could see that the building's rustic look was faked. Grey paint, cleverly applied, gave the wood a weathered effect.

Cowboy shoved open the faux barn door. A rush of icy conditioned air greeted us as we stepped into a lobby the size of an elevator. A woman in a shapeless black dress was crowded next to a small table stacked with menus.

"Good evening. Two for dinner?" The woman lifted two menus the size of serving trays from the pile and cradled them in her left arm. The deep wrinkles of a permanent frown belied the smile she offered us.

"We have a reservation," Cowboy said.

"You're in luck. I can seat you now." The Hostess hugged the menus to her chest and signaled us to follow.

Obediently, we trailed behind her, through the archway and into the dining room. Only a few diners were seated on the far side of the room, away from the long wall covered with dark draperies. Otherwise, the room was an expanse of empty tables draped with crisp white tablecloths. The Hostess marched us towards the other diners and stopped by a small table set for two. She pulled one of the chairs out and I sat.

"Uh, Ma,am?" Cowboy said. "We'd sure rather sit by the window." He gestured at the drapery. "And I wonder if we could open the curtains."

The Hostess shook her head. "Sorry. We're not seating anyone in that section. Suzanne will be your server tonight," she added as she dropped the oversized menus on the table.

Cowboy's eyes flashed with anger. He seized up a menu and gripped it with both hands, as if he were testing the heft of a plank of wood. For an awful moment, I was afraid he was going to hammer the menu down on the woman's skull. But the Hostess turned and made her get-away, quick-stepping across the dining room and then disappearing into the lobby.

"She's sure in a hurry," Cowboy said, dropping his frame into the other chair. He still held on to the menu.

I watched him, already doubting what I'd seen.

"I don't know," Cowboy said, shaking his head. "Last summer, you couldn't get in the door unless you had reservations." He glanced in the direction of the lobby. "She's new, that lady. I never saw her last year." There was a frown on his face as he pulled a pair of reading glasses from his shirt pocket and slipped them on, about half-way down his nose. That done, he flipped the menu open and studied it before heaving a dramatic sigh of relief. "Thank God. At least the menu's the same."

I propped the huge menu on the table and opened it. The entrées Cowboy had described were listed in large, spidery calligraphy on one side. The other side displayed a pen and ink sketch of the Homestead's exterior. The perspective was off-kilter, so the building looked to be collapsing on one side and swollen on the other.

My stomach growled, a beast threatening to turn on me unless I fed it, and soon. Even so, I had a hard time choosing between hazelnut halibut with garlic-mashed potatoes or salmon with marionberry salsa and couscous. I decided ask the server which entrée took less time to prepare. Unfortunately, she was nowhere in evidence. Cowboy had already swiveled his head several times in search of her and I noticed that people at the other tables were doing the same. One man made a show of looking at his watch. He wore a pastel pink golf shirt exactly matching the shirt worn by the woman seated next to him. The other couple at the table was dressed in identical navy blue shirts.

"We've been waiting fifteen minutes," the pink-shirted man said in a loud gravelly voice. His wife reached over and patted him on the hand. I could imagine her muttering, "Watch your blood pressure, dear."

As if on cue, one of the double doors from the kitchen flew open, banging hard against the wall. Startled, I turned my head in the direction of the sound. Everyone else must have also. The room got silent. Framed in the doorway was a blonde woman wearing a white blouse and a short black skirt topped by a frilly white apron. On her left shoulder, she balanced a tray loaded with glasses of water. The tray swayed ever so slightly, up and down, up and down. Ice cubes clinked in the glasses.

Someone at another table gasped. The door was closing. We could all see that it was going to smack against the tray. The woman holding the tray turned her head. She saw the door coming at her. As if in slow motion, the tray tilted lower and lower. Dangerously lower. I held my breath, mesmerized by the unfolding Charlie Chaplin skit.

And then it was over. Somehow, the woman scurried through the opening without dropping the tray or getting hit by the door. She crossed the room and settled the tray on an empty table without major mishap.

A relieved murmur of conversation started up. The server gave a quick tug on her thigh-high hemline and began carrying frosty water glasses to each table, two at a time. When the tray was empty, she tugged her skirt, pulled a pad and pencil from the apron pocket and held them aloft, poised to take an order.

"Okay," she said, her high-pitched voice cutting through the other noise. "Who's first?" I was sure the pink golf shirt man would claim this role. Instead, two women at the furthest table raised their hands, like good schoolgirls with the right answer.

Cowboy leaned across the table. "I'm starvin'. Let's order any kind of appetizer they can make real quick-like."

I nodded hearty agreement. While the server made her way from table to table, we surveyed the menu and decided on the demi-platter, described as an array of cheeses from the Northwest, accompanied by the restaurant's secret recipe rosemary bread. By the time the server got to our table, I was ready to settle for Saltines and Velveeta. Up close, I saw her blonde hair was streaked with gray. Fine lines puckered her upper lip and fanned out from the corners of her mouth. The server licked her thumb and turned to a clean page in the pad.

Cowboy gave the appetizer order. I decided on the hazelnut halibut and he ordered the seafood medley. The tip of her tongue poked from the server's mouth as she concentrated on writing down our order. When she finished, she slapped the book closed and gave her skirt a tug. "I'll go get these started," she said.

Cowboy held up the wine list. "Would you also bring us a bottle of the J and K pinot noir?" He turned to me. "Is that okay with you?"

Before I could answer, the waitress had grabbed the wine list from Cowboy and was squinting at it. "I don't see it on here," she said.

Rather diplomatically, I thought, Cowboy tapped the underside of the list. "It's under the Oregon wines section on the back."

She looked at Cowboy, her eyes wide with surprise, as if he'd just told her the world was really flat. "I never heard of no wines from Oregon," she said, flipping the menu over and scanning the page. "Huh. There's a lot of them. Hey, what kind did you say?"

"J and K." Cowboy repeated the name slowly.

She pulled the order pad from her pocket and flipped it open. "J and K," she echoed, tapping the end of the pencil thoughtfully on the pad. "You know, I used to live in Napa with this guy who was into wine. I must've drunk a lot of good wine in those days. A lot." She closed the pad and reinserted it in her pocket. "California wine, of course."

After she walked away, Cowboy smiled at me uncertainly and gestured at the table. "For now, I guess we've been condemned to bread and water, except without the bread." He shook his head in mock puzzlement. "They used to put bread and butter on the table right away, soon's you sat down. And I sure wish you could see the view. Oh well. What's important is the company, right?" He leaned forward. "I was kind of hoping we could just have a good ol' time, like we did when I met you."

"We did have a good time that night. And a lot of wine. Just like our server."

"Ain't that the truth." Cowboy lifted his water glass. "Here's to the good times. Good times with good friends."

I clinked my glass against his and took a long sip of cold water. He didn't drink from his glass, just sat there looking at me. Finally, he said, " I get the feeling you're different, somehow. You're not like most women. I think we really could be friends."

"If you're saying you're okay with just being friends, that's cool with me," I said.

Cowboy held his palms up. "Whoa. I never said no such thing. Truth is, I was hopin' for something quite different." He gazed at me with his Paul Newman eyes.

"Oh," I said. I felt my crotch grow warm and damp, melting my resolve.

Just in time, the kitchen door thumped against the wall. There was Suzanne the server, her left shoulder once again balancing a tray, this one holding a bottle and a couple of wine glasses. As she moved forward I could see there was a young guy behind her, wearing black jeans and a white shirt. Probably a busboy. His left arm supported a small tray holding a fat green bottle and several delicate champagne flutes.

It was eerie how the waitress once again scooted through the doorway, magically avoiding the swinging door. The busboy wasn't that lucky. Thwack. The closing door banged the boy's left elbow. His mouth and eyes rounded in surprise. Belatedly, he reached with his right hand to steady the tray. Time stopped, the way it does during emergencies and really good sex. Tray, bottle and champagne flutes, all seemed to drift languidly in the air, until suddenly, everything came down, clattering and shattering with a noise like someone banging discordantly on the high keys of a piano.

Several of the diners scraped their chairs back and stood to get a better look. The floor near the kitchen door glittered with flecks and shards of broken glass.

The champagne bottle rolled on the floor and settled against the wall. Still holding her tray aloft, the server stared at the boy. Both of them were wild-eyed and unmoving.

The hostess rushed into the dining room, hurrying past the server, and stepped carefully into the disaster area. Her shoes crunched on the glass. She halted in front of the boy and eyeballed him. Satisfied with her inspection, she turned to the group of diners.

"Everything's okay," she told us with a weak smile. "We'll have this cleaned up in a sec." With that, she and the busboy hustled through the doors and into the kitchen. A few seconds later, the hostess returned alone, carrying a broom and dustpan. She walked up to the server, who was motionless. "Keep serving," she hissed at the waitress.

Shaking her head, the server came over and set the tray with the wine bottle and two small wine glasses on the table. I saw Cowboy's eyebrows lift.

"Um, ma'am? Can you bring us those tall wide-rimmed glasses? I know they have some here."

She shrugged. "This is all the kind they got now. Do you still want the wine?"

Cowboy sat back in the chair with a resigned shrug. "Sure."

She dug a corkscrew from her apron pocket and positioned it on the bottle. A nub of pink tongue poked through her lips as she twisted the corkscrew down into the cork and then carefully pulled it from the bottle neck. "I usually have trouble with these little buggers," she said, dropping the corkscrew back in her pocket. She lifted the bottle and hurriedly splashed pinot noir to the brim of each glass. With a quick tug on her short skirt, she was gone.

I knew she was supposed to give Cowboy a taste first and then fill the glasses a third or maybe half-full. I eyed my full glass, wondering how I would lift it to my lips without disaster.

Cowboy shook his head. A piece of cork floated on the surface of his wine, a light-brown raft on a purple sea. He used a finger to fish the cork from his glass, splashing a few drops of wine on the tablecloth. His tight lips and the vee of his eyebrows made it easy to see he was not happy. Wordlessly, he lifted the glass by its stem and lifted the glass to his nose. Like a dog inspecting a new tree, he sniffed and sniffed again, considering the aromas. He took a sip, and then another. His eyes rolled up in his head as he considered the taste.

"Drinkable," he finally pronounced. "But damn. Sure would be better in the other glasses."

Carefully raising the over-filled glass to my lips, I took a small swallow. The wine was soft on my tongue and tasted like raspberries. I set the glass down, leaned my elbows on the table and changed the subject. "Have you ever listened to MaryLou's radio program?"

"Whew. Where'd that question come from?" He shook his head. "Fact is, I never have. Why?"

"Just curious. Me either."

Cowboy raised his eyebrows. "Really? I thought you were a big fan. Maybe not fanatic like those Betty SETII ladies. But still."

"SETII Betties," I corrected.

"Whatever." He paused a moment, scrutinizing me with his fiery blue eyes. "So how come?" Before I could answer, he slapped his forehead lightly. "I forgot. There's no radio at the cabin."

"Yeah, but I could just drive up to the top of the road." Wouldn't Sondra love hearing me now, I thought. "I'm not sure why I haven't done that. I guess I should. It's no big deal. Show's only on for five minutes or so."

"Tell you what." Cowboy gave me one of his Texas-sized smiles. "After dinner, I'll drive you up there and we'll listen together." He glanced at his wristwatch. "She's on at 10:00, right?"

I nodded. By this time my stomach was howling the hungry blues. The waitress had been back and forth twice, the first time bringing salads and a basket of bread to the table with the two women, the second time, a replacement serving of champagne to the table of the twin shirts.

Pink Shirt's voice rose above the chatter of the other diners. "These aren't champagne glasses, for god's sake."

Cowboy and I turned to look at the man, sitting at a table only a few feet from ours. The man was pointing at the glasses, which were definitely not champagne flutes. In fact, they looked to be the harp-shaped red wine glasses Cowboy had asked for earlier. While his wife tried to calm him, Mr. Pink Shirt was going on, loudly voicing his unhappiness. Ignoring him, Suzanne the server stood looking at the glasses with a puzzled expression, as if they'd appeared by magic. She shrugged. "Hey. It's my first night working here."

The Hostess returned to the dining room. "Let me see if I can help you," she said, as she approached the table. With a curt nod, she directed the waitress to the kitchen and set about quieting Mr. Pink Shirt and the others at his table.

Bam. The kitchen door slammed against the wall. For me, the sound was almost musical because I saw that Suzanne was heading towards us with a plate in each hand. When she stopped at our table, it was all I could do not to grab one of the plates and gobble the food ala Clarence.

"Here you go," the server said, setting my plate in front of me. I stared at it. The halibut was shiny white and raw-looking. Next to the fish, three small red potatoes floated in a lake of melted butter. The rest of the plate was occupied by a giant stalk of broccoli, overcooked to an unappetizing khaki color. I poked at the potatoes with my fork. Too hard. Next, the limp broccoli. Too soft. "I think my fish is still raw," I said.

"And this isn't what I ordered." Cowboy was looking at the pasta bowl in front of him, heaped with Pasta Alfredo.

"Are you sure?" Suzanne flipped the pages of her order pad. "It says right here." She stopped. "Oh. Sorry." She scooped the bowl of pasta off the table and put it on the tray.

"Where's our appetizer?" Cowboy said. "Aren't we supposed to get that first?"

She shook her head. "You didn't order an appetizer."

"Okay, forget it. But take that plate back to the kitchen and have them cook the fish."

She looked uncertainly at the plate. "She ate some already."

"No, I didn't," I said. "Do you think I want to die of salmonella?"

"You ordered halibut, not salmon." She pointed at the order pad. "It says right here."

"I'll take care of it, Suzanne," said the Hostess, stepping over to our table. She lifted my plate, stared at it for a moment, and frowned. She looked at Cowboy. "I'll check on your order too, sir," she said. "Suzanne, serve that plate before it goes cold."

"I'm so hungry, I almost could have eaten that fish raw," I said to Cowboy, when the Hostess and Suzanne hustled off.

He shook his head. "I can't believe it. Last summer, this place was great."

The door banged on the wall, signaling another appearance from the kitchen. Gingerly carrying a plate with the tips of her fingers, the server hurried to our table. She set the plate in front of me on the table. "Shit, that plate's hot," Suzanne said. "I think I burnt myself." She headed to the kitchen, shaking her hand in the air to cool it.

I took a nibble of the fish. It was overcooked and seasoned with a spicy red sauce. There was not a hazelnut to be found on my plate. The potatoes were soft now but the broccoli stalks had melted into a puddle of pale green ooze.

"Go on and eat," Cowboy urged me. "No need for both of us to suffer."

I took a couple of bites before laying down my fork to wait for his food to be served. The halibut was like spicy cardboard, the potatoes were soggy and the broccoli was inedible. Cowboy and I sipped the wine and several times attempted conversation, but mostly we waited for that kitchen door to announce itself. Minutes ticked endlessly by. Finally, the door banged open. The server emerged carrying a steaming plate of food. Silently, we watched her approach our table.

"Here's your order," she said, setting another bowl of pasta in front of Cowboy. This one was smothered in a red sauce dotted with brown things, maybe sausage.

"Darlin'," Cowboy said to the waitress. "I ordered a fish platter. Not spaghetti."

"Oh no." Her lower lip trembled and tears dewed on her eyelashes. When she lifted her hands to her mouth, I saw they were trembling.

"Hey. Don't worry, darlin'." Cowboy's voice was gentle. "I'm way too hungry to send another plate back to the kitchen." I liked him better for the kindness he showed to the waitress.

"Oh thank you," she said, wiping her eyes with her fingertips. "It's my first night. To tell you the truth, I hardly know what I'm doing."

As if we couldn't tell, I thought.

"Besides, it's not just me. The regular chef walked out yesterday so they have a new guy in the kitchen who I don't think ever cooked an egg before. And now the busboy went home just because he got cut from that glass. Wimp. Like some kind of fag or something. And now I have to do his job too." Her face tightened with anger as she turned away from the table.

"Hey you. Miss," Mr. Navy Blue Shirt called out. "Where's our dinner?"

Not to be outdone, Mr. Pink Shirt threw out his own challenge. "How come they got served before us?" He pointed at us.

Cowboy looked at me. "I must have one of their dinners." He leaned toward their table and called over. "One of you order spaghetti with sausage?"

Mrs. Pink Shirt turned our way and shook her head. "We all got steak."

"Phyllis, come on. We're going." Abruptly, Mr. Pink Shirt scraped his chair back and stood, followed quickly by his buddy. More reluctantly, the two women rose from their chairs and trailed after the men.

When he got to the door of the dining room, Pink Shirt halted and did an about face. His face was almost as purple as our wine. "I can't believe the rest of you aren't walking out with us," he yelled, shaking his fist at us. His wife tugged on his arm and he turned away. They followed the other couple from the room.

"Whoa," Cowboy said. "So they're having a bad night. No need to get so extreme. Bad service means a bad tip, that's all."

I smiled. "Well, maybe the situation doesn't deserve a 'Give me liberty or give me death' speech but this," I waved my hand to indicate not just our meals but the entire restaurant, "this is more than just a bad night."

Cowboy stared down at his plate. "'Fraid maybe you're right," he said, eyeing the pasta.

We turned our attention to our plates. I ate enough to quiet my belly - one potato and half of the fishy, tabasco-flavored cardboard - before I pushed the plate away. Cowboy only finished half the pasta before doing the same. We had, however, drained the wine bottle. When I stood up, I knew I'd consumed more than I should've.

By the time we left the restaurant, the sky was dark and studded with stars, some of which were probably satellites. We got into the truck and Cowboy flipped open the glove compartment.

"Let me try to make that fiasco up to you," he said, pulling out a small brown bag. "Here," he offered the bag to me. "Desert."

I reached inside. "Peanut brittle. Yum. My favorite."

"And a little after-dinner drink too." Cowboy lifted a plastic water bottle from the console cupholder.

I had to laugh. When he turned to start the truck up, I eyed Cowboy's profile thoughtfully, wondering if there was more to him than I'd assumed.

92

CHAPTER 11

Cowboy drove up the road beyond the cabin, to where the pavement ended. We parked at the flat spot with the great view I'd discovered on my first hike around the property. Although Cowboy's extended-cab diesel pickup was roomy enough for wild sex, we sat primly apart on the soft leather seats.

"I'm still surprised you never heard MaryLou's show," I said, continuing our earlier conversation.

"I've always been more Devin's friend." Cowboy's focus was on the console between us. He tapped on a couple of buttons and the side windows rolled down, letting in the warm evening breeze and the jingle-bell clatter of chirping crickets "What station is her show on?" Cowboy jabbed at the radio's on button.

"I'm not sure. I remember something about the far end of the AM dial. A local station."

"Seek and ye shall find," Cowboy said, poking at another button. Snatches of music alternated with the baritone buzz of static.

I leaned my head against the car seat and took a deep breath, inhaling the musty smells of summer, the lingering odor of newness inside the truck cab, whiffs of Cowboy's after-shave and my own cologne. The radio hissed. I heard MaryLou's voice. "That's her," I yelped, sitting forward.

"Said before. . .SETII. . . Seeking Energy, Truth, Infinity," said MaryLou. Her voice sounded thin and distant, although she was broadcasting from ten or fifteen miles away. Every few seconds, a wave of static drowned out her words. "Know truth? . . . Your heart and your mind."

"Lemme see if we can't get that in a little better." Cowboy poked at yet another of the buttons. On the hood, the truck's antenna glided upwards. The signal was stronger but spits of static still interrupted the flow of MaryLou's talk.

"Some people," said MaryLou, ". . . living a lie. The lie . . . never being open to the truth . . . deaf and blind to the truth that is inside . . . the truth that is all around. But by doing so, they can never . . . infinite wonder . . . infinite wisdom of the cosmos."

"What's she saying?" Cowboy gave me a puzzled look. "What little I can make of it sounds like B.S. to me."

"Shh."

He shrugged and slouched into the seat. His left arm was draped over the steering wheel, the right stretched along the seat back.

"How . . . know truth? By opening your eyes . . . looking around you . . . your ears and really listening . . . paying attention to the feelings you've ignored all your life." In the pause that followed, I heard the soft echo of another radio station. A man was speaking Spanish, way too fast for me to understand a word.

"Next time, I'll talk about . . . how to discover your internal truth . . . your eternal truth. This is MaryLou Hunter . . . understanding of SETII, you can be in charge of your own life."

"Geez almighty." Cowboy said, clicking the radio off. "No wonder Dev thinks she's throwing her money away, making that God awful show."

I considered this for a moment. "You mean, she has to pay to do the T.V. show?"

"You didn't know?" He arched an eyebrow in disbelief. "You betcha' she's paying. Using up tons of her inheritance money, from what Dev says."

"Well, it's her money. I guess she can spend it however she likes."

"You mean to tell me if you had a rich husband and you needed money, you wouldn't mind if he kept it all to himself to make some silly show?"

"It's not silly."

Cowboy shook his head. "I think it is. Silly and kind of selfish. Keeping the money for what she wants and not using it for what her family needs."

"What do you mean? I never noticed that the Hunters were living in poverty or anything like that."

Cowboy didn't answer right away. "Well, maybe I'm talking out of school, but Dev's business could use some help."

Probably true. I'd never seen a client climb the stairs to visit Devin's Capitol Investment nor had I ever taken a phone message for him. I doubted any amount of money would make a difference. Devin's personality would chase any prospective client out the door faster than a hound after a rabbit. Personally, I found it puzzling that Devin and Cowboy were such good buddies.

I turned to Cowboy. "How long have you been friends with Devin anyway?"

"We go back a ways," Cowboy said. "Met at college. Same fraternity."

"Fraternity? I thought you were a Texas Ranger or something like that."

He offered me a sheepish grin. "I've never exactly been to Texas. Grew up in West L.A., went to college in Arizona, moved here in the '80's. Got a job with a Dodge dealership, selling cars and trucks. Been there ever since."

I wanted to know where he got the Texas drawl, but I couldn't think how to ask the question without sounding bitchy. I tried another tack. "So how'd you get the name Cowboy?"

Rubbing his chin, Cowboy considered his answer. "Well," he finally said, "seems my little sister couldn't pronounce my name, which is Colby. Colby Winchester Butler the Third. Anyhow, she called me 'Coboy' instead. After a time, Coboy became Cowboy and that's what folks've called me ever since." He took his arm from the seatback and reached to turn the key in the ignition, ending the conversation.

We drove the mile or so back down the road to the cabin without exchanging another word. The truck's diesel engine made up for our silence, rumbling and pinging down the road and into the driveway. As soon as the truck rolled to a stop, I had the door open and one foot on the running board. "Thanks," I said. "See you."

"Wait," he said, touching me gently on my left shoulder. "How 'bout Labor Day weekend? There's a big barbeque and fireworks on the riverfront."

"Oh, I don't know." He probably thought I was acting coy. Really, I was being a wimp, not telling him no straight out.

"How's about I call you tomorrow or Friday? Maybe by then you'll know you want to say yes." He winked at me. "Take care, darlin'."

I slid from the seat before he could lean over to kiss me or anything else that would be awkward. My short legs dangled in the air a moment before I touched solid ground. Pushing the heavy truck door closed, I turned and darted up the pathway to the cabin porch where Clarence waited for me like an anxious father. As soon as I climbed the steps and knelt to hug the dog, Cowboy backed the truck out of the driveway and took off down the road. The stink of diesel lingered in the air long after the rumble and ping of the truck faded in the darkness.

The next day at work, just as I turned on the telephone answering machine so I could take my lunch break, MaryLou rushed into my little office. She was wearing a white tuxedo shirt with black pants. A turquoise pendant hung from her neck on a wide silver chain. She came around the desk and surrounded me in a hug as strong as a wrestling hold. "I can't wait," she said, squeezing me tighter. "How was it? Do you like him? You're going out again, right?"

"I'll tell you everything," I gasped. "Just let me go."

Releasing her hold, MaryLou took a step back and scanned my face. "I heard you listened to my show, finally."

I nodded, unsure which question I didn't want to answer the most.

"So?"

"So what?"

She smiled. "You're teasing me, aren't you? Tell me about your date with Cowboy first."

"It was fine."

"Okay. You don't have to tell me if you don't want to. You know I only ask because I care about you. I just want you to have happiness." MaryLou shook her head. "All right then, tell me what you thought of the radio show."

"Ah. Well, it was interesting to hear you. Your voice sounded so different. I was surprised."

"A.M. radio." She waved her hand in the air, as if she were swatting away a pesky fly. "It'll be better when we do those spots on TV."

"Not long now," I said.

MaryLou nodded and glanced at her watch. "Oh dear. I'm supposed to pick Devinda up early today. I'd better go." She headed to the door, then stopped short and veered back to stand in front of me. "I really value your opinion, Ruby," she said. "Thanks so much for being honest. I'm glad you liked what you heard."

"Sure," I said, feeling a guilty relief that she'd taken my comment as a compliment.

MaryLou cocked her head slightly to one side. "Ruby? You've kept your promise haven't you?"

"Of course."

She nodded approvingly. "Why don't you take the afternoon off," she said. "You've been working hard. You deserve some time."

"What about the phones?"

MaryLou waved my protest away. "Don't worry about it. Just keep the answer machine on." She turned and went to the doorway. "I'll see you tomorrow," she said, and disappeared from view.

I took a bit of time straightening the desk before I left. My first stop was the deli on State Street. I got a turkey and cheese sandwich on rye and a cup of coffee and slid into a corner booth. While I munched and sipped, I surveyed the bulletin board on the wall in front of me. The board was a crazy jumble of hand-printed index cards selling cars, washing machines, lawnmowers and dining room sets. On the wall next to the board, brightly colored flyers promoted local events, some of them for dates that were many months past. I ate almost the entire sandwich before I spotted a bright orange flyer for last October's Halloween party at the Kids Klub, the after-school place my uncle headed up. I jotted the address on a napkin. Maybe I'd take a side-trip on my way home.

The address was on Mission, in the area known as Felony Flats because of its proximity to the state penitentiary. Most of the houses I drove past were old and tired looking, with peeling paint, boarded up windows and weed-choked yards. More than a few had junky-looking trucks and cars parked in the front yard. Even in the moist, mild climate of the Willamette Valley, there wasn't much green grass on those lawns. Years earlier, the neighborhood made national news when the notorious Diane Downs, convicted of shooting her three kids and killing one of them, escaped and hid out in Felony Flats until she was recaptured.

I found the Kids Klub at the corner of Mission and Fourteenth, housed in a big pink building that had once been a supermarket. I turned and drove up the slope of the driveway into the parking lot. When I got out of the Golf, my heart was beating fast and I had a nervous tickle in my stomach. Half the parking lot had been fenced off and converted to make a couple of basketball courts. The area was empty now, except for a lone figure shooting baskets at the far court. The sound of the ball hitting the backboard had a metallic edge to it, like maybe the hoop was loose.

I was almost to the building when I heard my name being called. Startled, I looked left and right before I saw Uncle Mike jogging towards me, a basketball cradled in the curve of his arm. He was wearing gray sweats and a tight powder blue tee shirt that was darkened with sweat stains. A black sweatband with a Nike insignia circled his head like a crown.

"Hey," I greeted him. As he got closer, I could see that his upper arms were well-muscled and there was no extra fat on his frame. Self-consciously, I straightened my spine and pulled in my stomach muscles.

"Hey yourself," he said, stopping a few feet from where I stood. He was breathing heavily but not out of breath. "This is a surprise. How are you?"

"Okay. And you?"

"Okay." He bounced the ball once on the ground and tucked it under his arm again.

"I should have called," I said, regretting my impetuous decision to drop in on him. "I'm sorry. I shouldn't just pop in on you without warning."

"Oh, Ruby, you have nothing to apologize for. I'm the one who's been negligent." Glancing down at his sweat-soaked shirt, he grimaced. "Why don't you let me get out of these duds and take a shower? We really need to talk." He hesitated a moment. "I'm sorry. Do you have the time to wait?"

I nodded. "I can wait." Something in his manner convinced he was going to tell me something awful. Was he sick? Could someone this healthy-looking have cancer?

"Come on," he said, shifting the ball to his other arm. "You can wait in my office. You want a soda? Ice cream?"

"That's okay." Minutes ago, eyeing my uncle's trim form, I'd resolved to shed the extra pounds that rolled above my waist when I sat.

Uncle Mike set a brisk pace as he headed into the pink building. I had to scurry to keep up with him. "I won't be but a minute," he said as we went inside. "That way's the cafeteria and the gym." Without breaking his stride, he pointed at a row of doors on our left. The doors were painted bright red. "We're going this way," he said, heading to the right. "By the way, how's Clarence?"

We chatted about the dog and the weather as Uncle Mike ushered me to his office. It was at the end of the hallway, a windowless cubbyhole that had probably served as the mop and broom closet back in supermarket days.

Photographs of kids lined the walls, from floor to ceiling. One side of the narrow room was taken up by Mike's desk, a piece of plywood straddling two short metal file cabinets. Stacks of paper were spread across the desktop, barely leaving room for an ancient rotary-dial telephone and a portable computer that was folded closed. A metal folding chair sat in front of the desk. Aside from the small open space in the center of the office where the two of us stood, the rest of the room was crowded with a sagging couch draped with a green and blue and yellow India print bedspread.

"Do you mind waiting here?" Uncle Mike said. His blue eyes were fixed on me, as if my response mattered.

"This is fine." I arranged my face into a reassuring smile. Much as I wanted to know what he had to say, I didn't mind delaying the delivery of bad news, at least a bit.

"You sure you don't want anything?" When I shook my head, he lifted his eyebrows. "Okay. I'll be back in no time."

I scanned the walls, looking at the smiling boys and girls, all ages, all sizes. Many of the kids were blond and blue-eyed but the newer-looking photos showed bright-eyed kids who were African-American, Native American, Hispanic, Asian and Caucasian. The background in the photos was usually the Kids Klub building. Some of them had scribbled messages, telling Uncle Mike he was the best, the greatest, the dad they never had.

Once more, I experienced the dizzying sensation that my world had slipped from its orbit. Had Mike changed so drastically from the way I remembered him? Or was this always the real Mike? If so, what was wrong with me that I hadn't seen the truth? The office was too small for pacing back and forth. Instead, I sat on the sagging couch, crossing my legs, uncrossing them, crossing them again, unable to find a comfortable position, physically or mentally.

Uncle Mike reappeared in only fifteen minutes. His silver hair was wet and slicked back. He had on jeans and a blue sweatshirt with the Kids Klub logo. The color gave extra intensity to his eyes. He pulled the door shut and came to sit next to me on the couch. He inhaled deeply, like someone getting ready to sing the "Star Spangled Banner."

"This isn't easy to say." Uncle Mike's voice was tight. "I guess I've been avoiding you. I knew the next time we saw each other I'd have to tell you about me."

This was it. The big C. Or worse, if that's possible. I reached for his hand.

He stared at our intertwined fingers. "I thought you'd already guessed. But maybe not."

"Just tell me." I held my breath. My body was rigid.

"I'm gay, Ruby."

CHAPTER 12

"I'm gay." Uncle Mike's words ignited an explosion of emotions, firecrackers going off in my brain. I knew he was watching me, waiting for my response. Unsure how to translate my mixed-up emotions into words, I blurted the first thing that came to mind. "I'm glad you're not dying," I said. My voice was high and squeaky, a cartoon mouse voice.

Uncle Mike widened his eyes, startled. "You thought that's what I was going to tell you?"

I nodded. "You've been avoiding me. When I didn't hear from you, I figured you didn't want to see me. But when you said you had something to tell me, I thought, if you were sick it explained everything."

"I'm really sorry." Uncle Mike reached over and gently touched my arm. "I wanted to be honest with you. But I was afraid to tell you, afraid I'd lose you again. That's why I didn't call." He shook his head. "I was so caught up in my own issue, I didn't think clearly about how you'd be feeling."

"Why are you telling me now?" As soon as the question burst from my lips, I realized how childish it sounded.

He took his hand away, letting it rest on his knee. "I guess I want to start over. I'd get to know the real Ruby and you'd get to know the real Mike." He gave me a crooked smile. "What do you think?"

My response came slowly. "We could try, I guess. But what about Aunt Elaine?"

Mike nodded his head. "Fair question. Back when we got married, people said being homosexual was a choice. I tried to ignore my feelings but as time went on, it was getting more difficult. At one point, I even talked to a doctor about it and he told me a good woman and a few hours on a psychiatrist's couch would cure me. Cure me. As if I had an illness." His mouth trembled. "When I finally admitted to myself who I really am, I asked Elaine for a divorce. That's about when your folks died. She pleaded with me to stay, to help raise you."

"She knew." With a little epiphany, I remembered their separate bedrooms and the polite, almost formal manner they used with each other.

"She knew and she blamed herself," he paused and wiggled his fingers, drawing quotation marks in the air, "for failing to reform me. I kept telling her it had nothing to do with her but she never quite believed me."

"Oh." I wanted to say more but I was tongue-tied and my brain felt tangled in knots. My childhood, my memories, things I thought I knew, had suddenly become a jigsaw puzzle I'd put together before except now the pieces were different shapes and made a different picture. Almost right away, I fit a couple of the new pieces together. "So Barry? I mean, you and Barry . . . ?"

Uncle Mike's expression brightened. "He makes me feel good. He makes me laugh."

"Are you living together?"

The sunshine disappeared. "We've been seeing each other for a couple of years. Barry wants us to live together but I'm afraid to be that open." He gestured at the walls of photos. "It would hurt the Kids Klub. I can't take that chance."

I wanted to argue but I knew he was right. There were people who would see a gay man working with children as a bad thing. In fact, he'd worried I was one of those people."You were afraid to tell me you're gay?"

Uncle Mike lowered his eyes. "I thought you'd hate me. And I didn't want that."

This time, I was the one who reached over to touch him, placing my hand over his. "I'm not sure how I feel except maybe like I've been through an earthquake. It's not because you're gay. It's because of everything changing from the way I believed it was." I took a deep breath. "You know, when I was a kid I didn't think you liked me very much."

"I know. I wish I could make it up to you." He stared at the wall as if he could look through it and into the past. "I felt trapped but I couldn't break my promise to Elaine, especially after she got sick. I guess I was so wrapped up in feeling sorry for myself, I didn't have the time or patience for a spirited kid like you."

"Spirited? I guess I was pretty much a brat."

"You were angry, but you had every right to be." Uncle Mike turned to give me a warm look. His eyes were the blue of a June sky. "Elaine thought if we didn't talk about your parents taking off and then the way they died, you would forget. And I went along with it. So you grew up in a house where we didn't talk about the truth of things. And I apologize for that."

I gulped back the sudden swelling of sadness in my throat and nodded, not trusting my voice. I was sorry for all of us, but mostly my uncle. For one reason and another, he'd spent a lifetime having to hide a part of who he was.

"You know," Uncle Mike said, "it's really because of you that there's a Kids Klub. After you disappeared, I spent some time looking for you, including on the street, and I was shocked at how many kids were living out there. I went back to college, got a degree in Human Services and started working for a homeless shelter. After a few years, I helped start this place." He gave my hand a little squeeze. "I'm so glad we found each other. We have a second chance to make it right."

I squeezed back. "I want that," I said, realizing as I spoke the words how much I really meant them.

Suddenly the office door flung open. A chunky woman with dark hair appeared in the doorway. "Mike, we need you out here." Her voice was shrill, on the edge of hysteria.

He was up and out the door before I could struggle from the couch. I tracked Mike and the woman down the hall and through a red door leading into the gym. In the middle of the floor, a crowd of kids clustered around Mike and the dark-haired woman. As I got closer, I saw that each of the adults had their arms wrapped tight around a struggling boy. The angry red-faced boy in Mike's arms looked familiar. A trickle of blood leaked from his nose. The other boy appeared in worse shape, even though he was bigger. He had a red, puffy right eye and a jagged, Mark of Zorro scratch on his cheek.

"Okay everyone," Mike said. His commanding tone echoed in the large room. "Go find something else to do. We'll take care of business here."

At that moment, a young man wearing a red shirt with the Kid's Place logo came into the gym. Dangling from his neck was a jock's necklace, a black braided cord with a silver whistle . The man grabbed the whistle in his fist and lifted it to his lips, making an ear-piercing screech that got everyone's attention. "C'mon kids," he yelled. "Let's hit the courts." He started walking to the doors. The girls and boys reluctantly followed him, without the chatter and buzz that kids usually make.

In the interval, I'd grabbed another look at the familiar-looking boy. Of course he looked familiar. He was Lyman Hunter, MaryLou's son.

He recognized me too. "Ruby?" he said. "What are you doing here?" His voice was hoarse. Either he'd been yelling or he'd been punched in the throat.

Before I could answer, Mike spoke up. "Ruby? You know this boy?"

"I do."

"You gonna tell my mom?"

The look on Lyman's face reminded me of the first time I'd met him, when I caught him hurting Clarence. "Tell her what?"

Lyman narrowed his eyes and studied the other boy, as if he were mentally debating how much to reveal.

"I didn't do nothin'," the other boy declared. "He started it." He thrust his chin in Lyman's direction and sneered. The hard expression was incongruous with his pudgy face. He muttered something under his breath.

"What was that, George," the woman asked harshly. "What did you say?" She tightened her grip and gave the boy a shake.

"Ma," he whined.

"Connie," Uncle Mike said.

She shrugged and let go of the boy. George rubbed his arms, as if she'd hurt him, but I suspected he was faking. "I just called him Lyme the Slime," George said. "All the kids call him that."

"That's not all you said." Lyman lurched forward but Uncle Mike was faster and stronger. Lyman wriggled like a wet dog to escape Mike's grasp. Finally, gasping for breath, he gave up the struggle. But not the fight. He fixed his glare on George. "You called me a faggot. You take it back."

Uncle Mike focused his blue eyes on George. "George. Look at me." Uncle Mike was gentle but firm. I admired that, especially when I knew those words must hurt. Personally, I wanted to slap and shake both boys.

"George," repeated Uncle Mike.

The boy finally lifted his head. I could see he was blinking back tears. He swallowed hard. "Yeah?"

"You know the rules here. No name-calling. No fighting. What do you have to say for yourself?"

"Sorry," George said, looking at Uncle Mike, not Lyman.

"Tell him," Uncle Mike nodded in Lyman's direction.

George wiped the back of his hand under his nose. "Sorry," he mumbled.

Connie folded her arms across her chest. "Sorry isn't good enough, young man. You're 14-years-old but you act like a child. What am I going to do with you? What am I going to do?"

"Hey, Mom. Don't cry," George said, and hesitantly patted his mother's shoulder.

Uncle Mike turned to Lyman. "Are you calmed down?" Lyman nodded. Uncle Mike looked at Connie and me. "Lyman and George and I are going to talk about consequences now," he said.

Together, Connie and I walked out of the gym and through the large foyer. The front doors were open wide. Outside, we were greeted by a warm breeze that carried comforting playground sounds to us. The basketball courts teemed with kids, littlest ones closest to us, older kids at the far end.

Connie pointed at the first court. "That's my younger boy. Lucas." She dug a bedraggled tissue from the pocket of her pants and dabbed at her eyes. "We moved up here from California because of the gangs. I didn't want them growing up that way. But George just wants to fight." She crumpled the tissue in an angry fist. "He's just like his father."

I offered her a sympathetic look. "I guess it's pretty hard, being a parent these days."

"That's no joke. Thank God for Mike and the Kids Klub. The kids love him and so do us moms." She narrowed her eyes. "Say. You know that Lyman?"

"He's a neighbor kid. I don't really know him that well." It was too complicated, I thought, to explain that he was also the son of my employer and benefactor.

"That boy is very troubled. Not to excuse what George did, but that boy is seriously mental." Connie shook her head. "Being his mother would be pure hell."

We heard footsteps behind us and turned to see George emerging from the building. He plodded over to us, his shoulders rounded and his mouth turned down. "I have to leave," he said to his mother. "I can't come back until next week. And then I have cleanup duty the whole month."

Connie nodded. "Sounds fair," she said. "I'll take you home and then come back for Lucas." She turned to me. "Hey. I never asked which one was your kid."

"None of them. I'm here to visit Mike."

She eyed me suspiciously. "You a social worker?"

"Uh uh. Mike's my uncle." I felt a little rush of pride. My uncle.

"Okay then," she said. "Nice to make your acquaintance. And you," she addressed her son. "You get a move on. Now." She followed the shuffling footsteps of her son over to a faded blue Ford Taurus parked a few slots from my Golf. George went to the driver's side. Connie stopped, put her hands on her hips, and said something I couldn't hear. The meaning was obvious from George's reaction. Dejectedly, he walked around the car to the other side, got in and slumped in the seat. Connie got behind the wheel and started the engine. As the car pulled away, she waved at me. I waved back.

"Ruby?" Uncle Mike's voice turned me around. He and Lyman were waiting just in front of the entry, a few feet from where I stood. Already, Lyman was taller than my uncle, but he looked slight and unfinished next to Mike's sturdy frame. A backpack was flung carelessly over Lyman's right shoulder. He'd cleaned the crusted blood from his face, combed his hair and tucked in his shirt.

"Ruby?" Lyman echoed Uncle Mike. "Um. I need to leave." He glanced at Uncle Mike. "I mean, would you take me home? Please?"

"Sure." I also looked at Uncle Mike for guidance. He nodded approval. "I guess I'll see you soon," I said to him, making it not quite a question, not quite a statement of fact.

"You bet," he said. "If you don't call me in a few days, I'll call you. I think we have a lot to talk about." He reached out and took my hand, squeezing it gently.

I squeezed back. "I'll call you. I promise." Reluctantly, I let go and turned to the boy. "Come on, Lyman. Let's go."

Lyman trailed behind me as I crossed the parking lot. As soon as I unlocked the passenger side, he opened the door, tossed his book bag on the floor and slouched into the seat the same way George had.

"Seat belt," I instructed him.

He pulled the belt across his chest and snapped it closed with only a small sigh of protest at my adult caution.

I put the key in the ignition and paused. "Hey, Lyman, what about your mom? Won't she be coming here to pick you up?"

"Uh uh. Mike made me call her to say I was being sent home. She's the one who said you should take me." He delivered this little speech without looking up, as if he were talking to his shoes.

"You must've told her I was there."

He gave me a contemptuous sneer. "Duh."

"You want to walk home?" I shot back.

Slumping even lower in the seat, Lyman mumbled "Sorry."

We drove without speaking for several blocks. "Radio?" I asked. He shook his head. Let him be, I thought, remembering my own sullen adolescence. Maybe if I kept quiet, he would eventually want to fill the silence. By the time we got to the turn for Seven Hills Road, however, I decided it was up to me to start the conversation if I wanted to have one. After the Clarence episode, I'd never followed up on my intention to give him a good talking-to and this was a good opportunity. But how to say it so he'd really hear me? I was so busy searching the file cabinets of my brain for words that blended both wisdom and coolness I was startled when Lyman actually spoke.

"How come you changed Snoopy's name?"

"What? Oh. I knew another bulldog called Clarence. Besides, he seems to like his new name better." I glanced sideways, to see how he reacted to this, hoping he wasn't the one who'd chosen the name Snoopy.

"Devinda named him. I wanted to call him Tank." He looked up, surprised, when I laughed. Encouraged by my good humor, he continued talking. "Clarence is a good name too. Can I come see him? I kind of miss him."

"Sure. But don't be surprised if he's not thrilled to see you. Dogs are more forgiving than people but he'll remember that you hurt him and he might keep his distance."

Lyman got thoughtful, biting at his lower lip and furrowing his forehead. "I didn't mean to hurt him. Would he understand if I told him I was sorry?"

We were just rounding the last curve, only a half-mile from the Hunter place. Impulsively, I pulled onto a wide, graveled turnout and switched off the ignition. I faced Lyman, who sat watching me warily. "I think Clarence understands actions better than words. If you're serious about feeling sorry, you need to be gentle and kind with him from now on."

"Okay." He looked down at his hands resting on his lap. "Are you going lecture me about the fight too?"

"I'm not good at lecturing," I said. "You must already know that kicking dogs and getting in fights are not admirable qualities in a person."

"I know. But sometimes I get so mad." His hands tightened into fists. "I get mad at everybody and everything. And especially at my." His voice faltered. "Never mind."

"Look, Lyman. I was a mess when I was your age. I was angry and maybe I had some pretty good reasons to be. Trouble is, anger by itself doesn't solve anything and misdirected anger just creates more problems. Like today."

He gave me a skeptical look. "You were a mess?"

"It's nice that you find that hard to believe," I said. "But yes, I was."

"I know I should've ignored that dumbhead George but it was like he was poking my eyes with a stick. I wanted to beat the shit out of him." He eyed me, watching my reaction to what he'd said.

"I can understand that kind of feeling. But I think part of growing up is learning when it's worth it to fight and when it's not. I don't think George and his name-calling was worth it."

"Yeah, I guess I was a dumbhead too."

I was smart enough to keep quiet, giving him time to say what he had to say and time to trust me, too. It was late afternoon, the hottest time of the day. There was no breeze anymore, just the stifling air. The only movement I could see was waves of heat rising from the blacktop.

"You really were mad at everything when you were my age?"

"Yeah. I still feel that way sometimes."

"Really? I thought grownups weren't supposed to get mad anymore."

"Personally, I think there's plenty of shit in the world that people should get angry about. It's how you act on your anger that matters."

Lyman grinned. "You sound a lot like Mike, you know?"

I was surprised at how good that made me feel.

CHAPTER 13

I awoke before dawn, tangled in the sheets and too sweaty to sleep. All summer, the usually temperate Pacific Northwest had baked under an unrelenting sun. That Labor Day was no exception. Clarence was curled up near the bed, snoring contentedly, his legs twitching slightly. Maybe in his dreams he escaped his short chunky body to run sleek as a greyhound and with the endurance of a sled dog. I tiptoed past him and went into the kitchen to make coffee.

As soon as the Italian roast was brewed I poured a mug and went out to the porch, dressed only in underpants and an oversized, sleeveless cotton shirt. Savoring the relative coolness of early morning, I sipped the strong, earthy coffee and watched the night sky give way to a rosy-grey dawn. In the trees, birds began to twitter merrily, perhaps planning their own holiday from hunting seeds and worms. I was so overcome with happiness at how lovely and perfect everything was, I resolved to get up early all the time.

It didn't take long before my euphoria evaporated under the hot glare of reality. As the light increased, I saw that the garden and flowerbeds were drooping from yesterday's 100-plus degrees. I emptied the coffee mug with a few quick gulps, set it on the railing and went to fetch the watering can. Conditions were so dry the Governor had issued a plea for voluntary rationing of water use. Hand-watering was my way of not wasting a drop, even though it took many trips schlepping the heavy can back and forth, from faucet to plants. A few days earlier, when Cowboy showed up at the office with a latte for me, I'd complained about stiff shoulders and sore arms. He said he'd help set up drip irrigation for the flowers and garden if I still lived in the cabin the following summer.

"I'll be there," I declared. "I can't imagine being anywhere else."

"Never say never," Cowboy drawled. I rolled my eyes at the cliché.

By the time I finished watering the flower beds and the tomatoes, peppers and corn, I was a mess. My feet were dusty and my shirt was ripped up the side, the result of a fight with a blackberry vine that had sneaked into the garden overnight. I yanked off the tattered shirt to inspect the damage.

Because I'm probably the world's worst seamstress, I became totally absorbed in the challenge of how I might repair the rips in my shirt. I was surprised when MaryLou's Suburban chugged into the driveway. The monster vehicle rolled to a stop. MaryLou opened the door and climbed out, leaving the engine running. She wore a faded tee shirt, baggy sweat pants and rubber thongs. When she got closer, I saw that her hair was a nest of tangles and, without the usual makeup and mascara, her face was pale and undefined.

MaryLou was breathing hard when she reached the porch. She climbed up the steps and confronted me, hands on her hips and an angry burn in her eyes. "Where've you been? I tried calling you a bunch of times, but there was no answer."

"I was outside."

MaryLou frowned.

"What?" I said, defensively.

"Honestly, Ruby. You're prancing around half-naked where anyone could see you." Her nose wrinkled, as if I smelled bad. "Plus, you look like you've been rolling around in the dirt."

"MaryLou, come on. Who's going to see me? You're the only neighbor for a mile except for old Mrs. Hallmark and she can't see more than a couple of inches in front of her on a good day."

"That's not the point. Women shouldn't expose themselves like that. It's so, I don't know, so wanton." She glanced suspiciously at the cabin. "Is Cowboy here?"

"No, he's not." I shook my head slowly, puzzled by her behavior "Why did you come up here? What's going on that's so important at 6:00 in the morning, for God's sake?"

"I've been up for hours," she said. "I almost called you in the middle of the night to evict you."

"Evict me?" I couldn't hold back the note of horror in my voice. "Why?"

"I'm so angry at you, Ruby. Why didn't you say anything about Lyman? I thought you were my friend."

"What do you mean? What should I have told you?"

"About his fight at that place, that Kid's something-or-other."

"But you knew about it. Lyman called you and told you."

She waved an arm, brushing away what I'd said. "You never told me he came up here to see you."

"What's the big deal? It was yesterday. He helped me groom Clarence and get stuff out of the garden."

She blinked. "He did? I can never get him to do work for me."

"I didn't tell him it was work. He just thought he was having a good time."

MaryLou gave me a sharp look. "What about that fight? You should have said something to me."

"But Uncle Mike made Lyman call you and tell you about it. What more could I add?" I looked down at the empty cup in my hands. "MaryLou, I've got to get some more coffee." I made a face. "And put a shirt on."

She combed her fingers through her hair, making it even messier. "I guess maybe I over-reacted a bit. About evicting you and all."

"It's okay. You want some coffee?"

"No. I've only got a minute. Devin will be wondering where I am. But you go ahead." She flicked her hand, gesturing for me to go inside.

I turned and went in, blinking at the sudden change from bright to dark. MaryLou followed me into the kitchen. I poured coffee into the mug and took a quick, grateful sip.

"For goodness sakes, Ruby. Will you please get dressed?" MaryLou snapped.

Taken aback by her Jekyll and Hyde act, I set the mug on the counter a little more forcefully than necessary. Several drops of coffee splashed out and beaded on the tile. They looked like chocolate M & M's, my favorite. I wiped at the drops and took a deep breath, recalling my advice to Lyman. I decided to be patient with MaryLou. She was never this abrupt and demanding with me. Something else had to be wrong, something she wasn't talking about. I stepped into the bedroom and quickly dressed in shorts and the wrinkled blue linen top I'd worn the day before.

"MaryLou, what's going on?" I asked when I returned to the kitchen. "I've never seen you so jumpy and upset. Is there something wrong?" I picked up the coffee mug and took a long slurp of lukewarm Italian, eyeing MaryLou's reaction over the rim.

MaryLou cocked her head to the side. "Ruby," she said at last. "What did you say about your uncle before?"

"Mike? He runs the Kids Klub, remember? He's the one who told Lyman to call you."

"You were there visiting him?"

I nodded and swallowed another gulp of coffee.

"I didn't know you've been meeting with him. I thought you told me he wasn't interested in seeing you."

"Well, I decided to try one more time. And I'm glad I did."

"I know I encouraged you to see him, but now I'm not so sure. After this fight Lyman got into, I decided to do a little checking." She shook her head. "I'm forbidding Lyman to ever go back to that Kid's place."

"What do you mean? Why?"

"I asked around and I don't like what I found out. I'm thinking maybe I should do something about it."

"What're you talking about?" Something in MaryLou's voice raised goose-bumps on my arms even though the gauge on the kitchen window thermometer showed 75 degrees.

The phone shrilled, startling both of us. I picked up the receiver. "Hello?"

"She there?" It was Devin's voice.

Silently, I held the receiver out. MaryLou took it and turned her back, the telephone cord coiling around her like a shiny black snake. She murmured soothingly, trying to charm Devin, but it didn't work. I could hear his angry response through the earpiece.

MaryLou clicked the phone off and turned around. "Ruby, I've got to go. Maybe I'll come back later and we can talk some more."

"Sure. Cowboy isn't picking me up 'til afternoon sometime. We're going to the Labor Day celebration at the park."

"Then maybe I'll catch you there. See you later." She rushed out the door.

Moments later, I heard the SUV roar out of the graveled driveway. Sometimes, noise carries a long way in the country. I could follow the progress of the Suburban as it whooshed down the road. A mile later there was a squeal of tires as MaryLou hit the brakes to make the sharp left turn into the Hunter's driveway. MaryLou always braked hard and at the last possible moment. The back wall of her garage had been repaired several times because she'd pulled in too fast.

The clicking of Clarence's nails on the wood floor diverted my attention. He tended to stay in the bedroom when MaryLou visited. Anyway, he'd never been an early riser. I fed him and made my breakfast – a bowl of granola and another mug of coffee. Usually, I read a magazine or a book when I eat breakfast but that morning I found myself staring into space, cereal spoon in mid-air, mentally replaying the scene that had just occurred. I was still puzzled by MaryLou's anger and threat to evict me. Even more disturbing was the nagging suspicion my response had been too nice. After my divorce from Bob, I vowed no one would ever speak down to me in that know-it-all tone of voice. The very same tone MaryLou had used this morning. For the second time in an hour, I felt chilled, wondering if I'd developed a Bob-like relationship with MaryLou. Except, Bob wouldn't have minded my shirt being off.

Clarence rubbed against my leg, interrupting my mental self-flogging. Dropping gracelessly to the floor, I wrapped my arms around his sturdy neck. Hot tears erupted from my eyes and flowed down my cheeks, the salty lava of self-pity. Even with my nose stuffed from crying, I could smell Clarence's musty bulldog scent. I started to feel better. Dogs give the most wonderful comfort and sympathy. Cats, horses, guinea pigs and even fish will do in a pinch. Personally, I bet we could double the recovery rate if there were resident pets in every hospital and convalescent home.

"Thank you, Clarence," I whispered. As quick as an anteater, Clarence's sandpaper tongue slurped the last tears from my cheek.

We dozed off, side-by-side on the carpet. I awoke with a start hours later. Once again, I got up and tip-toed past my sleeping dog. That's when I caught a glimpse of the clock and jumped into rush mode, showering and dressing and feeding Clarence an early dinner. The adrenaline rush got me ready on time, but I felt groggy and irritable when Cowboy arrived to pick me up.

I was still moody a few hours later, slowly walking alongside Cowboy, eyeing the booths filled with crafts and artwork. The walkway was jammed with people and the humid air was suffocating. I was wearing my red sandals, a lightweight denim skirt and a white tank top, but I might as well have been wrapped in fur. Sweat bubbled out of every pore, from my scalp to the soles of my feet. Even my underwear felt soggy and I couldn't wipe away my sweat moustache fast enough before it grew back again.

Maybe that's why none of the pottery, jewelry or art displays lured me. When Cowboy halted to check out a display of silver belt buckles, I found my attention wandering from the offerings to the commotion attracting a growing crowd the next aisle over, where the political booths were situated. All I could see was a crush of people. Then I noticed a long red, white and blue banner being hoisted on a pole. As it unfurled, a John Phillips Sousa march blared patriotically from a loudspeaker somewhere.

"Whatcha' think, darlin?" A silver buckle nestled in the palm of Cowboy's hand, sparkling in the sunlight. The tiny price tag tied to the buckle with a red string said "$450." Behind the counter, a thin man with a ponytail stood watchfully, arms crossed on his chest. He had three small silver hoops in his left ear lobe and a thick silver band on his right wrist.

"It's different," I said. "I kind of like it. But it's so expensive."

Cowboy grinned at me. The buckle made a clicking sound when he laid it down. "Thanks, man. Maybe later." He looped his arm in mine as we walked away. "I've got to confess, I worked up a sweat just thinking about spending so much money on a belt buckle. Let's go get something cold to drink."

"I'm with you," I said, feeling more lighthearted.

"Hold it. There's Dev." Cowboy pointed to the end of the aisle. "Come on. We'll catch up with him and then get something wet."

Without much enthusiasm, I searched the crowd for Devin's figure. "I don't see him."

And then I did. Devin and Devinda were at the last booth. Devin's right elbow was propped on the booth's high countertop where his daughter sat, her skinny legs sticking straight out. Devinda was clutching a double-scoop ice cream cone with both hands. As she carefully lifted the cone to her lips, Devin's left hand slithered up the little girl's leg. His fingers disappeared under the hem of her shorts.

I squeezed my eyes shut, sure there was something wrong with my vision. I looked again, and saw the same stomach-sinking scene: the girl holding the ice cream cone to her mouth, her father's hand on her bare leg, his fingers hiding up her shorts. I imagined her pink tongue licking the cone and the cold, creamy sensation as the ice cream melted on her tongue and slid down her throat but I shut out the picture of what Devin might be doing.

Cowboy was several long strides ahead of me, moving towards Devin and Devinda. I scurried to catch up and grabbed at his shirt sleeve. "Did you see that?" I demanded.

"Huh?" He looked down at me, eyebrows forming a puzzled vee. "See what?"

"Devin and Devinda." I pointed in their direction but now our line of sight was blocked.

A clump of people was moving towards us. Except for the two men leading the way, the small mob was mostly made up of gray-haired women with pinched, angry faces. Many of them held hand-lettered cardboard signs. "No Special Rights" was in crayon, with the word "special" in red letters. "Save our Families, Yes on 13," and "Gays = Anti-family" were done with black markers. The largest and most imaginative sign had big letters reading "Leviticus 20:13" on a background of red and blue stripes. At the bottom was the word "SIN," all in caps. As the group came closer, I realized they were chanting "Keep Oregon clean with Measure 13."

Much as I wanted to scream profanities at the demonstrators, I was more frantic to stop Devin from groping his daughter. "Let's go," I shouted.

Cowboy nodded and grabbed my hand. Together, we plunged into the crowd. People moved aside without resistance, the way the Red Sea parted for Moses. No wonder, if Moses was over six feet tall and had an intimidating scowl, like Cowboy. I held tight to his hand and kept my head down.

"There they are," Cowboy said, his height giving him the advantage. "MaryLou's there. Lyman too."

I wondered at this. If MaryLou was there, Devin couldn't possibly have been touching his daughter that way. Perhaps my dislike of the man had tricked my eyes into seeing what wasn't really there. I slowed, unsure of myself, and Cowboy gave my arm a little tug, urging me forward. I could see them easily now.

The Hunters could have been posing for a family portrait. Devin's left arm circled MaryLou's waist. Devinda, holding the dripping ice cream cone, now stood pigeon-toed in front of her mother, whose hands rested lovingly on the little girl's shoulders. Only Lyman didn't fit the image, slouching against the booth, his lips curled in a surly expression. He wore a black tee shirt with a silk-screened image of a skull, a rose and Jerry Garcia's round face.

"Hey," yelled Devin, waving his right hand. "Over here." He was different when Cowboy was around, happier and friendlier, even to me. That afternoon, he was almost jovial, greeting Cowboy with a playful slap on the back and awarding me a weak-wristed pat on the arm.

MaryLou was her usual effusive self. She enveloped me in her arms as if our last meeting happened years and years ago instead of earlier that day. "Sorry about this morning," she whispered into my ear. "I wasn't thinking straight."

I pulled back from MaryLou's grasp and studied her face. "What's going on? Are you okay?"

"Of course." Her eyebrows arched with surprise. "Everything's fine. I just over-reacted to Lyman's fighting but Devin reminded me that boys will be boys."

I wanted to tell her that clichés weren't good guidelines for child-rearing and I wanted to tell her what I'd seen but before I could figure out how to say anything at all, the hum of noise grew louder. I looked right, left, right. There was no escape from the swarm of Measure 13 marchers. They were coming straight at us. I was seized with helpless panic, the way I would probably feel if I had a hornet's nest fall on my head.

"Mommy, it's too loud. I'm scared." Devinda dropped the ice cream on the dusty ground at her feet. She muffled her ears with her small hands and puckered her face to show her pain.

"It's just Mr. Sykes and his friends," MaryLou said, bending to pull Devinda's hands away. "You like him. He gives you candy all the time."

Devinda resisted MaryLou's tug. "No," she screamed. "My ears hurt."

"Don't be silly." MaryLou yanked a little harder on the slender wrists. "Don't you want Mr. Sykes to give you candy anymore?"

"Ow." An ear-piercing shriek was the little girl's answer. "Ow. You're hurting me."

The crowd of marchers had halted a few feet from where we stood and formed a half-circle, facing our direction. They didn't pay attention to our drama and kept up their chanting and sign-waving. Even Devinda's screams went unheeded. Maybe they weren't human. Maybe they'd been taken over by aliens, like Invasion of the Body Snatchers.

MaryLou stood up. "I didn't mean to," she told Devinda. "Mommy didn't want to hurt you." She backed away, a helpless look on her face and in the slump of her shoulders.

Devinda thrust her bottom lip out, pouting. "I want Daddy."

Devin was already there. He crouched to the girl's eye-level. In a surprisingly gentle voice, he asked Devinda what was wrong. She leaned to whisper in his ear and he nodded. "Okay. But you need to apologize to Mommy for yelling at her," Devin said.

Devinda bent her head down. "Sorry, Mommy," she said, her voice barely audible.

One of the men stepped away from the crowd and came over to us. He was movie-star handsome, with a boyish mop of blonde hair. He nodded hello to Devin and Cowboy, then turned to smile, first at MaryLou, then at Devinda. "Why is our little girl looking so sad?" he asked, in a soft baritone voice that was like the purr of a lion.

"Devinda honey, say hello to Mr. Sykes," MaryLou said.

I regarded the man with more interest. So this was Howard Sykes, MaryLou's secret patron. Apparently immune to the heat, he wore a light gray suit, a crisp, powder blue button-up shirt and a dark tie. He was fairly young, compared to most of the Measure 13 group, and way better looking than any of them. I was surprised that he would hang out with that crowd.

"Won't you come and give me a hug?" Sykes asked Devinda.

The little girl scooted behind Devin to hide, refusing to budge despite repeated urgings from both parents and from Cowboy too. Finally, MaryLou offered an exasperated apology to Mr. Sykes.

"It's no matter. She's just young and silly," Mr. Sykes said, turning his attention to Lyman. "And who is this young man?"

Lyman straightened himself and offered his hand to Sykes. "Lyman Hunter, sir." He reminded me of a cocker spaniel, earnest and anxious to please.

Mr. Sykes shook Lyman's hand. "Well, well," he said, his voice hearty and loud so we could all hear. "And are you a good Christian lad, son?" He had a tight hold on Lyman's hand. I had the urge to pry the hand loose, to rescue Lyman and take him away.

Lyman Adam's apple bobbed nervously. "I guess so, sir."

Sykes glanced at MaryLou and gave her a sly wink. Turning his head slightly, he winked again, including all of us in his fun. He turned back to Lyman. "Son, do you honor and obey your parents?"

I was already sweaty and over-warm, not to mention hot and bothered about where I'd seen Devin's hand. Now, an angry heat was smoldering in my gut. I didn't care for the man's politics but I positively despised the way Sykes was playing to the crowd at the kid's expense. I glanced at Lyman's parents, first MaryLou and then Devin, but neither of them seemed concerned.

Lyman stared down at his hand, still captive in Sykes' grip. With a condescending tone, as if Lyman had missed a cue, Sykes repeated the question. "Tell me son, do you honor your parents?"

This time, Lyman's head jerked up, his eyes round with surprise and something else I wasn't sure of. Slowly, Lyman turned his gaze on his father and kept it there, ignoring Mr. Sykes. Devin returned the stare, dark and unblinking.

The moment passed. Lyman turned to Mr. Sykes. "Yes, sir. Of course, sir," he said.

Sykes was a handsome devil, emphasis on the second word. Personally, I couldn't take him anymore. Acting on impulse more than thought, I walked over and linked my arm with Lyman's free arm. "Come on, Lyman. We need to go find a spot to see the fireworks."

Lyman's look was hard to decipher but Sykes glared at me and reluctantly relinquished his hold.

"Cowboy and I will bring Lyman home later," I told MaryLou as we walked past her, heading for the lawn.

Cowboy had to run a bit to catch up with us and when he did, he pulled me aside. "Hey," he whispered in my ear. "I was kind of hoping for a more romantic evening than babysitting." For an answer, I only gave him a smile.

"Thanks," Lyman said to me as the three of us settled on the blanket, with me sitting in-between Cowboy and Lyman. And then, so softly I almost couldn't hear, Lyman added, "I hate him."

"What do you mean," I asked.

Cowboy must have thought I was talking to him. "Guess," he said.

"Nothing," Lyman muttered at the same time.

It was only later - after the fireworks, after we brought Lyman home, and after I'd once again side-stepped Cowboy's amorous intentions – that I wondered about what Lyman had said, and whether the object of his hatred was Mr. Sykes. Or Devin. Or even Cowboy.

CHAPTER 14

After Labor Day, we started the countdown to MaryLou's TV premiere. The atmosphere at SETII was frenzied as a kennel full of yapping Yorkies. The Crew worked long hours rewriting and editing and rewriting again, barking at each other over every detail. Even the SETII Betties were snippety with each other about whose turn it was to do the dishes or sweep the porch.

One morning, I was in the kitchen fixing a pot of French Roast, one of my usual tasks. It wasn't just that I almost always arrived the earliest. I'd gladly volunteered to be in charge of SETII's java detail because most people skimp when it comes to brewing coffee. My recipe for a twelve-cup pot of good coffee involves fourteen generous scoops of dark roast, one scoop for each cup of water plus one for extra measure and one for good luck.

I'd started counting off, carefully dumping each scoopful into the basket, when the kitchen door thudded open. Startled, I did an about-face and held my arms up in self-defense, a reflex that linked me with the ancient ones. Personally, I don't mind having such a root connection with a Cro-Magnon grandmother. On the other hand, she wasn't measuring scoops of Peets into a Mr. Coffee. When I whipped around in self-defense, ground coffee scattered everywhere. It looked like an invasion of sugar ants marching across the white linoleum. I stared at the floor, unnerved by the odd sensation of seeing something one way when all the while you know very well it's not that way at all.

"Leave me alone, will you?" Devin's voice snapped my attention back. He marched into the room, followed closely by Sondra. She wore another expensive-looking pants suit and high heels.

"I won't leave you alone," she was saying. "If you don't stop, you're going to ruin everything. Don't forget." She blinked her eyes furiously. "You owe me."

Devin halted mid-stride, spinning around to confront her. His quick move caught Sondra off balance. She grabbed at Devin's arm to steady herself. Devin shrugged loose of her grip. "Lay off me," he said. "Leave me alone." I wondered if the petulant tone in his voice was an echo of their childhood. Poor Devin, having Sondra as his bossy older sister.

Sondra was a typical bully. When she knew she wouldn't win the skirmish with her brother, she turned her aim on another target. A sneer curled her lips as she swiveled her head in my direction. "Who's answering the phones, Ruby?"

"It's only 8:45," I said, failing to keep a smug tone from my voice. "Office doesn't open until 9:00."

Sondra's eyes narrowed. She knew I was taunting her with the facts. "Clean that up," she said, a forefinger jabbing in the direction of the French Roast spill. "How dare you leave a mess like that?"

"It just happened," I pointed out. "I'll clean it, don't worry. When I'm finished making the coffee."

She raised her scolding finger higher, aiming at my chest. "You'd better. And don't think you're off the hook. We'll discuss this later." With a final wag of her finger, Sondra turned her back on me, a move immediately copied by Devin. In unison, they trooped out of the room. Apparently, they'd silently called a truce with each other to join forces against a common enemy. Me.

With a self-pitying sigh, I got the broom and dustpan from the closet. Anticipating a confrontation with Sondra was like anticipating a colonoscopy or having your teeth drilled. Lately I'd experienced too many of these moments with Sondra. She was one reason I'd lost my enthusiasm for getting up in the morning and coming to work at SETII. But not the only reason.

Like an emotional earthquake, the events of Labor Day had me all shook up. Questions tumbled like loose boulders in my brain, eroding my self-confidence. I'd seen Devin's hand crawling under Devinda's shorts. But I couldn't have. Surely MaryLou would know if something like that was happening in her own home. Wouldn't she? I had doubts too about the handsome but slimy Mr. Sykes. How she could hook up with someone like him? And why had she been so mean, threatening to evict me from the cabin over the Kids Klub incident? I didn't have any answers and the heap of questions kept growing. More than once, I thought about the check I'd finally deposited in a savings account. I was tempted to take my stash of money and run. But at night, when I sat on the cabin deck with Clarence, watching zillions of stars sparkle above us, I promptly forgot about leaving.

"Ruby? Are you busy?" Laura and Janet were standing just inside the kitchen doorway.

"Come in," I said, waving them into the room. "What's up?"

The women approached tentatively, practically shuffling their feet. They were both dressed in Northwest casual - jeans, tee-shirts, clogs.

Laura spoke first. "We need to talk."

I looked at them. The frown lines on Laura's face were Grand Canyon-sized. Janet looked even worse. Her body drooped like a wilted sunflower stalk and the skin on her face and neck was blotchy.

"This looks serious," I said.

"It's Sondra," said Laura. "You know what she's been doing?" She paused, darted a paranoid glance over her shoulder and lowered her voice to almost a whisper. "Bad stuff," she said. "Really bad, un-SETII kind of stuff. Like, well, like false chaos. And misusing energy."

I hadn't the least idea what she was talking about but I nodded encouragingly.

Words tumbled from Laura's mouth, a verbal landslide. "She makes us do her work, so then we have to stay overtime to get our own jobs done. That's bad energy." Half-a-sentence into her complaint, she forgot about keeping her voice lowered. "I've been working late every night. While she does nothing. Just because she's MaryLou's sister-in-law, she thinks she can get away with it."

"False chaos," Janet cued.

"Oh. And false chaos because she yells at us all the time." Laura paused "Yesterday, she made Janet get down on her hands and knees to clean a spill on the kitchen floor."

"You're kidding me." I looked at Janet.

She bent her head slightly and shook her head "She ordered me to. Said it was part of my job and I should be grateful to do it. I know I'm blessed to work for MaryLou, it's not that." She gave me an intent look, her eyes pleading with me to believe her. "It's Sondra. It's how she treats me. How she treats all of us."

"Not only that," Laura said. "Sondra was the one who spilled the coffee cup."

"Maybe you should confront her," I said to Janet. I could hear the doubt in my own voice.

Laura shook her head. "Janet can't," she said. "She's too soft."

Janet grimaced in agreement. "I need to work on my core," she said, flushing unevenly. "MaryLou says I should try breathing deeper."

"Anyway," Laura said, reclaiming my attention. "We did go talk to Sondra. But she just laughed, and when I said we'd tell MaryLou, Sondra said she'd get us fired first."

"I don't want to lose my job," Janet said. "Except for Sondra, I like working here."

"Me too," Laura said. "I love MaryLou."

"I wish I could help you," I said, "but I don't know how."

"We were thinking you could go to MaryLou, tell her about Sondra. MaryLou would listen to you. You know she would. Wouldn't she, Janet?" Laura turned to Janet, who nodded. "See?"

I shook my head. "I'm not as sure about that as you are. Besides, I've got Sondra problems too."

"It's different." Laura said. "She doesn't push you around the same way because she knows you're MaryLou's favorite."

"I'm not."

"Yes you are," Laura said. "The SETII Betties are all really jealous of you."

I shrugged. "That doesn't prove anything. Let's get back to this Sondra thing. If I did go talk to MaryLou, what else should she know?"

"Just tell her how horrible and mean Sondra is. And she's the meanest to Barry," Janet said. "Even worse than she is to me." The pink blotches on her neck darkened to red.

Laura bobbed her head. "That's true. She's always picking on him, making these little comments, saying stuff just low enough so we can't hear. And Barry just takes it quietly, just sits there and suffers. I don't know what's going on exactly. He won't talk about it."

"You could ask me," Janet said in a small voice. Something in her tone made us both pay attention.

"So?" Laura asked.

I kept quiet. My stomach was queasy. Somehow, I knew what she was going to tell us.

"She thinks Barry is a homosexual," Janet said, dropping to a whisper on the last word.

"Oh," Laura said, a puzzled expression lowering her eyebrows. "He can't be. Otherwise, how could he do that script?" She clamped her lips closed, gulping back the rest of her words.

"Laura." Janet was wide-eyed but I couldn't tell if she was surprised or afraid.

"I know, but I didn't say anything, not really."

I interrupted them. "Where is Barry, anyway? Why didn't he come with you?"

"He's been out sick the last few days," Laura said. "It's a wonder we're not all sick from over-exhaustion."

"All right," I said. "I'll talk with MaryLou."

They both hugged me. Janet cried quietly. I had to promise several times I'd let them know how it went with MaryLou.

When they were gone, I hurriedly swept up the spilled coffee and rushed down the hall to my office, managing to switch on the phones only seconds before 9:00 AM. No sense in giving Sondra something real to complain about. I zipped through all the first-thing-every-morning tasks before I gave myself permission to call Barry, but for all my rush there was no answer at his place, although I let the phone ring a long time. Mentally rehearsing what to say, I punched in Uncle Mike's telephone number at the Kid's Place.

He answered on the first ring, as if he'd been waiting for a call. "Yo?"

"It's Ruby."

"Ruby, dear. What's up?"

"Not much. Well, maybe a little something. Barry's been sick and I wondered if you knew how he's doing. I tried calling him just now, but there's no answer."

Uncle Mike was slow to respond. "I didn't know he was sick. He said he was working all kinds of crazy hours to get everything just right and he'd call me when he was done."

"He's probably sleeping and he's got the phone unplugged," I told Uncle Mike, trying to convince myself as well.

"I'll run over there on my lunch hour and check on him."

"Let me know how he's doing, okay?"

"Sure," he said. "Call you later."

I disconnected and simultaneously reached for the super-size container of Tums I'd started keeping next to the telephone. I shook out two tabs, a mint green and a pale tangerine, popped them into my mouth and crunched. Chalky sweetness masked the sour taste in my mouth but my gut still churned with acidic worry.

For a couple of hours, I was distracted by a slew of incoming calls and visits, mostly from one or another of the SETII Betties. One of the Betties, a new woman with faded blonde hair and the paleness of someone who doesn't get outdoors much, really tested the limits of my patience. Every twenty or thirty minutes, she'd pop into my office to ask if MaryLou was in yet. She looked familiar, but maybe I'd just seen her around the SETII building. Besides, I had too much on my mind to puzzle out who she was.

At lunchtime, I wandered into the kitchen, intending to grab a yogurt from the refrigerator. I was unlucky as old Mrs. Hubbard's dog. The refrigerator was bare. Grumbling to myself over the inconvenience, I got my purse and jacket from the office and set out for the Metro Café a few blocks away. Overhead, a grey sky threatened rain. The sidewalks and lawns were covered with red and yellow leaves scattered by a cool breeze. Summer was being pushed out by a blustery autumn, even though it was only September.

A half-block from the cafe, I saw two skateboarders surfing the sidewalk, heading towards me. They were young teenagers, androgynously dressed in loose black pants, black tee-shirts and black baseball caps turned backwards. Prudently stepping aside to avoid a head-on, I stood admiring their grace and skill on the flimsy-looking boards with rollerskate-sized wheels. Suddenly both skateboarders jumped in the air and somehow simultaneously kicked at the back of their boards. The boards flipped up and over, like miniature poodles trained to do somersaults. In synch, the skateboarders landed on the sidewalk, easily catching the boards as they descended. Nonchalantly, as if they hadn't just defied gravity, they strolled forward, skateboards tucked sedately under their arms.

"Hey Ruby."

"Lyman. I didn't recognize you. I didn't know you could skateboard so well."

Lyman shuffled self-consciously. "Carleen's way better," he said, glancing sideways at his companion.

"Carleen." I smiled at her. "I sure admire your skill. Looks like fun."

"You've never skateboarded?" Carleen's tone made it clear this was the same as never having breathed.

I shook my head. I felt a thousand years older than her.

"Wow." She pulled her cap off, shook out a thick mane of brown hair and scratched her scalp.

"We could teach you, Ruby. It's not that hard, really," Lyman said. He bent down and put his skateboard on the sidewalk in front of me.

I took a step back. "I don't think so. Besides, I don't have time. I have to grab some lunch and then get back to the office. Maybe some other time?" I hated how grownup and uptight I sounded.

"Sure," Lyman said. He put one foot on the board, ready to roll. "Later."

Carleen dropped her board onto the sidewalk. The board landed next to Lyman's with a clatter, sounding like tin cans falling on the cement. She tucked her long hair under her cap with quick hands "Come by the skate park sometime," she called as she pushed off and glided away, followed by Lyman. I waved goodbye, although neither of them turned to look.

When I got to the Metro, most of the noon crowd had already come and gone, so there was no wait. I assembled my lunch at the salad bar and went to pay for it. All the while, my mind lurched from thought to thought like a drunk clutching lampposts on her way down the sidewalk. Worry about Barry turned to nagging doubt about what I'd seen on Labor Day to puzzling over the Sondra problem and whether I should talk with MaryLou, and what I should say if I did, then back to my encounter with the two young skateboarders.

Lyman had seemed a different person. The only other time I'd seen him so relaxed and happy was after Clarence awarded a slurp of approval on the boy's arm. And yet, as quiet and depressed as he usually acted, Lyman wasn't as difficult to be around as his sister. I could still hear the venomous way she'd hissed at me: Jesus hates you. Was she screwed up because her father molested her? Or was she just a spoiled brat? Maybe her behavior wasn't proof of anything except her mother and father's weak parenting skills.

"Four dollars, please." The cashier interrupted my busy brain. I dug four bills out of my purse and turned to scan the room. There was a clean, unoccupied table in the corner and I carried my tray over to claim it. As soon as I sat down, I began pitching forkfuls of greens into my mouth, mechanically chewing and swallowing, without tasting anything. I was trying to gather my thoughts, but still they skittered from one thing to another.

"There you are." MaryLou rushed up to the table. She was flushed and sweaty. "Lyman said you'd be here."

"What's going on?"

She pressed her hands against her heaving chest, as if that would help her catch her breath. "Need to talk."

"MaryLou, sit down." I gestured at the empty chair across from me. "Please."

She dropped into the chair. "It's terrible. One of the scripts is missing." MaryLou took a deep breath. "Barry must've taken it. What're we going to do?"

"But he's at home. He's sick."

She shook her head. "Sondra said she called his house and he's not home. He's hiding somewhere."

"Hiding?" I laughed. "You mean like 'ready or not here I come' hiding? Like 'oly oly in free' hiding?"

"I'm serious," MaryLou said sternly.

"So what can I do?"

She leaned forward. "Maybe you know where he is?"

"I haven't the slightest," I said. A piece of lettuce was stuck in the tines of my fork. It looked like a wrinkled green flag on a silver pole.

"Do you know any of his other friends? Or where he hangs out?"

I shook my head. I couldn't say why my gut feelings silenced me, but something kept me from naming Uncle Mike.

"Hm." MaryLou made a face. "Somehow, I thought you'd know." She started to rise from the chair.

Impulsively, I decided to bring up the Janet and Laura issue. At least I would have one less thing to worry about. "MaryLou? Before you go, could I talk with you about something?"

She sat again and rested her hand on my arm. "It's Cowboy, isn't it? I told him you were vulnerable right now and he should just be patient. He can be pushy, just like Devin. But you can't blame him, you know. Men are like that."

I shook my head vehemently, disagreeing with everything she'd said. "It's not Cowboy. It's not men at all. It's Sondra."

"Sondra?" MaryLou sat back in the chair and regarded me with a puzzled expression.

"She's driving everybody crazy the way she's acting, ordering us around, picking on us. I know she's got it in for me, but this morning I even saw her arguing with Devin."

MaryLou nodded thoughtfully. "We have to be understanding with Sondra," she said. "She's had a difficult life."

"Who hasn't?"

"Not like Sondra. She's had a terrible tragedy in her life, one most of us can't comprehend."

"Yes," I said, "you told me about her son."

"So sad," MaryLou shook her head. "Nobody knows how it happened exactly but he took Devin's motorcycle, went out on the highway going the wrong direction and got hit by a semi-truck."

I blinked away the image of a young boy looking a lot like Lyman, pasted like bugkill on the front grille of a truck. "I didn't realize it was Devin's motorcycle he stole."

"Yes. Devin felt guilty for years but I told him he didn't need to shoulder that burden. It was drugs that caused Dustin's death. It wasn't Devin's fault or Sondra's. Sondra is learning to understand it was Dustin's karma to die young."

You owe me. The way Sondra had spit those words at Devin, I wasn't sure she accepted Dustin's death as easily as MaryLou seemed to think. Personally, it wouldn't comfort me to know my child died too young in a horrible accident because it was his fate. I voiced my thoughts. "It must be awful to have your child die that way. Even so, it's no excuse for being mean to the rest of us."

MaryLou waved a hand in the air, swatting away my pesky complaint. "I'm sure everything will be great again, just as soon as we get the show on the air. We're all a bit edgy right now. Even you, Ruby."

"Me?" My stomach chilled. Did she guess I was more worried about Barry than I'd revealed? Did she know I was suspicious of Devin?

She smiled. "I can tell you're feeling unsure about Cowboy even if you can't admit it to yourself yet. Don't worry. Everything will be fine. It always is." She pushed away from the table and stood, giving a quick glance at her watch. "I've got to go. We'll talk later."

Annoyed at her dismissal of the Sondra problem and her assumption that my problems were Cowboy-related, I managed only a half-hearted wave goodbye. I stood and carried my tray from the table to the bussing area. I stacked the salad plate on top of other dirty dishes in an industrial-gray rubber bin, tossed the fork in a bin filled with soapy water and swept the crumpled paper napkin into the waste basket. If only life's troubles could be disposed of so easily.

CHAPTER 15

My mood darkened as the day dragged on and I was less patient than usual at the constant interruption of telephone calls from the SETII Betties. Martha was looking for Evelyn, Shirley had a message for Emma, and everyone wanted to find Suzanne. I tried to picture the women but I still had trouble telling one SETII Betty from another. Probably because I didn't much like them. Their subservience and uncomplaining willingness to do even the most menial task made me grumpy.

When there was a moment's lull in the phone calls, I managed to dial Uncle Mike's office phone. It was in message mode. There was no answer either at his house or Barry's. That didn't make sense, unless Barry was so sick Uncle Mike had taken him to the doctor. At 5:00, as soon as I forwarded the phones to the answering machine, I tried each of the numbers again. No luck. I decided to stop at the Kids Klub on my way home.

When I asked for Mike at the reception desk the volunteer told me he'd taken the afternoon off. I backtracked across town and over the bridge to the West Hills and Uncle Mike's place. The driveway was empty. All the windows were dark. On the back of a paper scrap I dug out of the glove compartment, I scribbled a note reminding Mike to call me and slipped it under the door. I didn't know what else to do. I was frustrated as a hound on a short leash.

As soon as I got home, I called again. It occurred to me that the loneliest sound is a phone ringing endlessly on the other end of the line. Even so, I couldn't restrain from dialing Uncle Mike's phone number and then Barry's, over and over and over. If only they had one of those mobile cellular phones. The last decade of the Twentieth Century seemed to be all about computers and other techno-gizmos. I'd seen more and more people carrying mobile phones. The idea of others having a cell phone when I needed to reach someone was appealing. Perversely, I didn't care for being that available if someone was looking for me.

In between dialing, I paced the floor, unable to settle myself. Clarence regarded me with a bemused cock of his head. My last attempt to reach Uncle Mike was at midnight, with the same dismaying non-result. I got into bed. Dark thoughts troubled my sleep. Finally, at 5:00 AM, I gave up, abandoning the warmth of the bed for the cold floor of the kitchen. I flicked the lights on and quickly did the makings for a pot of coffee before I picked up the phone. With no expectation of success, I punched in the telephone number.

Uncle Mike answered on the first ring. "Hello?" His voice was husky.

"Uncle Mike. I've been so worried."

"Ruby?" He yawned. "Excuse me. I was up half the night. I'm sorry I didn't call."

"What about Barry? Is he okay?"

There was a long pause before he spoke. "I don't know."

The raw pain in his voice shocked me. For the first time, I comprehended how much Mike cared for Barry and how they were emotionally wedded in a way I'd dreamed of for myself but never experienced.

When my uncle first told me he was gay, my world went atilt. Childhood memories were unbalanced, and so was my sense of the way things were ordered. As time went on and I examined my past more clearly, I understood that Uncle Mike wasn't an ogre and my aunt hadn't been a saint. At the same time, I was growing more fond of Mike and Barry and I enjoyed their company tremendously. All of this made me feel I was betraying Aunt Elaine. One way I'd handled my confusion was to regard Uncle Mike and Barry's relationship as something one-dimensional. I'd ignored the flesh and blood and tangled emotions of their real love for each other. Until now.

"I'm sorry," I said, although he had no idea what I was apologizing for.

"He's gone. I looked everywhere I could think of. I even went to see his parents, thinking maybe they'd know. Awful people. I don't know what I was thinking."

"Why?"

"They said if he was missing it was God's will, that he was cursed. And then they slammed the door shut on me."

"His parents said that?" I remembered the Measure 13 people at the Labor Day picnic. Maybe Barry's folks had been part of that crowd, carrying a sign with screaming red letters calling homosexuality an abomination.

The first time I came across that word was in a comic book where the main character – Little Lulu, as I recall – defeats the Abominable Snowman by tricking him into standing too long under the sun, thus melting the monster. When the word appeared again, it was at the Sunday School my aunt made me attend the winter I turned ten. I puzzled over the new way the word was used. According to our group leader, Mrs. Walker, abominations consisted of a variety of sins, from unmade beds to touching yourself you-know-where and other things little girls had no need to know about. I couldn't reconcile this long list with the cartoon monster.

Besides, I didn't trust Mrs. Walker. She had bad breath and always wore the same navy blue dress with half-round stains of sweat that showed whenever she lifted her arm to write at the blackboard. By February, I refused to go back. Come to think of it, Uncle Mike had helped me convince Aunt Elaine to let me off the hook. Except for my temporary return to the church when my aunt was dying, I considered myself religion-free. Maybe that's why I couldn't understand a religious fervor strong enough to compel a mother and father to reject their child.

On the other hand, were Barry's parents any worse than my frivolous, fun-seeking folks, who had pretty much abandoned their baby daughter? Ah well. My feelings about my parents had condensed into a hard pebble. Sometimes, I held the pebble in my hand, rubbing the smooth surface with the edge of my thumb. Other times, I put the pebble in my shoe and a sharp pain walked with me all day long. I wondered how Barry dealt with his feelings.

"Does Barry know his parents say that stuff?" I asked.

"I'm afraid so." Uncle Mike sighed. "Look, Ruby, I've got to find him. It's my fault he's missing."

"What do you mean?"

"He thinks he's protecting me by disappearing."

"Protecting you from what?" An image of Sondra popped into my mind.

"Look, I can't really talk now. I'd better get going. I want to take off as soon as it's light out. But I promise to call later."

"Please. As soon as you find him. And good luck." I held the receiver in my sweaty hand after Uncle Mike said goodbye. The phone beeped a reminder to hang up. I couldn't shake the strange feeling that Sondra was somehow involved. Janet and Laura said Sondra had harassed Barry. Were her threats about homosexuality scary enough to send him into hiding? Could be, if he thought Uncle Mike would get hurt. I wondered about the missing script too. Was Barry holding it hostage? Or maybe he'd taken it in revenge.

When I got home that night, the phone was ringing insistently. It was Cowboy asking me to dinner on Sunday, a couple of days away. I breathed a coward's sigh of relief. I had an excuse, couldn't go, because that night was the first airing of MaryLou's TV spot. As soon as I hung up, the phone rang again.

The second call made my heart ache. Uncle Mike voice was low and dispirited. He told me he was driving to the southern part of the state, on the chance of finding Barry. Barry had always liked that part of Oregon and his family owned some property down there. Mike said he had to do something to hunt Barry down, even if it was an iffy something "Otherwise," he said, "I'll be crazy with frustration and worry."

Like me. I drifted aimlessly from room to room. I sat down and stood up, I picked up a book and immediately laid it down. I thumbed through a magazine and tossed it on the table, unable to focus. My nervous pacing finally drove Clarence to hide in the bedroom.

In the morning, there were dark circles under my eyes and even a couple of double-double lattes didn't jolt me alert. I was getting ready to collect phone messages when I heard cowboy boots clomping on the wood floor outside my office.

"Hey, darlin'. How's Miss Ruby Doobie this fine morning?"

His cheerfulness made me feel like squinting. It was too bright. "Good morning," I said, thinking there was nothing good about it.

"Plans have changed," he told me. "We're invited to Devin's on Sunday for dinner and watching MaryLou's show."

It was hard to keep from rolling my eyes in dismay. I never enjoyed being with the entire Hunter Family. Also, I'd resolved to have an honest talk with Cowboy the next time we were alone. The dinner gathering would delay my opportunity and probably be unpleasant. On the other hand, it was the easiest choice. I did not rise to the occasion. "Okay," I said, regretting the word as soon as I spoke it.

"Good girl." Cowboy slapped the edge of my desk. "I'll pick you up 'bout 5:30."

Sunday evening arrived much too soon and was everything I dreaded it would be. Dinner, prepared by Devin, was a store-bought macaroni and cheese casserole, pulled from the freezer and nuked. My serving wasn't fully defrosted. I picked at the edges, avoiding clumps of orange cheese that looked too much like globules of fat in cheap canned dog food.

I looked around the table. The others, MaryLou, Devin, Cowboy and Lyman, were halfway to cleaning their plates. Devinda, however, sat back in her chair with her arms folded across her skinny chest. She was wearing the Grateful Dead tee-shirt I'd seen Lyman wear before, a tee-shirt that was big as a nightgown on Devinda. Based on the shirt Lyman had on that evening, his tastes had changed drastically, from the Dead's trademark grinning skull with a rose in its teeth to graphic images of blood-spattered corpses.

MaryLou noticed her daughter's pout. "Devinda. Why aren't you eating? We made your favorite."

"This is not my favorite," Devinda said, her queenly tone leaving no doubt. "I hate this."

"But yesterday when you wouldn't eat your nice steak you said you would only eat mac and cheese."

Devinda stared at her mother. "I did not."

"Devinda," Devin said. "Start eating. Now."

Devinda regarded her plate with a mix of disgust and disdain. "I can't. It looks like dead worms that someone puked on."

I looked down. The kid was right. A giggle almost escaped my lips. Quickly, I grabbed the wine glass and gulped some of the Chianti Cowboy had poured for us.

It was Devinda, of course, who busted me. "Ruby's not eating either," she said, pointing a small, accusing finger at my plate. "Whyn't you make her eat?"

"That's enough." MaryLou stood. She reached across the table and removed the little girl's plate. "If you don't want to eat, fine. You won't eat. But don't go telling on other people. That's not good energy."

Devinda's eyes moistened. A single tear glistened on her smooth cheek, like dew on a rose petal. The teardrop slid down until it neared the corner of her little mouth. Suddenly, Devinda's pink tipped tongue darted out and licked the teardrop away. Devinda the frog.

"C'mon little darlin'." Cowboy reached across the table and patted Devinda's shoulder. "Don't you cry, now. I can't stand to see girls cry."

The little girl's head tilted flirtatiously. "Does it make you sad?" she said, fluttering long eyelashes still dewy with tears. Devinda the sexpot.

"I'm very sad," Cowboy said, contradicting himself with a big smile.

"I won't cry anymore. I don't want you to be sad." With the awkwardness of a little girl, she rubbed the moisture from her eyes. I was astonished at how quickly she changed from child to coquette and back again. She was still clumsy at seduction but in a few years, she'd have more finesse.

Cowboy turned to Lyman. "What's up, man? What's that cool shirt you're wearing? I can't quite read what it says."

A sneer of contempt curled Lyman's lip for a moment and was gone, replaced by the bored gray look he usually wore at home. "It's nothing." He lowered his gaze to a neutral spot on the table.

Devin's fist pounded the table, rattling the plates and silverware, startling all of us. "Damn it, Lyman," he thundered. "Someone asks you a question, you answer them."

With insolent slowness, Lyman lifted his head. He looked his father in the eye and arched one eyebrow quizzically, James Bond-style. "Of course," he said. He turned to Cowboy and opened his arms wide, revealing the full impact of the shirt's silkscreen design. I was seated across from Cowboy and alongside Lyman, so I caught only a glimpse of the gore, but I could tell from Cowboy's wide-open stare that he thought the shirt was shocking and grotesque.

"Cannibal Corpse," Cowboy finally said. "Never heard of 'em. What do they play?"

Lyman shrugged. "Music."

"All that off-key shouting and moaning and drums," Mary Lou said. "What'd you tell me it was called?"

Lyman sighed. "Death Metal, okay?

"Isn't that awful?" MaryLou addressed the adults. "And they said we were terrible when we listened to the Beatles and the Rolling Stones. Except, I only listened to the Beatles." She pushed her chair back from the table and stood. "Let's just leave everything on the table and clean up later. It's almost time."

Obediently, we trooped into the living room. Devinda scurried to sit next to her mother on the couch, in the center of things. The rest of us arranged ourselves on the floor. The TV was tuned to a shopping network. Devin pointed the remote at the screen. We watched a dizzying blur of changing channels until MaryLou lost patience. "It's Channel Twelve, Devin," she said, her lips clenched so tightly she could've hired out as a ventriloquist.

The local news show was almost over. The male announcer, a plump, middle-aged man with big ears, was talking about Columbus Day, 1962, when storm winds raced through the Northwest going more than a hundred miles an hour. I was twelve that year. I remember huddling in the basement for two days with my aunt and uncle and Clarence the First. Despite the inconvenience of having no electric lights, eating mostly peanut butter and jelly sandwiches and having to use the increasingly stinky basement bathroom, my youthful ignorance allowed me to think of the event as an adventure, something unique in my otherwise humdrum life. Afterwards, when we went upstairs, the living room carpet and all the furniture glittered with pieces of shattered glass. The windows had been blown out of their frames by the wind. Outside, fallen trees and limbs were scattered like a game of pickup sticks, only these sticks were big enough to squash cars and rooftops.

"They say there wasn't a barn left standing in all of Western Oregon," the newsman said cheerfully.

"Is that so?" twinkled the female newscaster. "That must have left a lot of cows and horses shivering out in the rain." Her fellow newscaster nodded his head and laughed. I didn't think it was funny. What did they think the barns fell on when they blew over? I scanned the room. None of them got it, except Lyman, who was sitting on the floor next to me, on my right.

"Dead cows and horses can't shiver," he said, keeping his voice low.

"Damn it, Lyman. There you go whispering again," Devin snapped.

"Shh," MaryLou said. "It's almost on."

And there she was, wearing the same blue robe-like outfit she'd worn for her appearance on the People and Places show. MaryLou stood in front of a powder-blue and silver curtain. Her hands were clasped in front of her breasts, which looked round and matronly in that dress. She looked straight at the camera, smiled softly and began to speak.

"Welcome friends and strangers. I feel so blessed to be here with you. To-night, I want to tell you a little about how you can get anything and everything you want."

"Hey, MaryLou," Cowboy said. "Does that include sex?" He gave me a nudge.

I ignored him. The MaryLou in the living room said for him to hush. The one on TV kept talking. "It's not a secret," she was saying. "If you've ever heard the story of Peter Pan, the answer will be familiar. All you have to do is believe." MaryLou's voice trembled with passion. "Believe you can do it."

"Clap your hands," Devinda squealed. "Like Tinkerbelle. Right Mommy?"

"That's right dear. Now don't interrupt anymore."

"You behave now," added Devin. "Sit still."

"It's boring," the little girl whined. "I can't sit still anymore."

"Just believe you can, Devinda," said Lyman.

Cowboy snickered but Devin wasn't amused. Out of the corner of my eye, I saw Devin's arm reach out to deliver a hard smack on the back of the boy's neck. Lyman stifled a gasp. Otherwise he showed no reaction. No one said a word except for the TV MaryLou, who kept on talking about how God wants us to be happy. Surreptitiously, I reached over and patted Lyman's shoulder. He didn't acknowledge my gesture. After a few moments, my attention was pulled back to the show.

On the screen, MaryLou took a step toward us at the same time the camera moved in for a close-up. Something more than TV makeup showed on MaryLou's face, reminding me of the caring woman I'd encountered on Seven Hills Road. "You must remember that you are one with God. And since you are one with God, it stands to reason that unhappiness and anger, dishonesty and fear, all the negative emotions and all the badness, all these are merely illusions. They are illusions because everything is perfect." MaryLou lifted her arms. The blue gown shimmered like satin under the camera lights. "You are already perfect."

MaryLou brought her arms down. Ever so slightly, she leaned forward. There was something so intimate in her gaze I felt she was staring right at me. For a moment, I forgot the real MaryLou sitting behind me on the couch.

When she began to speak, her voice was soft and hypnotic. "I want to show you how SETII can light your divine inner spark, the spark you need to manifest the happy, successful, wonderful you. Some of you know that SETII stands for Seeking Energy, Truth, Infinity. For those of you who are joining us for the first time, I know these mere words cannot describe the immensity of what they represent. Let me paint you a picture."

"Like the universe, our own creation begins in chaos. In order to survive, in order to turn that chaos into controlled energy, we have to learn how to eat, how to walk, how to talk, how to behave and a multitude of other things, including false and negative beliefs. We get so busy learning these things we forget the most important thing we know. We forget that we're perfect already."

Mentally, I was scratching my head, trying to decipher the fuzzy words and wispy ideas. MaryLou, however, was becoming more impassioned. However vague her message was to me, it obviously held a lot of meaning for her.

The pitch of her voice rose as she continued her speech. "As we grow and age and figure out how to make our way in this world, we begin to seek something more than mere survival, we begin to seek the truth. Sometimes, we seek it willingly and sometimes life forces us to ask the right questions. And that is when we're open to knowing our oneness with the One Who Is Perfect."

MaryLou paused for a dramatic moment. "I hope I've tickled your memory a little bit and I hope you'll join me again next week at this same time. I'm MaryLou Hunter and this has been "Spirituality for Success" on your local news station TV Twelve." She waved at the camera with a funny back and forth motion, like the Queen of England. "Goodbye. Thank you."

"Well. What did you think," the real MaryLou asked, as her image faded into an ad for Hailit's Chevrolet.

Everyone else started talking at the same time, congratulating her. Devinda climbed onto her mother's lap to give her a big hug. Devin moved from the carpet to the sofa, filling the space the little girl had occupied. He draped an arm around MaryLou's shoulder and deposited a noisy kiss on her cheek. Cowboy was standing by this time, offering MaryLou his praise. Personally, I thought it was obvious he was being a polite liar. Even Lyman got up and offered his mother a quick, stiff hug. All the while, I stayed where I was on the floor, wondering what to say. How could I tell MaryLou what I really thought?

I became aware of a difference in the room. Silence. Reluctantly, I turned and looked at the others. You'd have thought I turned chartreuse and grew lavender wings, the way Devin and the kids and even Cowboy stared at me. I looked at MaryLou. Her face was pale, a spot of pink on each cheek. The way everyone was looking down at me, I felt small and wrong. I scrambled to my feet.

"You didn't like it," MaryLou said. "Tell the truth."

"Actually," I said, drawling like Cowboy, stretching the word out. I needed time to think of the right words. But my brain was empty as Clarence's dog bowl three minutes after feeding time. I couldn't come up with anything except the truth. "Actually, you're right. I didn't like the show. I heard a bunch of pie-in-the-sky words with a couple of scoops of God on top, but I'm not sure what you really said."

MaryLou's lips formed an O of surprise.

"It's probably just me. Everyone else liked it."

"Damn right," Devin said. His eyes glittered angrily. "You apologize to MaryLou right now."

"Hey, Dev," Cowboy interjected. "Ruby was just answering the question."

Devinda looked up at her father and then at Cowboy. "Does this mean you're going to fight," she asked, her voice pitched with anticipation.

"Quiet, all of you." MaryLou pushed herself up from the couch. "The fact is, Ruby's the only one who tells me the truth." She took a few steps to where I stood and gathered me in her arms, squeezing me into the bulge of her breasts. My nostrils filled with the scent of her perfume. Chanel No. 5, same as my mother wore.

MaryLou leaned back. "Ruby. I just had a wonderful idea. I know you'll love it. She pulled me into another tight embrace. "You can take Barry's place," she said, in my ear. "Help write my little talks. Isn't that a great idea?"

I struggled out of her arms. "No way."

"You can't say no, Ruby. I need you too much." MaryLou reached over to brush her fingertips on my cheek. "Just for a little bit, until Barry comes back."

"That reminds me," Devin said. "Sondra called earlier, said she'd heard some news about Barry."

"What?" MaryLou and I chorused.

"He was in an accident."

CHAPTER 16

"Oh no," MaryLou wailed, her voice high-pitched and nerve-jangling as a fire alarm. "Now I'll never get my script."

I stayed silent. Couldn't move. Couldn't breathe. Fear grabbed hold of my heart and gave it a fierce squeeze. What had happened to Barry? And what about Uncle Mike?

"Who's Barry?" said Cowboy.

"One of MaryLou's writers," Devin said. "And, as it turns out, he's a flaming fag."

"Devin. That's not a nice word," MaryLou scolded. "Devinda, we don't use that word."

"What's a fag, Daddy?" Devinda asked, ignoring her mother. "Why's he on fire?"

Devin snorted contemptuously. "A fag is a queer. A sicko creep."

"No, that's not right." I struggled to find words of protest, but nobody paid attention to me.

"Anger, be my fire," chanted Lyman. "My blood runs cold. Anger, be my fire. My blood runs . . . ."

"Lyman, stop that," MaryLou broke in. She returned her attention to the little girl. "Devinda dear, that's a word about some people who make a misguided choice."

Somehow, she was able to ignore her son's dramatic display of contempt. Lyman lifted his upper lip in a sneer, sniffed disdainfully and then turned away to slouch from the room.

The little girl wrinkled her nose and frowned. "What kind of choice?"

"A wrong choice."

"Like what?"

"Wrong. That's what," MaryLou said. "Now, why don't you go get ready for your bath? Mommy will meet you in the bathroom, okay?"

Devinda's lower lip curled in a pout. She crossed her thin arms and shook her head. "I want Daddy."

"Okay." Devin unfolded himself from the couch and stood. "Come on then. Daddy will give you a bath."

I watched Devinda take the hand he offered her. A raspy protest escaped my lips. "No. Oh no."

This time, someone heard me. Devin raised his left eyebrow and regarded me. "You have something to say, Ruby?"

I shook my head. I had only suspicion. I'd started to wonder if what I'd seen was only a trick of my eyes. There was no evidence I could offer to keep a father from giving his child a bath. On the other hand, he wasn't going to get away that easily. Before he could turn away, I started flinging questions at him. "What about Barry? Do you know what happened? Do you know where he is?"

Devin glared at me, transmitting beams of hatred with his Dr. X-ray eyes. He didn't say anything.

"Devin, tell us," MaryLou said. "Please?"

"C'mon, man," Cowboy added. "Quit your teasin'."

Devin shrugged. "All Sondra told me was something about a car crash. Somewhere in Southern Oregon. Roseburg, maybe. He's at the hospital there."

Adrenaline pulsed in my veins. I rushed from the room, slowing only to grab my jacket and purse from the halltree before I shoved open the door and ran out of the house.

Behind me, Cowboy called my name. "Ruby. Wait." I let him catch up and gratefully accepted his offer of a ride up the hill to the cabin, since the night was moonless and I had no flashlight. We were there in minutes. As soon as the truck rolled to a stop, I jumped out and scurried up the path to the cabin. In the quiet, I heard the phone start ringing. I took the steps two at a time, pounded across the length of the porch, and flung open the door. Clarence stood in the middle of the living room, staring at the tall counter where the phone shrilled insistently. I lifted the receiver up and breathed a frantic hello into the mouthpiece.

"Ruby? Are you okay?"

"Uncle Mike? Did you find Barry?"

"No. No, I didn't."

I took a deep breath, trying to slow the thumping of my heart. "I might know where he is."

"Tell me," he groaned.

"Well, I don't exactly trust the source." I glanced over at Cowboy, who was just coming in the door. He hadn't heard me. "Devin Hunter said Barry was in some kind of accident and that he's in a hospital in Roseburg."

"What hospital?"

"I don't know. How many hospitals can there be in Roseburg?"

"You didn't call yet?"

"No. I just got . . . ." The dial tone buzzed in my ear. He'd hung up.

"What's wrong now, darlin'?" Cowboy stood in the passageway to the kitchen.

"I forgot to ask where he was."

"Who?"

"My uncle." I pressed my lips together, regretting I'd said anything. My reluctance to pair my uncle's name with Barry's was growing into something more than a gut reaction.

Cowboy leaned forward, his body language screaming curiosity. "This Barry guy knows your uncle?"

I kept my tone casual, my expression neutral. "Oh sure. He knows everybody in town, practically." I studied Cowboy's face, and was relieved when he smiled and changed the subject. He asked if I wanted a glass of wine. I said yes. At the time, it seemed a good idea.

"Sparkling?

I lifted my eyebrows. Even in my dazed state, I knew Cowboy always drank red wine and if he couldn't get a red, he drank dark ale.

He chuckled. "I brought them for MaryLou. To celebrate."

"Sparkling. Sure."

"Your wish is my command." He headed across the room. "I'll just fetch them outta' the truck."

Clarence stood, gave himself a quick shake and trotted after Cowboy, following him as far as the front door but no further. As soon as Cowboy stepped outside, I called directory assistance and got the telephone number for Roseburg General. The frenzied tone of Uncle Mike's voice echoed in my mind. I had to find out if Barry was okay. For my uncle. And for me. My hand trembled slightly as I dialed the number.

An electronic female voice greeted me with instructions: "Press one for English or el numero dos por Espanol." I stared at the keypad. Stress makes my mind do funny things. I got caught up wondering why the number one has its very own button, unlike all the other numbers that have to share the space with the alphabet. Even 0, which is really an O for oper(ator) has letters after it. I guess it's true that one is the loneliest number. I pressed it.

This time, an asexual voice delivered a litany of information I didn't need, all about visiting hours, permitted use of parking lots A and B and so on. This is a good example of what's wrong with modern medicine. After all, when people telephone a hospital it's because they're in trouble or someone they know is in trouble. What they need is a compassionate person who can direct the call. What they get is a machine.

Impatiently, I punched the O button. A comforting male voice responded. Finally, I had a real person on the other end of the line but he had bad news. There was no Barry Adams registered as a patient at Roseburg General.

"Are you sure?" My voice quivered with barely contained hysteria.

"I'm sorry," the man said. "Perhaps your friend is in another hospital?" He gave me the telephone numbers of smaller hospitals in some of the nearby towns. "Hope you find him," the man said. "Good luck."

"Thank you," I said. "I hope so too."

Cowboy came out of the kitchen, carrying two juice glasses filled with white-gold bubbly. "Drink," he instructed, handing me a glass. I took a small sip, letting the sparkling wine tickle my tongue before I swallowed. After I took a few more tastes, Cowboy took my glass and set it next to his. Gently, he guided me about-face. "Let me get some of those knots out," he said.

I felt the soft pressure of his hands, massaging my shoulders. It did feel good. Reluctantly, I stopped him. "I've got to make more calls," I said.

"I'll help you." Cowboy reached into his pocket and pulled out a palm-sized cell phone. "I just got this gadget." He held it in the air and squinted at the small display screen. "Yup. I got service. Three bars."

Not more than twenty minutes later, our combined dialing had failed to locate a Barry Adams who was a patient in any hospital within a 50 mile radius of Roseburg.

"You know," Cowboy said, pouring the last of the bottle into my glass. "Devin never was much good at details. What if he disremembered the name of the town? Maybe it's not Roseburg."

"Will you call him?" Hope fluttered in my chest.

"Nah. I'll do better'n that. I'll call Sondra." Cowboy flipped his cell phone open. "Lemme see if I've got her number." Using his thumb, he pressed one of the keys a couple of times. "Whatya know?" He grinned at me. "I do have it."

I folded my arms across my chest. Maybe there was a false note in his voice or a guilty twitch on his lips that gave him away. Or maybe I'd played this scene too many times before, with other men. I was positive Cowboy knew all along he had Sondra's phone number. What was the big deal? It was perfectly logical that he have it. After all, she was Devin's sister and he was Devin's best friend.

Cowboy threw a wink at me, signaling that she'd answered. "Sondra? Listen, Babe. Help me out here. You told Dev this Barry guy was in the Roseburg hospital." Cowboy paused, listening to the buzz of words on the other end. "Uh huh," he repeated, more than a couple of times, but he said nothing to reveal Sondra's side of the conversation. At last, he murmured his goodbye and snapped the cell phone closed. "Cunt," he said.

I stared at him, momentarily taken aback. Even if I think she is one, I hate hearing a man use that word about any woman. Maybe it's like white people using the "N" word, or straight people calling a homosexual a fag or a dyke. But I was too impatient for news about Barry to dwell on anything else. "What'd she say? Is he all right? Where is he?"

"Whoa. Slow down." Cowboy lifted his hands in mock surrender to my attack of questions. "He's not in Roseburg, just like I thought."

"Where is he?"

"Rogue River. At least Dev got the first letter right." Cowboy shook his head, clearly amused by Devin's lack of geographic intelligence.

I thought of Uncle Mike, searching for Barry. "Isn't that in Southern Oregon?"

"I think so." Cowboy gave me a puzzled look. "Why?"

The little bell that had been jingling in my brain started to clang. I'd finally figured out what it was trying to signal. "Wait a minute. How come Sondra knew about Barry?"

"Well, see, that's the good part," he said. "I guess he lost control of his car coming through the mountains."

"What? That's the good part?"

"He's okay." Cowboy laid a reassuring hand on my arm. "See, this Barry guy had one of those near-death things, so then he called Sondra and told her off." He snickered. "He really got to her."

"You mean he's not hurt?" I reached for the telephone and then hesitated. "Where is he? Where can I call?"

"I don't know. She didn't say. At least you know he's okay." Cowboy picked up one of the juice glasses and handed it to me. "Here, finish this and I'll open the other bottle."

I lounged on the couch, resting my head against the pillow back. I was light-headed from pouring too much alcohol into my empty stomach and from relief that Barry had been found. I thought about his phone call to Sondra, wondering what he said to anger her. I grinned. Whatever he said, good for him.

Cowboy returned to the living room, carrying the second bottle. "Here, darlin'," he said, pouring another glassful. "What's that big smile for?" He walked around the coffee table and sat on the couch, his leg touching mine.

"Nothing really. Just smiling." I scooted slightly, until there was a gap between us again. Both of us pretended not to notice.

"Aw. Come on. You can tell me."

"Okay. I had this picture of Barry giving Sondra hell," I said, "and Sondra holding the phone, getting all red-faced and sputtering."

"That is kind of amusing," Cowboy said, touching his glass to mine. "Let's drink to that."

I raised the glass to my mouth. The bubbles tickled my lips but I didn't swallow anything. Carefully, I set the glass down. Immediately, Cowboy poured more sparkling, filling the glass to the top.

"Lemme finish that massage, huh?" Cowboy's hands landed on my shoulders. His strong fingers began to manipulate my tight muscles. I purred contentedly, like a fat cat on a sunny window ledge. Vaguely, I was aware of Clarence signaling his disgust with me by leaving the room.

Cowboy inched his left hand downward until his fingertips almost touched the slope of my breast. I tingled with anticipation. Cowboy's other hand moved on my arm, squeezing me closer. It was at that moment my sex-starved body staged a coup, seizing control from my alcohol-soaked brain. Like someone in a trance, I turned to Cowboy. Our lips met and pressed together. We kissed, his tongue exploring my mouth. We kissed until we were panting with lust. And then my shirt was off and my bra and Cowboy had one hand cupping a bare breast, his lips sucking my nipple, his other hand reaching into my pants to get at the rest of me. I reached down and felt his penis grow with my touch. And then he was undressed and unrolling a condom and he slipped inside me and we rocked and we rolled so hard we knocked all the pillows off the couch.

I awoke with a start much later, sandwiched between Cowboy and the sofa back. For a few moments I lay there, shivering from nakedness and regret, before I slowly extricated myself from the couch, careful not to wake Cowboy. I grabbed my clothes and retreated behind the locked door of the bathroom. Stepping into the shower, I turned the faucet on, enduring the first icy shock of water as a kind of punishment. Again and again, I soaped my body, from my scalp to my toes and in every crevice and fold. The water turned so hot my skin was day-glo pink when I finally stepped out of the shower and reached for a towel.

I was confronted by my blurry reflection in the medicine chest mirror. I leaned over the sink until I was almost nose-to-nose with my image. "Idiot," I hissed. The face in the mirror mimicked me.

"Telephone," Cowboy called through the door.

I glanced at the little clock on the window ledge. It wasn't even midnight. Maybe Uncle Mike was calling. Or Barry. "Who is it?" I asked him.

"MaryLou. And she's hysterical."

CHAPTER 17

My flannel bathrobe was missing from the hook on the back of the bathroom door and I remembered carelessly tossing the robe on the bed that morning instead of hanging it up. Cursing myself as both a fool and a slob, I converted my bath towel into a sarong. Belated modesty. With my arms pressed tightly against my sides, I clutched the towel closed with one hand and cautiously opened the door with the other.

Cowboy was waiting, slouched against the wall opposite the bathroom, dressed only in his Jockey shorts. His upper arms and chest were pale and blue-veined compared to the healthy tan on his forearms and face. In his outstretched arm, he hefted the phone like a fifty-pound barbell. When he handed it to me, he couldn't resist flexing his biceps and puffing out his chest.

Ignoring Cowboy's boyish display, I grabbed the phone from him. "MaryLou? You okay?"

"Ruby? I'm so excited. Ever since you left, I've been thinking," MaryLou said. "I've come up with a great idea for next week's show. You're going to love this, I promise. Anyway, I want to get started early. Tomorrow. Around 8:00, maybe?"

"But tomorrow's Saturday." I'd toyed with the idea of driving to Southern Oregon for the weekend, to look for Uncle Mike and Barry. My plan was vague and a little scary. The practical part of me knew it was best to wait for Uncle Mike's call but I was overwhelmed by my need to do something.

"We need to get right on this."

I stifled a yawn. "What's the big deal?"

"Oh, Ruby, I can't wait until Monday to come up with another script. I really need your help. Please. I can't do this without you."

I babbled a weak defense. "I'm sorry, but I just can't. I'd like to help you out, really I would, but the thing is I need to stay by the phone. I'm waiting for a call. A really important call." Once again, I found myself reluctant to mention Uncle Mike's name.

"No problem," she said. "We'll just meet at the cabin. It's perfect." Her voice gained enthusiasm. "I can bring everybody up there in the van. And Ruby, don't bother about food. I'll bring stuff up from the house."

"But I still don't know why you need me to. . . ."

"I can't talk now," MaryLou cut in. "I promise I'll tell you all about it in the morning. Listen, I've got to go. I still have to call Janet and Laura." She hung up.

I stood there, clutching the receiver in mid-air, suddenly struck by the realization that MaryLou never mentioned Barry's accident or my abrupt departure from her house hours earlier.

"What's with her?," Cowboy said.

"The missing script must be for next week," I said, more to myself than Cowboy. "That's why she needs me."

"Hey, Babe. I need you more." Cowboy held out his arms. "Come to Papa."

"Uh uh," I said, shaking my head. "I'm pretty much done in for the night."

"Aw c'mon." He pushed away from the wall and leaned toward me.

I stared at him, stunned that I'd never before noticed his resemblance to Donnie and Bob and countless other men I'd been attracted to, men with easy charm and careless smiles. Men who wanted things on their terms, who didn't know how to meet you halfway. Fighting the urge to retreat, I pulled my spine straight and looked him in the eye. "No."

"Hey. You don't mean it."

"I do mean it. I'm really tired and I have to work tomorrow. It's time to say goodnight."

Cowboy gestured toward the living room and the couch. "You sure liked it an hour ago. I know you want more." He arched an eyebrow, trying for a sexy-Tom Selleck-as-Magnum P.I.-look. Instead, his wrinkled forehead reminded me of a worried Shih Tzu. Any lingering romantic urge quickly evaporated.

"Good night, Cowboy."

Cowboy's hands tightened into fists. "You can't do this to me." In the small hallway, the threat in his voice was magnified.

"This isn't about you. It's about me."

"You're a cunt," he snarled. "Just like all the others."

My heart thumped with sudden fear. I started thinking about how to defend myself. One hand was white-knuckled from clutching the towel closed. My other hand was wrapped around the telephone. I gripped it even harder and wondered if I could use it to hammer him, if I needed to. My palms were so sweaty I worried the phone would slip from my hand. Cowboy had the advantage in height, weight and strength. Probably, he'd overpower me. But I didn't have to make it easy for him. Narrowing my eyes, I put on my meanest face.

Cowboy's eyes widened. He's afraid of me, I thought, gleeful and amazed, until I heard the click of toenails on the wooden floor behind me. Cowboy was afraid of Clarence. I fixed my glare on Cowboy as Clarence trotted into my field of vision. He stopped beside me and gave a low growl. Oversized lower canines jutted from Clarence's mouth like little swords. His ears were back and an angry stripe of fur bristled along his spine.

Cowboy leaned forward slightly. Clarence snarled, vicious as a thirsty werewolf.

"Does it bite?" Cowboy asked, staring at the dog.

It? I looked down at Clarence. He cast his eyes up at me and I swear he lowered an eyelid to give me a devilish wink.

"He might," I said. "Bullldogs were bred for fighting, you know."

"Good boy, good boy." Cowboy fanned his hands, protecting his crotch. Slowly, he backed out of the hallway and into the living room. "Okay, Ruby," he said. "You win."

Clarence and I stood side-by-side in the passageway. We watched Cowboy scurry to gather his clothes and clumsily put them on. Still tucking his shirt into his pants, Cowboy shuffled over to the coffee table and grabbed the half-finished bottle of sparkling wine. He opened the front door and paused, one hand cupping the doorknob the way it had held my breast an hour before. "Just tell me one thing," he said.

"What?"

A puzzled expression showed on his face. "Didn't you like it?"

"Goodnight," I said. Clarence backed me up with a bark from deep in his barrel-shaped chest.

"Fuck you, bitch." Cowboy yanked on the doorknob. The door swung outand hammered his foot,. "Shit," he screamed, as high-pitched as a little girl. He limped through the doorway, turned around and slammed the door shut, rattling windows and my nerves.

I held my breath until I heard Cowboy's heavy footsteps cross the porch and go down the stairs. Then I ran to put the safety chain on the door. My heart pumped with anger and fear. Clarence followed close on my heels. Outside, there was the noise of the truck engine starting. Cowboy gunned the motor, using probably a gallon of diesel. The truck spun out of the driveway, scattering gravel like birdshot. Moments later, the tires squealed as the truck sped onto the pavement. I held my breath until the truck's noise faded into the distance.

Wobbly with a mix of emotions, I sank onto my knees and wrapped my arms around Clarence. More than anything, I owed him a huge hug and about a million liver snaps.

After securing all the window locks and checking both doors twice, I rummaged in the kitchen drawer until I found a package of sandlewood incense. I pulled out a stick and lit it "Okay, Clarence," I said. "Follow me." Even though I was still wrapped in the towel, I paraded through the cabin, waving the incense stick in the air like a wand, hoping to smudge away the unpleasantness of Cowboy's visit. After several tours through each room, I felt better. I stuck the remaining half stick of incense in the geranium flowerpot and stumbled into the bedroom. Dropping the towel on the floor, I crept under the covers.

Exhausted as I was, sleep wouldn't come. I flipped from one position to another. Comfort eluded me. In my brain, a voice whispered incessantly about how I'd made a mess of my life again. Alongside the bed, Clarence breathed heavily, almost panting. He was awake too, still on guard. I wondered if I merited such devotion but I was grateful to have it. Finally I was calm enough to doze, although I was too uneasy to sink into deeper slumber.

My eyes fluttered open as usual, before the alarm. Huddled under the covers, I listened to rain dripping from the eaves above the bedroom window, where the rain gutter was rusted and cracked. After a few minutes I threw back the covers and climbed out of bed, shivering in the chill air. My robe was tangled in the blankets at the foot of the bed. I quickly extricated it and wrapped it around my goosebump-covered body. Reversing my opinion of last night, I forgave myself for leaving the bathrobe on the bed. Einstein was right: everything is relative.

Groaning like an old man, Clarence heaved himself up and followed me. While the coffee perked, I went into the living room and made a quick job of collecting the scattered pillows and rearranging them on the couch. I carried the dirty glasses to the sink, quickly washed, dried and put them away. Finally, I surveyed the cabin, deciding it was presentable enough for MaryLou, Janet and Laura. Spending the morning in a SETII meeting was the last thing I wanted to do. If only I had the guts to pick the phone and tell MaryLou.

The java machine gurgled to a conclusion. I fed Clarence, poured myself some coffee and carried the hot mug to the kitchen window. In the rain-splashed glass, I saw another ghostly image of myself, this one superimposed on the dark landscape. Staring at the blurry me, I took a sip, and let the spicy, exotic Sumatra roll on my tongue like good wine. I heard the comforting sound of Clarence chomping down the dog food, his dog tag clinking against the side of the metal bowl. I drank more. The caffeine dripped through my veins. My sanity began to awaken.

I felt better but I still had worries. I dialed Uncle Mike's telephone number. No answer. I returned the handset to its cradle and almost at once, the phone shrilled. I grabbed it up again. "Uncle Mike?"

"Ruby. It's MaryLou. Listen. We're going to meet at SETII, okay?"

"But I can't. My phone call . . . ."

"Listen, I can't talk now. I just need you to get here. Please?" Her voice hiccupped with a little sob.

"What's wrong? Are you okay?"

"No." She sniffled. "I need you. You're the only one I can count on."

I hesitated, torn by conflicting loyalties. "Okay," I sighed. "I'm on my way."

"Oh, Ruby. You're a dear." She hung up.

"Another crisis," I grumbled to Clarence. "Just what I need."

He raised his big head and regarded me with milk chocolate eyes.

"Sorry, boy. You have to stay home. Too bad you can't answer the phone for me." I got on my knees to give him a back scratch, to make up for leaving him alone on a Saturday. Clarence gave me a loving slurp in return. Ten minutes later, I rushed out the door, a thermos of coffee tucked under my arm.

I had on jeans, a red sweater, a pair of clogs and my black raincoat. It wasn't fully light yet and a misty rain contributed to the gloom.

Without much traffic to get in my way, I arrived at SETII in half the usual time and found a parking spot only half-a-block away. I was surprised to find the front door unlocked. I went inside and into the office area. "MaryLou?"

"In here, Ruby," she called from her office.

I hung my raincoat up and rushed down the hallway, practically running into the room. And then, mid-stride, I stopped so fast that if I'd been wearing rubber-soled shoes I would've made skid marks. MaryLou's tearful plea for help, only thirty minutes earlier, hadn't hinted there would be a crowd of people sitting in the room with her. Especially this crowd of people.

MaryLou sat behind the desk, her hands clasped and at rest on the desktop. She had on a black turtleneck sweater that turned her complexion a deathly pale. On the couch, Devin and Sondra were perched side-by-side like two hungry buzzards on a fence. The biggest surprise was Mr. Sykes sitting stiffly in the overstuffed chair. Handsome as ever, he was dressed in a dark business suit, a starched white shirt and a gray tie, in contrast to everyone else's casual attire. At the side of the room, crowded into the area on the other side of the desk, there were several folding chairs. One of the SETII Betties sat primly on the last chair. Her blonde hair was quickly going gray and heavy makeup couldn't hide the smoker's-mouth wrinkles radiating from her lips. I'd seen her before but whether it was around the SETII offices or elsewhere, I couldn't recall.

Voices sounded in the entryway. Moments later, Janet and Laura bustled into the room with apologies for being late, even though it was 7:45 AM on their day off. I turned to smile hello but they nudged past me, heading to the folding chairs.

"Psst," Sondra hissed at me. "Go sit down. We're waiting on you."

Like a dreamer trapped in a nightmare, I made my way to the last empty folding chair and sat down.

MaryLou unclasped her hands and sat back in her chair. "Good morning." She looked around the room, her gaze lingering on each of us. "Thank you for being here."

"C'mon, MaryLou," Devin said. "Let's get on with it."

MaryLou turned to Mr. Sykes. "Would you tell them, please?"

Sykes nodded and smacked his lips together, as if he had something tasty to say. "Measure 13," he intoned. His baritone voice was too loud for the small room. "That's what it's all about. Measure 13 is a test that we don't dare fail. Because if we fail, we're doomed." He smacked a fist sideways into the open palm of his other hand. "Doomed," he yelled, making me jump an inch or two off my chair.

"But I'm not giving in so easy," Sykes went on. "That's why I got this measure on the ballot, to protect decency and marriage and family values." Dramatically, he paused and gestured at MaryLou. "Me and this little lady here, we're putting up a heck of a fight. And we're going to win."

MaryLou nodded. "Mr. Sykes here is going to help us do a special show. I was so worried about the missing script and then Ruby gave me a wonderful idea last night. It's a miracle. And Mr. Sykes loves it."

"What idea?" I couldn't imagine Mr. Sykes liking any idea of mine.

"No, no, my dear," Mr. Sykes talked over me. "Your Rudy or Ruthie or whatever may have been the vehicle, but God was the driver. God gave you the idea, not a mortal sinner."

How dare he call me a sinner? Athough I'd called myself worse last night, I glared at him before I turned my attention to MaryLou. She was the one I was angry with anyway. "What're you talking about, MaryLou? What idea did I give you?"

"You said I was talking, but not doing."

"Well," I groped through my memory for the exact words I'd spoken. "I think I said it was a lot of words that didn't mean much to me."

"Same thing." MaryLou waved her hand, making it so. "After you left, Howard here called," she gestured at Mr. Sykes, "to ask me to take action."

"I asked MaryLou if she would stand up for decency," Sykes interrupted. "And when she said yes, I asked her to testify right on her show that she supports Measure 13." He rose from his chair and looked down at the rest of us. "She said yes again."

Slowly and deliberately, Sykes moved his gaze around the room, pointing his finger first at Devin and Sondra and then at the SETII Betty, at Janet, Laura and finally, at me. "And you? Will you stand up for what's right?"

"We will," Sondra said. "Right, Dev?"

Devin nodded.

The SETII Betty scooted to the edge of her chair and raised her hand, eager to be called on. "I will."

"Good. Now tell me. How many of you will be voting yes for Measure 13?" There was no response. "What's this?" He frowned. "Are you voting no?"

Sondra shook her head. "I can't vote. I forgot to register."

Sykes looked around the room again. Under his gaze, MaryLou and Devin shook their heads and Janet and Laura shifted uncomfortably on the folding chairs.

"I've got an excuse," whined the SETII Betty. "I just moved here a year ago."

"No matter," Mr. Sykes said, but his scowl contradicted the words. "It's enough that you convince others who can vote. Tell me you'll do that." He became more animated, hammering one fist on the other. "Tell me 'yes'," he shouted.

"Yes," chorused everyone. Everyone else.

Sykes narrowed his eyes at me. "You," he said. "I haven't heard you say anything."

"No," I said. "No you haven't."

"Ruby?" MaryLou had a puzzled expression on her face. "What's wrong?"

"I don't agree with Measure 13. I'm not voting for it."

Sondra leapt up. "What?" She turned to Mr. Sykes. "Don't worry. We're with you a hundred percent. Ruby gets stubborn sometimes but we'll set her straight."

"See that you do," Sykes snapped at Sondra. He gave MaryLou a curt nod and marched from the room.

The room filled with heavy silence. Everyone looked at me expectantly. "I won't do it," I said.

"It's no big deal," Sondra said. "We're just going to have all of us standing behind MaryLou while she tells the viewers to vote yes for 13. You don't even have to nod your head or anything. All you have to do is stand there."

"Ruby, please. He's going to give us a lot of money. We'll be able to do a lot of really good things."

"I can't, MaryLou. I can't support something that's so hateful." I glanced at Sondra. "Even if it only looks like I support it because I'm standing there."

Devin turned to face me. "I'll tell you what, Ruby. If you know what's good for you, you'll keep your mouth shut and go along with this."

Fear shivered my spine at Devin's words but I shook my head no.

Janet reached over and lightly touched my arm. "Why are you so against this, Ruby?"

"Because it's bigoted and unfair, that's why."

"But it just says they don't get special rights. What's so wrong about that?"

"Special rights?" I shook my head. "I think this measure makes it okay to discriminate against anyone who's gay. Or who you think is gay."

There was a chorus of denials. "Ruby." MaryLou's voice rose over the others. "Homosexuals are Chaos. They're out of balance and being out of balance threatens the stability of everything." She smiled sympathetically. "Even if your friends and relatives are confused about the truth, we have to help them make the right choice." Her eyes grew shiny with tears. "Sometimes people have to suffer a little bit until they understand they need to make a better choice."

"Being gay isn't a choice," I snapped. "It's not like deciding what to have for breakfast or what you're going to wear."

"What is this thirteen thing anyway?" The blonde SETII Betty leaned forward, waiting for an answer, the tip of her tongue poking from her mouth.

Something about that gesture tugged at my memory. I pushed the distraction aside and tried to find the best words. "It's on the ballot for the election next week. It says that homosexuality is a choice that's morally wrong. I don't buy that."

"So what? It's just words." The SETII Betty shrugged and sat back in her chair.

"It's not just words when you're trying to get special rights for your friends," Devin said. "And for your relatives." His eyes glittered nastily.

"I told you she was disloyal. I told you from the start," Sondra said, turning to MaryLou.

MaryLou's face was white as a winter moon. She sat back in her chair, staring at me. "I should have known when you told me that story about your last job," she said. "Something about a dog and how you were nasty to your boss."

"No, MaryLou, " I said. "You've got it wrong. And now, I think I'd better go." I was glad my voice didn't shake. I was scared and angry and worried about people I loved, but for once I felt entirely certain about what I had to do. I stood and made my way across the room, chin in the air and fingers crossed, hoping I wouldn't trip and ruin a dignified exit.

As soon as I was out the door, a frenzy of voices erupted in the room. I walked slowly down the hall, trying to hear what they were saying. With all of them talking at once, though, I couldn't make out much except my name, repeated over and over.

"Ruby. Ruby. Hold on a minute." MaryLou was half-running down the hallway to catch up with me.

I stopped.

"Whew." She fanned her face with her hand "I'm so out of shape."

I didn't say anything.

"You're mad, aren't you Ruby? Don't be. I didn't mean what I said. And I'm sorry about asking you to go against what you believe." She rubbed her eyes and I saw she was crying. "Please. I need you. I need to talk with you. Can I come up to the cabin tonight?"

"MaryLou, what's wrong?" My anger was washed away by her tears.

"Tonight. I'll tell you tonight. Please?"

No, I thought. I don't want to. But as usual, I felt guilty refusing her. "Okay."

"Bless you, Ruby. Don't worry about them." She gestured at the room down the hall, still noisy with raised voices. "Just say you forgive me."

I gave her a non-committal nod.

"Good." She turned to leave and then hesitated, looking back at me. "Cowboy's not going to be there tonight, is he?"

"Hell no," I said.

For a moment, as I watched MaryLou walk away, I had the dizzying sense that I was teetering on a narrow bridge stretched over a wide chasm. On one side of the deep divide there was my uncle and Barry, on the other was MaryLou.

Through the wall, I heard MaryLou's voice. Her tone was calm as a mother reading a bedtime story to her children. "Let's all take a deep breath. We need to turn this chaos into good energy." There was a rumble of protest but she talked over the voices. "We'll just go on without Ruby," she said.

I didn't want to hear any more. As I hurried for my car, my stomach rumbled, complaining that I'd skipped breakfast. Food. That was it. The SETII Betty looked familiar because she was the waitress at that horrible restaurant Cowboy had taken me to last summer. "Suzanne," I remembered out loud, startling the old man who'd just let his equally aged cocker spaniel lift a leg on the Golf's tire. The man yanked the dog away, and the dog, confused, lifted his leg and peed on the man's pants leg.

I had to smile. Every now and then, people get what they deserve.

CHAPTER 18

S till grinning, I switched on the ignition, swiveled my head to check for oncoming traffic and pulled away from the curb. Earlier, I'd driven to SETII in a wet gloom that was more night than day. Now, a buttery-yellow sun was shining in a startling blue sky. Rolling the driver's side window down, I inhaled deeply. The autumn air was crisp as a ripe apple.

The weather encouraged me to believe in possibilities. For the first time in my life I had a savings account with a respectable balance and I had a dream for what I wanted to do with the rest of my life. Ever since I'd worked at ARF, I'd had the idea of setting up my own animal rescue operation for dogs and maybe cats. I would talk to MaryLou that very night, tell her I couldn't work for her anymore. I would offer to pay rent so I could stay at the cabin. Not only that, my Cowboy problem had been solved, thanks to Clarence. And surely Uncle Mike would call soon to reassure me. I even dared to hope Measure 13 would be soundly defeated

On impulse, I decided to go by the Kids Klub to see if Uncle Mike had checked in. The Capitol was deserted on a Saturday. I zipped easily from the town center to Felony Flats and the Klub. Only a mile or so separated these two parts of the city but otherwise they were planets away from each other.

As soon as I approached the intersection of Mission and Fourteenth, I knew something was wrong. I braked, letting the Golf idle. A snarl of cars blocked the street. People wandered through the congestion, joining one or the other of the several groups huddled on the sidewalk in front of the Kids Klub driveway.

While I sat there debating what to do, I noticed several guys come bursting out of a house on the other side of the street. All of them were dressed in black jeans and black sweatshirts with the hoods up, hiding their faces. I watched them dodge through the maze of cars and shove past a crowd of women gathered by the fence. Pushed off balance, one woman stumbled, her arms flailing helplessly in the air. Just in time, a few women rushed to her aid and kept her from falling. One of them raised a fist and shouted something.

None of the guys looked back. They rushed up the driveway of the Kids Klub parking lot and disappeared from my view.

I put the Golf in reverse and checked the rearview mirror. Then I backed the car down Mission about a half-a-block and parked. Quickly as possible, I headed towards the Klub. The bottom of the driveway was mobbed. The small groups had congealed into one noisy mass of women and children. At the edge of the crowd, I stopped to ask a large woman with kind brown eyes what was going on.

"Some kind of demonstration," she said, waving a flabby arm. "Buncha' weirdos showed up and started yelling at people, calling names and like that. Some of the big kids didn't like it." She turned to the others. "Ask me, it was just another excuse for a fight."

There was a murmur of agreement but a skinny blonde woman shook her head. "Nope. They was saying stuff about Mike."

Stuff about Mike. The words chilled me. I tossed a hasty thank you over my shoulder and plunged into the mess of people. "Excuse me, excuse me," I repeated, as I maneuvered and elbowed and squeezed my way through the barrier of bodies. I was sweating by the time I burst free. I ran fast, up the driveway, dreading what I'd see.

Sure enough, at the top of the incline a frenzied mass of people filled the middle of the parking lot, blocking my way to the building. Some of them hoisted signs reading "Yes on 13" and "Yes for Decency," just like the group on Labor Day. I slowed to a walk, scoping the situation. I suspected some in the unruly crowd might try to stop me. I would have to sneak past them and make a dash for the Kids Klub. Cautiously, I angled along the back of the crowd, hoping to approach the building without anyone noticing.

As I got closer to the building, I saw there was a line of people in front of the Kids Klub, facing the angry mob. The black hooded guys stood guard at the front doors. Some of the Kids Klub volunteers and an older man wearing a black and white striped referee shirt were nearby. Behind them, I recognized Connie, her son George and a bunch of other kids. A few more adults, probably parents, hovered anxiously in the back.

Somehow, Connie spotted me. She waved her arms in the air. "Ruby. Over here, Ruby, over here." A few of the Measure 13 people turned to stare at me.

"Don't go there," a red-faced woman standing near me said. She pointed at the Kids Klub. "That's Satan's palace."

A thin man with a pale, narrow face stepped in front of me. The sour smell of sweat assaulted my nose. "I can't let you go to that place of evil," he said, crossing his arms and planting his feet.

"Let me through, please."

"No can do." His smile was definitely in the category of smugly superior, the kind of smile that used to make me crazy with helpless anger. I was helpless no longer. Clarence taught me what to do.

I wrinkled my face into a mean scowl, hunched my shoulders like a football player and started to move forward. "Out of my way," I growled, trying for a bulldog baritone. A surge of self-confidence made me stand tall.

"Hey, little lady." The man backed away, lifting his hands in surrender. "No need to be a bitch."

I snarled at him as I passed, enjoying the nervous blink of his eyes as he retreated further. There was no time for real gloating, though. My attention was quickly diverted.

"We've come to rescue the children," boomed a deep voice. "There's a man in charge here who's a homosexual deviate. Your children are being poisoned by his homosexual agenda. Help us save them."

Through the crowd, I caught glimpses of a man dressed in a blue business suit. He stood tall, an arm raised overhead. The pose reminded me of Charlton Heston as Moses in *The Ten Commandments.* I wondered if the image was intentional and then I realized who the man actually was. Just to make sure, I stood on my tiptoes and peered over the mostly white-haired crowd. It was Sykes.

If my eyes were blowguns, he'd have died from the sting of a million poison darts. Less than half-an-hour ago, when Sykes had stalked out of MaryLou's office, he was headed here. Did MaryLou know he was going to the Kids Klub? Did she know he would attack Uncle Mike? I thought about what she'd said: Special rights for friends and relatives. Friends and relatives. . . confused about the truth. Help them make the right choice. People have to suffer. And I remembered Devin's threat: If you know what's good for you.

And then, in one of those freaky moments that prove how weird life is, Sykes lifted the microphone of a portable sound system to his mouth and echoed those words. "If you know what's good for you," he shouted, "you'll let the children go."

The small group surrounding him took up the chant. "Let the children go, let the children go."

"Let. Them. Go," Sykes boomed into the microphone.

"You're the one who should go," one of the black-hooded guys screamed. "You should go fuck yourself."

Both groups erupted into a shrill and incoherent volley of name-calling. In the chaos of noise, I darted forward, circling wide around the Measure 13 group, and made a desperate run to the building. When I got close, arms reached out and pulled me into the protection of the people bunched against the wall. Connie squeezed next to me. "Are you okay?" she asked.

I grabbed her arm. "Is Mike here?"

With her free hand, Connie crossed herself. "Thank God he's been spared that." She turned to the people standing closest to us. "This is Mike's daughter," she explained.

Before I could correct her, a woman in a pink blouse reached over to pat my shoulder reassuringly. "Don't worry, honey," she said, her smoky voice offering comfort. "We'll get rid of this bunch of crazies."

Other voices joined in. "We won't let them get away with this," someone said.

Connie's son George made a megaphone with his hands. "You better get out of here," he yelled at the Measure 13 crowd, his teenage voice betraying him with a squeak at the end of his threat.

Across from us, the chanting got more strident and threatening. Sykes lifted his fist in the air, Zeus with a thunderbolt. "Homo lovers," he boomed at us.

Maybe I only imagined the momentary hush and the gasps of shock before the hubbub of noise was louder than before. Suddenly, the shriek of a referee's whistle cut through the uproar. The man wearing the striped ref's shirt walked forward until he was standing halfway between the two groups. He took the whistle from his mouth and held his hands out.

"Enough," he declared in a voice so commanding that even Sykes quieted. "You people," the Ref said, pointing at the Measure 13 group. "You need to leave quietly now. This is private property and you're trespassing. You're breaking the law."

A few of the people lowered their signs and started turning away.

"Wait," shouted Mr. Sykes. He pointed at the Kids Klub. "What about God's law? God says in the Bible that homos are a perversion. You're allowing a known homosexual to corrupt your children."

"Shut up, man," screamed one of the young guys in front of me. "Stop saying that."

Sykes ignored him. "Mike Lewis is a pervert and a homo," he declared. "He should be fired."

My gut churned acidly. "You're the pervert," I yelled. It wasn't the best comeback but at least it was the truth.

The whistle shrilled again. "I said enough," the Ref said. He looked at Sykes and then checked his wristwatch. "I'll give you five minutes to peacefully vacate the premises," he said.

"What're you going to do? Make me?" The taunt came from the skinny, smelly man who'd confronted me.

"Want to find out?" the Ref said. There was a long moment of silence. He lifted his arm and threw a meaningful glance at his watch.

The skinny man turned and scurried off, followed more slowly by the others. They were quiet now, their signs drooping toward the ground, the way dogs tuck their tails down when they've been scolded. Mr. Sykes brought up the rear, moving stiffly, like someone who doesn't do much walking. His blonde hair was golden in the sunshine.

"Mike Lewis is a fine man and a wonderful example to our kids," Connie shouted at his back.

Sykes turned around to glare at her.

"Jesus." Connie held out the three middle fingers of her left hand and made a spitting sound. "That man has an evil eye," she said.

There were murmurs of agreement from people standing nearby. "He owns half the town," someone said. "Thinks he can get away with anything he wants to do."

"He's crazy. I heard his wife left him to run away with a woman. She's one of them lesbos."

"Lesbian," someone else corrected.

"Whatever."

"You know, even if they're wrong about Mike," said the woman in the pink blouse, "they're right that we shouldn't let perverts near our kids."

One of the parents grabbed my arm. "They are wrong about Mike, aren't they," she demanded. "He's not a homo. Right?"

Connie pointed at me. "How can he be one of them if he has a daughter? Tell them, Ruby."

"Maybe she's one herself," someone said.

Moments ago, these people had fiercely defended Mike and the Kids Klub. If friends and supporters were so easily persuaded to condemn Mike for his sexuality, no wonder he kept that part of himself hidden.

"Wait a minute," I said. "You've trusted him with your kids and he's never betrayed your trust. That hasn't changed. Mike is still Mike." I looked at Connie and her son. "Mike helped you. He's helped all of you." I gestured at the building. "Look at the Kids Klub. Look at yourselves. If you're honest, you'll admit that your life is better because of Mike." I swallowed hard. What I'd just said applied to me as much as anybody.

Someone started to applaud, a girl with a mess of long brown hair. Then George put his hands together and after a moment's hesitation, so did his mother Connie, followed by the pink-bloused woman. One by one, people joined in, until almost all of them were clapping their hands and nodding agreement. I let out the breath I'd been holding.

"Okay everybody," the Ref yelled. "Party's over." He walked toward us, his stride full of authority.

The crowd began to disperse. Some of the volunteers herded kids back into the building, others headed through the parking lot to the street. Like hounds on scent, the black-hooded gangbangers dashed across the asphalt, disappearing like shadows down the slope of the driveway.

"Ruby?" It was the girl who'd started the applause. She shook her thick mane. "Remember me? Carleen?"

I smiled. "The skateboarder. How are you?"

"Okay, I guess. That was great, what you said."

"Thanks for the support. If you hadn't started clapping, I'm not sure what would have happened."

She shrugged and kicked at an invisible pebble. She was wearing torn tennies with neon pink shoelaces.

"Lyman with you?"

Her face wrinkled with disgust. "His mom won't let him come here, remember?"

Mentally, I slapped my forehead, remembering MaryLou's words. They reverberated in my head: "I don't like what I found out. Maybe I should do something." Maybe she had.

"Lyman thinks you're pretty cool." Carleen tilted her head and studied me, as if she was evaluating Lyman's opinion. "If I tell you something, will you keep it a secret?"

I gave her a sharp look, wondering what I would be promising, before I nodded yes.

"Don't worry. It's nothing illegal or anything, " she said. "It's just sometimes Lyman gets real sad. But then he gets all angry and crazy and I'm kind of scared he's going to hurt somebody. Or like, maybe himself." She gave a quick toss of her long hair.

"What about you? Are you afraid he'll hurt you?"

She sneered at my adult concern. "Me? No way." Another toss of her brown hair.

"Do you know why he's sad?"

She shook her head and bit at her lower lip. "Uh uh. He won't talk about it. But I think it's something with his dad."

I wasn't surprised. Devin's meanness to Lyman was the biggest reason I'd avoided visiting the Hunter home. "I'll try to get him to talk with me," I said.

"You won't tell him I said anything," Carleen pleaded.

"I won't. I promise."

She pulled a navy cap from a back pocket of her faded jeans and settled it on her head, tucking away her long hair. The front of the cap had the embroidered white NY insignia for the New York Yankees. She looked tough and vulnerable all at the same time. "I hope you can help him," she said softly.

"Me too. You're a good friend. Lyman's lucky."

Carleen awarded me a shy smile before she darted away, quick as a startled deer. On the run, she grabbed the skateboard leaning against the brick wall of the building, dropped it noisily onto the pavement and hopped aboard, gracefully balancing on one foot and pushing off with the other. As Carleen's skateboard picked up speed, the wheels clacked and clattered like a train going down the track.

I watched Carleen glide across the parking lot. When she disappeared down the driveway, I went to the Kids Klub entryway and rapped my knuckles on a faded orange door. One of the parents guarding the entry recognized me and opened the door, urging me to hurry inside. "Are they gone?" she asked.

I nodded and made the okay sign with my right hand but I kept walking. As I headed down the hallway to the office area, I fantasized I'd find Uncle Mike at his desk, catching up on paperwork.

The office door was decorated with yellow sticky notes, not a good omen. I knocked a couple of times before I twisted the knob. The door swung open. An empty chair faced away from the desk. Stacks of paper, leaning precariously, covered most of the desktop. The telephone's message light flickered like a fading star.

"Mike's not here." The Ref's easy-to-recognize baritone came from the dark depths of the office diagonally across the hallway. Moments later, he appeared in the doorway. "Can I help you?" Up close, I saw he wasn't much older than me.

"I'm Mike's niece Ruby. I've been trying to track him down."

He smiled and held out his hand. "I'm Dave. Pleased to meet you."

We shook hands and made eye contact. Something sparked between us, something I didn't have time for right then. I got back on track. "Have you heard from him?"

Dave nodded. "Called this morning. Should be back tomorrow. Seems to be okay."

"Oh good. I've been so worried." I babbled on. "It's not like him to disappear like that." As the cliché slipped out, I realized I had no idea if Mike's disappearance was in character or not.

"Yeah. I was worried too." Dave broke into a wide smile, transforming his stern appearance. "I like Mike. He's a fine man. You did good out there, standing up for him." The smile faded. "Sorry about what happened. People should mind their own damn business."

"I agree. The world would be a better place, and all that."

He laughed. Once again, our eyes locked in a warm gaze.

A phone rang, breaking the spell. His eyes shifted in the direction of his office. "I'd better go," he said. "Hope to see you soon."

"Thanks. Me too," I said and stepped further into Mike's office. The faint, spicy scent of shaving cream was mingled with the musty odor of a closed-up room. The smell conjured a memory, a memory I'd long suppressed.

It was a rainy day. Forced to stay indoors, I'd grabbed a favorite book, wrapped myself in a blanket and nested in my favorite spot, the alcove tucked under the stairs. The telephone shrilled, once, twice, three times before it was silenced. I heard the high-heeled tap, tap, tap of Aunt Elaine's shoes coming out of the kitchen and walking to the foot of the stairs. She called my uncle's name. I stayed hidden, curious but apprehensive about the tone in my aunt's voice.

"What's the matter," Uncle Mike called. Heavy footsteps thundered above my head as he rushed down the stairs. "What's wrong," he asked again. My aunt's expression must have previewed the bad news she blurted. A plane wreck. In the Atlantic. No survivors. My parents were dead.

Unaware of my presence, Aunt Elaine and Uncle Mike kept talking. My aunt said my mother and father died because they were selfish. "God is punishing them," she said. "The way God will punish you."

"Hush, Elaine. Don't start that now. We have to figure out how to tell Ruby. But how do you tell a young girl her parents are dead?" Uncle Mike sounded like his nose was stuffed up and I could tell he was trying not to cry.

"She hardly knew Marsha and Arthur," Aunt Elaine said. She was angry. "Once they found out being a parent was hard work, they couldn't wait to get away. They gave her to me. We're her parents now."

"Shush," Uncle Mike said. "Marsha was her mother and Art was her father. Ruby's just a girl. We need to help her."

"Nonsense. She'll get over it. At least now I won't worry about Ruby being influenced by my selfish sister."

The book fell from my hands. "Don't say that," I screamed.

I watched Aunt Elaine's legs march towards the alcove. She was wearing her ugly varicose vein stockings and a pair of black pumps. "Ruby, what are you doing down there? You know better than to be eavesdropping. You come out of there right now." The words were stern but her voice quivered.

Slowly, I crawled out from my hiding place. My Aunt's anger puzzled me. She was obviously upset, but why at me? She'd made it clear time and again that my parents were sinful heathens who constantly courted God's wrath. Maybe she was angry because now she was stuck with me for good. I sat on the floor and mutely looking up at Aunt Elaine.

Uncle Mike stepped into view. He placed a gentle hand on my aunt's arm. "I'm sorry about your sister," Uncle Mike said.

I watched Aunt Elaine pull away, rejecting his touch. She brushed at the place on her arm where he'd touched her.

He sighed and turned to look at me. "Ruby. Did you hear everything?"

I shrugged and stared at him, daring him to make me cry.

Uncle Mike crouched down so we were eye-to-eye. "I'm sorry you had to find out this way about your parents dying." He offered his hand. After a moment's hesitation, I laid my smaller hand in his and he gave it a gentle squeeze. "I liked your mother and father," Uncle Mike said. "Marsha and Art were full of life. They were exciting and fun and magical and they sparkled like champagne. I'll miss them." He wiped at his eyes.

That undid me. I broke into sobs. Uncle Mike gathered me in his arms. He held me a long time, until I was too tired to cry anymore.

I rubbed my eyes, momentarily surprised to find myself in Uncle Mike's office at the Kids Klub instead of the foyer of my aunt and uncle's house in Northeast Portland. The clock on the wall showed only a few hours had passed since I left home but in that short time, a lot had changed. I'd found strength to walk out of MaryLou's office and the courage to stand up for my uncle. I'd remembered the truth.

CHAPTER 19

When I got outside, the temperamental weather was throwing another fit. The bright sun that cheered me earlier had disappeared behind a mass of charcoal colored clouds and the valley sky was dark as dusk. Walking to the car, I was chilled by the first drops of rain. By the time I was driving along South Side Road, raindrops the size of BB pellets rat-a-tat-tatted on the car roof. Even on high speed, the windshield wipers were overwhelmed by the downpour, cutting visibility to near zero.

Hunched over the steering wheel like the captain of a trawler caught in an Atlantic storm, I guided the Golf home. When I finally parked in the driveway, my legs and arms ached with tension. I splashed my way to the house, surprised to see Clarence guarding the doorway. Usually he's not terribly alert and could snore his way through the end of the world. Not a bad way to go, when you think about it.

Inside, I stripped out of the wet clothes, including my underwear, and headed down the hall for a hot shower. When I came out, I found Clarence waiting. He tracked my steps as I scurried to the bedroom to dress in my sweats. He followed me to the kitchen, to the living room and back again. I was glad for his company. I couldn't shake the sense of something awful waiting to happen.

Glad I'd spend weekends gathering and storing small stacks of wood, I sat in the rocking chair, letting my hair dry in the heat from the small Franklin woodstove. Clarence was next to me, tucked into a furry ball. I began to feel drowsy and content.

Suddenly, an unfamiliar sound brought me to the edge of the chair. Alert to my movement, Clarence stretched and sat, ears cocked, muscles tensed. After a while, hearing nothing but the snap of wood burning in the woodstove and hard rain hammering the roof, we both settled into an uneasy rest. Absently, I scratched Clarence's back and resumed my mind's replay of the strange day.

I might have dozed off. A howling sound jerked me upright. Ghosts? Coyotes? Clarence was at the door before me, poised in a guard dog stance, bulldog version - legs spread wide, barrel chest thrust forward. He growled deeply.

I called out: "Who's there?" My voice sounded weak and fearful. There was no answer. Again I called, louder this time. Again no response, only the noises of the stormy night. I reached for the doorknob. No. I pulled my arm back. I wasn't going to be one of those silly victims who opens the door to the monster.

Clarence pushed in front of me. He snuffled at the doorsill a few seconds and then turned and walked away, back to the woodstove. He circled once, then plopped down and farted, making a noise like a balloon losing air. Apparently Clarence wasn't afraid of what was out there. I, on the other hand, could still hear terrifying moans and shuffling noises on the other side of the door. I put my ear by the crack. I held my breath. I heard rain and the gurgling of the drainpipe. And something else. Crying? Recklessly, I undid the lock and opened the door.

A dark mass huddled on the top step, rocking back and forth. For a moment I saw the fiend I'd imagined. The shape shifted and lifted its head. I released my terror in a long sigh of relief. This was no monster. It was MaryLou, huddled under a black plastic poncho. Her hair was dripping wet, pasted to her skull.

I stepped onto the porch and crouched beside her. Immediately, I was more soaked than I'd been before, maybe wetter than I was in the shower. I put my arm around her shoulders. She was shivering.

"Come on, MaryLou," I said. The noise of the rain drumming down was so deafening, I had to speak loudly so she could hear me. "What's the matter?"

"Shouldn't have come here." Her voice was muffled. "I'd better go." Clumsily, she tried to rise.

"You're sopping wet and shaking with cold. Come inside and get warm." I held my arm out to steady her. "Come on. We're drowning out here."

She nodded and let me usher her through the door. I kicked it closed behind us. Neither of us said anything. We stood in our wet clothes, staring at each other. MaryLou's face was puffy. Black mascara streaked her pale face, giving her the half-comical, half-satanic look of the KISS Rock N' Roll band member who called himself the Demon.

A drop of water rolled from MaryLou's soggy hair and ran down her forehead. She shook her head, splattering water like a wet dog. As she did so, a key ring holding a couple of keys dropped from her grasp and clattered on the floor, startling both of us. Right away, I recognized the old-fashioned style of the keys. I had a duplicate set to unlock the front and back doors of the cabin. It looked as if she'd planned to get inside whether I opened the door or not. MaryLou bent to pick up the key ring. Tossing it carelessly on the little table by the door, she turned and stared at me as if I were the intruder.

"Did you think I wasn't going to be here, MaryLou?" I didn't hold back the sarcastic edge to my question.

She shook her head. "No. It's not like that."

"Fine. Then let's get dry." I took charge, sending MaryLou to the bathroom along with a clean towel and the raggedy old bathrobe left over from Cowboy's residence or maybe before that. I got a towel for myself and went to the bedroom to change into dry clothes. Again. All the while, I couldn't help supposing a million different reasons for MaryLou having hysterics on the cabin steps in the middle of a semi-hurricane. None of my guesses came close.

"Ruby?" MaryLou called from the bathroom.

I came out of the bedroom and took a few steps down the hallway.

The bathroom door was open just enough for her head to poke out like a turtle's. Except for red-rimmed eyes, MaryLou's face was colorless now that she'd scrubbed away the ruined makeup. She smiled, giving me the same bright look I used to believe in.

"I was hoping I could have a little glass of wine. I think it would energize me," she said. When I didn't respond right away, her eyes clouded. "You're angry at me, aren't you?"

"Yes. I am." I was surprised how good it made me feel to say that. "You and your Mr. Sykes."

"What have we done?" Her eyebrows stretched in surprise.

"Thanks to you, my uncle's probably going to lose his job. And Barry almost lost his life."

Tears spouted from her eyes. "I'm sorry you're disappointed in me. Can't we talk about it?" she pleaded mournfully. She opened the door wider, revealing her fleshy nakedness.

I flashed back to that sweltering morning MaryLou had thrown a fit about my naked boobs. This was another inconsistency to add to the list, but I had more important issues to resolve. Maybe a glass of wine would soften her up, help me persuade her to call off Sykes before he made things even worse for a lot more people. "All right," I agreed.

"You're an angel." MaryLou retracted her head and shut the door.

I got my last bottle of wine, a nice Chianti, grabbed two glasses from the cupboard and carried it all into the living room on a tray. Carefully, I lowered the tray to the small table by the rocking chair and resumed my position near the woodstove. MaryLou took a long time in the bathroom. At last she emerged, wrapped in the well-worn robe. She pulled a chair next to me and sat. Clarence got up and retreated into the bedroom.

I poured wine into both glasses. MaryLou gripped the stem of her glass and took a big swallow.

"Mmm. Thanks," she said, holding her wine glass up to the light. "I think you're supposed to say something about the wine having nice legs." She gave me a playful glance. "I always thought that was kind of sexist, talking about wine like it's a woman."

"Men have nice legs too," I snapped, further irritated at the image that popped into my mind at the mention of legs - Cowboy's legs, long, shapely and firm.

MaryLou ignored my comment. She lifted her glass to her lips and chug-a-lugged the wine, as if she was drinking Coors instead of Chianti. Immediately, she grabbed the bottle and refilled her glass, almost to the brim. Her hand shook when she lifted the glass to her mouth. Wine splashed over the sides of the glass. She took another noisy gulp and clumsily set the glass down on the little table.

"I have to tell you something," MaryLou said. "I can't hold it in anymore." She took a deep shuddering breath. "First I need another drink." She reached for the glass and emptied it in a few swallows. She held the glass out. "More," she said, looking at the bottle.

"I think you've had enough."

She shook her head. "Not tonight I haven't."

I poured another half-a-glass full for MaryLou and shook the few last drops into my own glass. "So? What's going on?"

She drank some wine and bent over to set the almost-empty glass on the floor next to the chair. When she lifted her head, MaryLou's eyes glittered like black pebbles under water. "You can't tell anybody." Her voice dropped to a whisper. "Promise?"

I didn't answer her. She'd asked for my promise not to reveal Mr. Sykes as her secret sponsor. And look how that turned out.

But MaryLou interpreted my silence as assent. Words tumbled from her mouth, one on top of the other. "I wouldn't hurt my kids. Never. I didn't know. I swear I didn't know. He took them camping. I'm such an idiot, I thought they were bonding. All this time. All this time, he had me fooled." With a clumsy gesture, MaryLou wiped at her face with the sleeve of Cowboy's bathrobe. "I didn't find out until yesterday when Devinda told me."

"She told you she was being molested." It wasn't a question. The image of Devin's hand sneaking up Devinda's skirt still haunted me.

MaryLou arched her thinly tweezered eyebrows. "Why would you think that?"

"I thought I saw Devin touching her."

With a bark of laughter, MaryLou cut me off. "No, no, no. He's not interested in Devinda. Or me."

"What do you mean? What did Devinda tell you?"

MaryLou strangled a lock of hair in her fingers, twisting it tighter and tighter. When she finally spoke, her voice was so low I had to lean forward to hear her. "Devinda saw Devin with. . . . He was with Lyman." She covered her face with her hands, muffling her sobs.

"No." I wanted to deny the picture in my mind: Devin's face, twisted in a fanged grimace. Lyman, too weak to resist, his smooth neck exposed. The vampire swoops down, clutches the boy in a fatal embrace. Lyman stares at nothing. His eyes are old and sad.

I pushed the awful image from my mind. The room felt suddenly too warm and suffocating. I could hardly breathe. My mouth was dry.

At that moment, Clarence rushed from the bedroom, skittering slightly on the wood floor. He ran to the front door, barking gruffly.

"Devin," MaryLou whimpered. I almost felt sorry for her.

I got up and went over to stand next to Clarence. "Who is it?" I called. My voice was as quivery as my legs.

The answer could have been the squeal of a small animal or maybe a high-pitched voice. I couldn't tell for sure through the uproar of Clarence's barking. I bent down to pet him and then gently muzzled him with my hand. "Who is it?" I asked again.

"It's Sondra. Is MaryLou with you?"

I turned and looked the question at MaryLou. She touched her left pinky to the corner of her mouth, considering. I could see the finger move slightly, tracing the tiniest circle at the corner of her lips.

Sondra knocked again. "I'm getting soaked out here," she said, her voice muted, as if her lips were pressed against the wood. It was true the storm was fierce, sheets of rain tossed by winds blowing with hurricane strength. It was tempting but I really couldn't leave her out there. And I couldn't shove MaryLou out the door either, much as I wanted to.

"You might as well let her in," MaryLou said. She stood up. The wine glass she'd set on the floor fell over and shattered. Wine spattered like drops of blood on the floor and shards of glass gleamed in the light cast by the woodstove fire. Ignoring the damage, MaryLou came over to stand beside me.

First, I patted Clarence and told him it was okay. He didn't bark, but the trembling of his body meant he hadn't decided if things were safe yet. I un-latched the door and opened it only wide enough for Sondra to squeeze through. Even so, damp air came whooshing in. Without a word to me, Sondra stepped into the house. She wore a man's rain hat and a beige trenchcoat. Playing the detective, maybe.

Wet coat and all, Sondra surrounded MaryLou with her arms. "Thank goodness I found you."

"You're going to drown me," MaryLou said, pushing away. "You didn't have to come fetch me home."

Despite MaryLou's ungrateful response, Sondra smiled, plumping the two rouged globes of her cheeks. "We were worried," she said. "Storm's getting worse and the creek's almost at flood stage."

"I just needed to get out for a while, that's all." MaryLou turned to me. "I could use some more wine, Ruby."

I didn't say anything.

"Come on, MaryLou," Sondra said. "Let me take you home and then you can drink as much wine as you want."

"I'd rather stay here. Ruby and I were talking." MaryLou sounded whiney and petulant, just like her daughter, Devinda.

Sondra's smile was replaced by a frown. "What were you talking about?"

MaryLou ignored her. "C'mon Ruby. Gimme some more to drink." The words slurred together.

Sondra turned to me. "What did she tell you?"

I shrugged. "She's drunk."

"No I'm not. And I'm not going home, either."

Sondra cocked her head, considering. "It's pretty stormy out there. Maybe that wine's a good idea after all," she said. "Mind if I take my coat off and stay a while?"

"I think it would be better to persuade MaryLou to go home."

Sondra reached past me and yanked the door open. If anything, the rain was pounding down harder, sounding strangely like the roar of applause on a television soundtrack. "You're not sending us out in that?" Sondra's tone was heavy with incredulity. "Couldn't you at least let us stay until it lets up a bit?"

"Take off your wet coat," I said. "You can hang it there." Not very graciously, I gestured at the coat tree and walked away. I went into the kitchen, standing on tiptoes to peer into the closet above the refrigerator where the booze was stored. There was no wine, just a lonely half-bottle of cheap liqueur belonging to some previous occupant. I reached down the bottle and got three Looney Tunes juice glasses from the cupboard. The grouchy Yosemite Sam was for Sondra, the inept Elmer Fudd for MaryLou. I kept Bugs Bunny for myself, for good luck.

"There's broken glass by my chair," MaryLou said as I walked into the living room. "Remember the night we met, Ruby? There was broken glass all over. That was the time a deer jumped right in front of my van." She waved her arm in the air. "It jumped so high. Then it fell down and died." She sat back abruptly. "Whew. That made me dizzy."

A picture rose in my mind of the battered van, leaning on a tire rim. That night, MaryLou had told me a story about hitting rocks on the road. This wasn't a mere inconsistency. She'd lied to me.

"I'll get it. I'll get the glass. Don't move." Sondra bustled over and picked up the broom and dustpan from near the woodstove. She bent by the chair, gingerly sweeping pieces of glass into the dustpan. When she was satisfied she'd swept up every sliver of glass, she went into the kitchen to toss the broken glass in the trash.

"What kind of wine is that?" MaryLou said, eyeing her glass as I poured.

"It's liqueur. That's all I've got." My words came out sharp and distinct, like little bullets. I splashed some in Sondra's glass, then mine. I took a tentative sip. Was it possible someone had substituted red mouthwash for the liqueur?

Sondra came back into the room. She walked over to the table and picked up the Yosemite Sam glass, eyeing its contents suspiciously.

MaryLou swallowed the glassful down. "More."

"Here," I said to MaryLou. "Have mine." I handed her the glass.

"Love Bugs Blunny," MaryLou said, looking at the glass. "I mean, Blood Bunny." She giggled. "Bloody Bugs Bunny. Bloody buggered bunny. Bloody buggered boys."

"Come on, MaryLou, you really are smashed." Sondra set the Yosemite Sam glass down hard on top of the bookcase. It made a thunking sound but didn't break. "Maybe I'd better take you home."

"Don't touch me." Shuddering dramatically, MaryLou pressed herself against the back of the chair, away from Sondra's reach. "You're evil. You and Devin."

"I'm just trying to help you." Sondra shook her head and turned to me. "She gets a little crazy when she drinks."

"I'm not crazy," MaryLou shrilled. "You knew. You knew and you didn't stop him."

Sondra arched an eyebrow. "What's to stop?"

Angry blotches spread across MaryLou's neck and face. "You didn't stop Devin with my boy. Just like you didn't stop him with yours."

"What're you talking about?" Sondra's tone oozed with contempt but she couldn't hide the nervous blink of her eyes and the way her mouth twitched at the corner.

"What am I talking about? I'm talking about your son. I'm talking about why your son killed himself." MaryLou narrowed her eyes, fixing Sondra with the hypnotic gaze of a stalking leopard. "I'm talking about how you let your brother do it to your own son. And to your own nephew."

The accusation stunned me. I didn't want to believe any of what MaryLou was saying about Sondra, about Devin, about Lyman and about herself, but already my mind was amassing evidence. Again, I remembered the day I'd overheard Sondra and Devin in the SETII kitchen. You owe me, she'd said. My hand rose involuntarily to my mouth. I wanted to throw up. Nothing in my life had prepared me for this. And Lyman. What could have prepared him?

"You crazy bitch," Sondra shrilled at MaryLou. "You don't know what you're talking about. You need to shut up."

"Wait a minute." I had to shout to get their attention. "What about Lyman? Where is he?"

MaryLou blinked. "He's home."

"You left him alone? With Devin?"

"It's all right. Cowboy's there. Nothing will happen," said Sondra. MaryLou nodded confirmation.

"No. It's definitely not all right." I kept my voice calm, even though I wanted to scream. "We should call the police. Or Child Welfare. Or somebody."

The two women stared at me as if I were the one who'd done something wrong. As if I was the crazy one.

"Nobody is calling the police." Sondra used her condescending tone on me. "It would ruin SETII. You know that. Besides, this is a family matter and that's how we'll keep it."

MaryLou nodded agreement. She got up and took a few steps to stand next to Sondra.

"I don't believe it. You just can't do nothing."

"We won't," MaryLou said. "We'll help Devin get cured."

"Cured? Moments ago, you accused him of molesting your son and Sondra's. How do you cure that?"

MaryLou shook her head. "Ruby, you still don't understand." Her face radiated with that look of hope I had so much wanted to believe in. "I know we can turn his inner chaos into positive energy."

"What about Lyman? How will you cure his inner chaos?"

"We'll figure it out," Sondra snapped. "It's really none of your business. You'll leave it be, if you know what's good for you." She turned to MaryLou.

"Sounds like the rain's let up. Put your coat on. We can make a run for my car."
She shrugged into her wet trenchcoat and held up MaryLou's plastic poncho.

"My clothes," MaryLou said.

"Get them later." Sondra tugged on MaryLou's arm. "Put your poncho on.
Come on."

At the door, MaryLou held back. "Ruby." She fixed me with one of her
forceful looks. "Don't forget. You promised not to say anything. If you've ever
been my friend, you'll honor that." The door clicked shut behind her.

CHAPTER 20

The sound of the shutting door released something in me, in the same way the finger-snap of a hypnotist ends a trance. With sudden clarity I understood that MaryLou had lied to me from the start. When I found her on Seven Hills Road the day I almost committed suicide, she told me rocks had damaged her van. I knew now she'd hit a deer.

The lie about the deer was all part of the terrible pretense MaryLou maintained about her life, about SETII, about the Hunter home and the monsters who lived there. The deer, my uncle, my friend Barry, and MaryLou's own children were casualties of her hit-and-run style of dealing with the truth. As for me, I'd fallen under MaryLou's spell, ensnared by my own self-deception.

I had no magic sword or incantation, no garlic or stake to ward off the evil I'd discovered. But I had the telephone. I would find someone to rescue Lyman and Devinda, someone to stop Devin. Still, I hesitated, knowing what the call would cost me. I would have to leave the cabin. And yet, that wasn't my greatest concern. I worried more that the Hunters would retaliate, making things worse for my uncle, for Lyman and for me.

I was so edgy, the sudden shrill of the telephone levitated me off the chair seat. I hurried to the counter and plucked up the receiver but I didn't say anything, thinking it might be MaryLou.

"Ruby?"

"Uncle Mike. I've been so worried about you." I talked fast, wanting to get everything out. There was so much to tell him and no good way to tell it. "The Measure 13 people picketed the Kids Klub and Sykes told the parents to fire you because you're gay. I think Sondra or MaryLou told him. And MaryLou supports Sykes and is doing a pro-Measure 13 spot on her show. Worse than that, she confessed her husband is a pedophile. With Lyman."

"Whoa, whoa," Uncle Mike interrupted. "Start over from the top."

I repeated the story. It didn't get easier in the retelling.

Uncle Mike sighed deeply. "I should have recognized the signs in Lyman. I'm so sorry to hear this." He cleared his throat.

"I should report Devin. But I'm worried about what might happen. I don't know what to do."

"You have to do what you think is right. Are you afraid?"

"Well, yeah. I'm scared they'll get back at me by hurting you some more."

Mike's laugh was sardonic. "How much more can they hurt me?"

"You're probably right. God, I'm sorry. What're you going do?"

"About what? The Kids Klub?"

"Yes."

"I'm not sure. I think I'll sleep on it, see how I feel in the morning. What are you going to do?"

I sighed. "Call."

"Good. But I wish you'd clear out of there. Those folks sound pretty unpredictable. I'm not sure it's safe there for you. You and Clarence should come to my place."

"Thanks." I felt safer already. I had somewhere to go, someone who cared. "We'll pack up and leave in the morning."

"Are you sure? Maybe you should leave tonight."

"I'll be careful. Don't worry. I've got some things to finish up and a couple of errands to run. I'll see you tomorrow, probably early afternoon."

"All right. Barry sends his love and says he can hardly wait to give you a hug. Me too. And Ruby? Please be careful." With that fatherly admonition, he hung up.

I guess he had every right to be parental. He'd willingly become more than an uncle-by-marriage when I was orphaned, and in doing so, he'd sacrificed a part of himself. A rush of love flowed through my veins, warming my blood better than a shot of cognac. It gave me courage too. I got the telephone directory and looked up the county's Helpline number. Before I could change my mind again, I dialed. The person I spoke with – a woman with a serene and comforting manner – took the information and told me not to worry.

I did worry. I was ninety-nine percent sure I'd done the right thing. But the two percent nagging doubt gave me a headache.

I set the alarm for 6:00 AM, just in case, and crawled into the big bed. My last night under the down blanket was anything but restful. At 5:25, after a fitful night, I got out of bed, made a small pot of coffee and dressed. When the coffee was perked, I drank a cup and poured out the next one to keep me going while I collected my few possessions: clothes, three bags of French Roast beans, a copy of *Even Cowgirls Get the Blues* I'd picked up at the bookstore on Liberty Street, Clarence's bowls, his leash and a twenty-five pound bag of lamb and rice nuggets. I did a quick tidy-up of the kitchen and bathroom but I left MaryLou's wet clothes on the floor where she'd dropped them. It made me feel better. Then I started shlepping stuff to the car, taking extra care in the early morning darkness. The rain had stopped but the path was slick with wet leaves.

It took less than an hour to remove any evidence I'd ever lived in the cabin, except it was cleaner than when I'd moved in. The last thing I did was to lay my keys on the hallway table, next to the set MaryLou had left the night before. I left the door unlocked.

Clarence followed me on my final trip and happily climbed into the back seat with his blanket and bowls. I was more reluctant to say goodbye. I stood next to the idling car and recalled the endless hours on my knees while I weeded the flower and vegetable beds and the thrill of eating the food I'd grown. I could almost smell the rich, damp, freshly spaded earth, almost feel the juice of a fresh-picked tomato running down my chin.

I whispered goodbye to the gardens and trees and the cozy cabin with the eiderdown blanket on the wonderful big bed. Once again, I had packed up my life and was moving on. At least this time I wasn't penniless and suicidal. I had Clarence and my Uncle Mike and Barry. I was wiser too, at least a little bit. I got in the car and backed out of the driveway, onto the road. Slowly, I drove away, watching the cabin in my rear view mirror until it disappeared from sight.

A mile down the road, the Hunter house was still dark. I moved my foot, ready to step on the gas and hurry past when I saw that a tan Jeep with police lights mounted on its roof was approaching on the narrow road. I pulled the Golf to the side as the Jeep came closer. About a hundred feet from where I was stopped, the Jeep turned into the Hunter driveway.

"Stay here," I instructed Clarence. I cracked the window open slightly, grabbed the keys and stuck them in my pocket. With no further thought or

185

plan, I was out of the car and chasing after the Sheriff's Jeep. I was almost at the top of the Hunter driveway, in sight of the house, when I slowed my approach, belatedly realizing I would be smart to remain hidden. Moving quickly off the driveway, I forced my body behind the thick wall of rhododendrons planted alongside the pavement. I crouched low to the ground and darted from bush to bush until I was only a car length or so from the garage.

From there, I had a view of the front door where a uniformed deputy sheriff and a woman in a charcoal gray pantsuit were standing. Slung over the woman's shoulder was one of those big purses that doubles as a briefcase. She knocked on the door with her knuckles. In the early morning quiet, the sound was sharp and loud, like the retort of a gun.

The doorway filled with light and then darkened again as someone stepped forward. It was MaryLou. My heart quickened. The dense leaves made it hard for me to see her clearly but I recognized her shape.

The woman in the pantsuit said something. I heard her voice but not the words because her back was to me. But I saw the deputy take a half-step to the side. I saw his hand edge closer to his holster.

"I don't know what you're talking about," MaryLou said. She was good at projecting her voice and it carried easily to my hiding place. The woman must have spoken again, because MaryLou shook her head and placed a hand over her heart, pledging her honesty. "You don't believe me? I'll prove it."

MaryLou disappeared and light streamed from the doorway. The woman turned to the sheriff. He nodded but didn't turn his head in her direction. My knees ached. I was sure I'd never be able to straighten myself, but I didn't dare make a move or disturb as much as a leaf, for fear of being discovered.

The doorway filled with MaryLou again. Her right arm was wrapped around Lyman. Lyman's head was bent, almost resting on his chest. My stomach soured.

MaryLou faced the woman and the Deputy. "This is my son," she said. "He'll tell you." With her free hand, MaryLou touched Lyman's chin, urging him to lift his face.

Reluctantly, Lyman raised his head until his eyes were leveled at the woman. The way her head bobbed, I could tell she was talking to him. Every now and then, I heard her voice.

Lyman stared at the woman, his mouth curled in a sneer. "No way," he said. "You're a crazy bitch."

The deputy stepped forward. Hands on his hips, he addressed Lyman in a loud, commanding tone. "Young man. No need to talk like that. Now answer the question."

Lyman smoothed his face into a neutral look but his tone of voice remained defiant. "My dad never touched me. Nobody ever touched me." He glanced at MaryLou. "Someone's telling you lies. I bet it's someone who's jealous of my mom. She's famous, you know."

"Oh God," I groaned. Lyman was being a Hunter. Hunters always stick together.

MaryLou hugged him. Then she turned to the woman and the Deputy. "Now get out of here before I call my attorney and have you both fired for malicious harassment." The door slammed shut with a loud noise, like a rifle shot.

The woman looked at the Deputy. He shrugged. She made a gesture of resignation, dropping her hands to her sides. They were giving up. I watched them trudge back to the Jeep. I wanted to call out, but even if I stopped them, it was still my word against MaryLou and Lyman's.

As the Jeep drove past where I was hiding, I flattened myself on the soggy ground and squeezed my eyes closed, as if my not seeing them would insure my invisibility. Maybe it worked. They didn't stop. I waited until the sound of the Jeep's engine faded away before I pushed my way through the jungle of rhodies to the bottom of the driveway. I reached the road and ran to the safety of my car. My hand shook as I turned the key in the ignition.

All the way to Salem, I thought about Lyman. I had to talk with him. On Sunday mornings, MaryLou took the kids into Salem for church. I knew Lyman often finagled his mom into letting him hang out at the skateboard park by the bridge while MaryLou and Devinda went to the service. Was it possible the Hunters would keep to their usual routine for the sake of appearance? I hoped so.

According to the car clock, there were a few hours before I'd find out. I parked on Commercial Boulevard, made sure the front windows were open an inch or two so Clarence would have enough air, locked the car and walked the couple of blocks to the Courthouse Cafe for breakfast. I ordered a Greek omelet and flipped through the thick Sunday newspaper I found lying on the table.

There was little escape from the dark world. It wasn't just the Hunters. Most of the articles and commentary were about people doing harm to other people. Wars. Racial strife. A guy who was arrested a week or so back for shooting at the White House, trying to kill the president. A woman who drowned her kids in the bathtub and then tried to blame it all on a fictitious black man.

I'm sure the omelet was delicious but for all I tasted, it might just as well have been salt free oatmeal. I was nervous, mentally rehearsing what to say if I did find Lyman. Finally, I figured it was time. I paid up and headed north to the skatepark, crossing an expanse of wet grass to avoid a sizeable group of homeless people who'd set up camp on the sidewalk near the park restrooms.

As I approached the large cement structure built for skateboarding, I saw two figures riding their boards along the curved sides, looping around each other in an elaborate skateboard dance. Up and down, in and out, they flew along the arched walls, defying gravity. The skateboard wheels made a growling noise on the cement that got louder as I drew near. The skateboarders were Lyman and Carleen. I wondered how long they'd been aware of my approach.

Carleen continued her flight around the structure, spinning and jumping like a ballerina on wheels. Lyman pulled away. He shortened the arc of his skateboard until he slowed and came to a grinding stop at the edge of the cement near me. With one foot planted on the board, he gave me an unfriendly scowl. "What're you doing here?"

"I wanted to talk with you."

He crossed his arms on his chest. "What for?"

"I wanted to see how you're doing."

Lyman shrugged.

"I know about your father. I know what he does."

His jaw tightened, like he was clenching his teeth. "No," he said. "You're wrong."

"Lyman. I'm not wrong. Your mother told me."

"No. Go away."

"But, Lyman, I want to help you."

"I don't need your kind of help. You sent the cops to our house." His pose was defiant. He kept clenching and unclenching his fists.

"Lyman, I want to make your dad stop hurting you."

"No." He shook his head vehemently. "Leave me alone. Don't you see? They're my parents." He turned his back, lifted his other foot onto the skateboard and wheeled away.

Carleen waited for him at the crest of a small mound. He skateboarded past her and disappeared behind the deep, concave bowl. I heard his wheels spin on the concrete. Carleen shot a disappointed look at me before she hurried to catch up with Lyman.

"Lyman," I yelled, although I didn't expect an answer. All I heard was the distant sound of traffic on Commercial and the discordant shout of one of the homeless men, like the harsh caw of a crow.

CHAPTER 21

"We can't give up," Uncle Mike said, getting up to turn off the radio.

"Sykes won," I moaned.

"And MaryLou." Barry wrinkled his nose and pursed his lips, showing his distaste for this outcome.

We were in the living room. All night we'd huddled around the radio, listening to election return updates, sipping lukewarm green tea and munching Trader Joe ginger snaps, more to stay awake than from hunger or thirst. Beyond the huge windows, city lights twinkled in the 3:00 AM darkness. I was still in street clothes but I'd long ago slipped off my shoes and stretched my legs on the oversized couch, toe-to-toe with Barry, who sprawled on the opposite end. He had on sweatpants and a faded yellow and green Oregon Ducks tee-shirt. Across from us, Mike sat in the leather chair, the one that looked like something straight off the set of a cowboy movie. Clarence was nestled on the floor beside him.

"It's so depressing," I said. "I can't believe all those people voted yes."

"Just like you couldn't believe it when they accepted Mike's resignation at the Kids Klub." Barry sat up, suddenly invigorated. "Mike, we should fight them. Demand your job back. It's unconstitutional or something."

Mike leaned forward, forearms resting on his legs. "I couldn't destroy the Kids Klub to make political points."

"I know, I know. But it's a damn shame you have to walk away from your whole life," said Barry, flopping back on the couch like a rag doll.

"It's not my whole life," Mike gently corrected. "You and Ruby are my life too. And you, Clarence." Smile lines wrinkled at the corners of Mike's eyes. He reached down and rubbed the fur along Clarence's back.

Barry cleared his throat. His Adam's apple bobbed up and down. "It's my fault," he said. "I brought this on. How could I have been so stupid, believing all that garbage?"

I tried to comfort him. "Hey, it's not just you. MaryLou has a way of making people feel special."

"She didn't make me feel special at the end, when she fired me."

"She fired you?"

"Didn't you realize that? I told her I couldn't write that pro-Measure 13 garbage because it was like cutting myself with sharp scissors. So she fired me." A small smile lifted the corner of his lips. "Before I left, I grabbed up all of the new scripts and put them through the shredder."

I recalled the scene at the Metro Cafe, when MaryLou had come looking for me. Even then, I'd been almost as gullible as a SETII Betty. Although I'd been cynical about the chaos, energy, time, infinity stuff, I'd nibbled at the lures MaryLou had dangled in front of me - her friendship and the cabin in the woods - and I'd failed to recognize a thousand clues about the Hunters, clues that seemed obvious in hindsight.

"Hey, you two," Mike said. "Don't be so hard on yourselves. When push came to shove, you did great. You stood up for what's right." He looked at each of us. "Okay?"

"Okay." Barry nodded and smiled reluctantly.

"Ruby? Okay?"

"Sure."

Mike leaned forward. "So, what're you going to do now?"

"I don't know. Find a job, a place to live. Figure out my life." I shrugged. "The usual stuff." I hadn't gotten around to telling Mike about my idea. Maybe I'd look for some acreage, so the shelter could help large animals too. Lately, I'd been thinking I might name it Clarence's Emergency Treatment Institute. CETI.

Uncle Mike's expression was serious. "I'm thinking about selling this house, getting out of Salem." He glanced at Barry. "We want to talk to you about it."

"Uh huh," I said, blanking my expression. Was Mike warning me the guest bedroom was just temporary?

"We talked about fixing Barry's place up and moving there."

"Where's there?"

Barry sat up, wide-eyed awake all of a sudden. "God's Country. Otherwise known as The Rogue Valley. I've got about a hundred acres with an old farmhouse. Bought it when land was cheap, in the early Seventies."

"We'd love for you to join us," said Mike. He kept his eyes on me. His mouth hung open slightly, as if he were holding his breath for my answer.

"There's a fabulous little guest house you could have to yourself." Barry clapped his hands enthusiastically. "I know Clarence would love it there. Please say yes."

Clarence's ears stood at attention when he heard his name. He sat up, tilted his large head and gazed at me with soulful eyes. His stumpy tail twitched back and forth. Clarence was voting yes.

That made it unanimous. For once my heart and brain knew the same thing at the same time. This was what I'd wanted all along: a family, a home, a place I belonged, people who cared. Simple as a greeting card. Not so easy to find. I'd spent years stumbling in and out of situations, thinking maybe I'd fall over the right thing. Go figure. I never imagined I'd find what I was looking for with a bulldog and two gay men.

Like I've always said, life is weird. That's why you have to be ready when something good finally shows up.

"Yes," I said.

www.ingramcontent.com/pod-product-compliance
Lightning Source LLC
Chambersburg PA
CBHW030501260626
47157CB00005B/1599